Tryst

Murder and intrigue in suburban Hampshire

John Mitchell

2016

To my wonderful wife and constant supporter Jules.
Thanks for all your help and encouragement.

All the locations in this book exist, but none of the characters are based on real people. Some of the events are from experience, but most are the product of a vivid imagination.

CHAPTER ONE

"Tryst"

Kathy looked up and turned to the voice behind her. A tall man, about her age, was standing there, smiling inanely. He was not bad-looking, slightly tanned and wearing a suit with a formal shirt but no tie, which gave him a typical "just left the office" look. He held a half-empty pint glass. From the comfort of her sofa she gave him her best 'are you hitting on me?' stare.

"Excuse me?" she replied sharply, in a voice to match her stare. But then thought, maybe he'd said something different, or what he had said hadn't been meant for her.

"Eight across. Five letters, 'Attempt to join holy person for secret meeting'". He smiled again.

"And how long have you been looking over my shoulder?" she said, trying to sound unimpressed.

"Long enough to see you get most of the other clues. I guess you don't need me to explain it" She said nothing but held his gaze defiantly.

He waited, then soldiered on. "But I will. 'Attempt' is 'Try', 'Holy Person' is 'Saint', abbreviated to 'St', and joined up they make 'Tryst' which is a secret meeting." He could see that he was just digging himself in deeper. Sheepishly he thought he'd

try another angle. “Are you waiting for someone?”
“Can't a woman sit in the club bar without being hassled?” she maintained her defensive tone, and folded her newspaper so the crossword was hidden.
“Whoah, no offence intended. I'm new to the gym and just trying to be friendly. I'll leave you in peace”. He turned to go back to the bar, but couldn’t help but notice her slightly guilty look and paused.
“No, you don't have to do that, “she conceded, her voice softening, “but instead of standing there looking over my shoulder why don't you just sit down and talk to me?” She unconsciously pushed a strand of her blonde hair back behind her ear without seeming to recognise the intimacy of her action. “You could introduce yourself, for a start.”
“OK then”. He moved around the sofa and sat next to her.
“Sorry it sounded like I was coming on strong. Maybe I should have bought my own paper if I wanted to do a crossword.”
She smiled.
“My name's Jack.” He offered his hand and she shook it. “So you've been a member here a while?”
She seemed to relax a little, and took a sip from her glass, the remnants of a clear fizzy drink which had been on the table next to her untouched all the time that Jack had been looking

over her shoulder.
“I’m Kathy. I’ve been a member for a couple of years, since I moved up from Bournemouth. I'm here twice, maybe three times a week. I hardly ever venture into the bar, though. How about you?”
“Oh, I joined just a few months back, to play some squash. I joined the league, but I'll probably come last because I don’t really take it seriously enough. I go at it like a bull in a china shop, win the first couple of points but then I’m exhausted and end up losing against anyone with any experience. I seem to have this thing where I know exactly where my opponent is standing when I hit my shot and yet my brain makes me aim the ball directly at him so he can hit it without moving. I was supposed to have a game tonight but the other bloke called in sick, so I thought I'd have a beer or two instead. Somehow it's a bit more civilized sitting on these posh sofas than in some local pub. Although most of this crowd seem very serious about their keep-fit stuff – I haven't sensed much in the way of socialising yet”
He glanced around and Kathy followed his gaze. Small groups of fit-looking people, mostly in tracksuits with the obligatory Head bag at their feet, and a glass of flavoured water in their hands, earnestly discussing the next tournement. There weren’t

too many people sitting alone. Maybe there actually wasn't a social scene here, but he could invent one. "Actually," he continued, "the bar steward knows me by name"
"I think you'll find that's part of his job, Jack" Kathy smiled.
"Well, I suppose you're right." Jack returned the smile. But now we've met, maybe I can ask you again – are you waiting for someone?"
Kathy hesitated. "Well, to be honest, I'm just sulking. I wasn't really in the mood to work out. I got here early tonight after a furious row at home. I've spent all evening here doing my crossword and I'm determined to go home late to teach my husband a lesson."
Jack kept a neutral look. "Anything I can do to help?"
"Yes. You could get me another drink. It was a white wine and soda"
Jack downed the last mouthful of his pint and went to the bar.
"Same again, Jack?" asked the barman.
"Yes please. Steve, isn't it?" offered Jack
"Sam."
"And a white wine spritzer for the lady". Jack glanced up at the mirror behind the bar. Kathy was still sitting there, and gave him a friendly smile. He smiled in return, and was still smiling when Sam caught his eye with a "seen it all before" look.

Pretending not to notice, Jack added the drinks to his tab, carried them over to the table and sat down.
"So what was the row about?" he started , then thought maybe he shouldn't have. She seemed not to mind.
"Well, since you asked...." she began, "Let's just say it was me who started it, so it must have been about money." She took a sip of her drink, then smiled. "If it had been Mike who started it, the row would probably have been about sex". Some subconscious reaction caused Jack to take a long gulp of his pint. "So how about you", she continued. "What brings you here?"
He was happy to push his subconscious thoughts deeper, and gave her a potted history of his current lifestyle, as people came into the bar, mostly damp from a fresh shower and went, mostly refreshened by something cool and non-alcoholic .
"Home for me is in Bath, where I'm supposed to be based, but I'm not there too often. I'm working here in Fareham on a six-month assignment. I'm an IT consultant. There are always early morning meetings or late nights in the Computer Suite, so as it's eighty miles drive back home I stay at the local Travel Lodge motel during the week. The client pays for my food and lodging, although living on expenses always sounds grander than it is. The hotel bill is paid directly but I get a food

allowance which barely covers an evening meal in the hotel restaurant. I usually economise by having a massive breakfast at the hotel and a cheap lunch at the works canteen. In the evenings I just do a bit of exploring or go to the supermarket, then come back to the Travel Lodge for a pot noodle in my room."

"Is that a euphemism?" she interrupted.

He paused, then saw the joke and they both laughed naturally, although his face had reddened slightly.

"No, it's not. Well, not always" he smiled "Although it's not quite as sad as I've made it sound. The company pays for a gym membership so at least I can keep fit and not get too bored while away from home. Admittedly the arrangement isn't too good for family life, but you all get used to it after a while. I've got a wife and two teenage kids, but you have to go where the work is, don't you? "

Kathy let him ramble on and nodded in what seemed to be the right places. When it was her turn, she described the suburban life she currently lived with her husband, no kids, in Eastleigh, just out of town.

"My background is in accounting, and I worked for a bank in Bournemouth, just down the coast, for a good few years, but then I met my husband, who worked at the same place, then he

got a job up here in Fareham, so I quit my job and now I'm "exploring my options". For me, the gym is the same as it is for you, a social club without the social life, but normally I don't really need that side of it. Just recently, though, it seems that Mike and I argue about the most trivial of things. Don't get me wrong, he's a lovely bloke and I couldn't wish for a better husband, but he seems to have changed over the last couple of months and it doesn't take much to set him off. I've kind of put it all down to the move. Seems like he's feeling a lot of stress from the more challenging job, and I'm feeling a lot of sheer boredom from not having a job at all."
Jack listened attentively but was more interested really in just looking at her. She was a handsome woman, not stunningly attractive but beautiful in a natural way. She wore no make-up and didn't need any. Her natural blonde hair fell over a pink Nike sweatshirt which hung loose over tight-fitting designer jeans and did little to mask curves in some very interesting places. He was careful to avoid his gaze lingering, but he did wonder how someone as vivacious as her could ever get bored.
Eventually the bar became empty. Sam the bar steward came over. "Sorry folks, you'll have to drink up. The last bus home is in five minutes, so I need to close up." He picked up their glasses, hurriedly rinsed them and started locking up

cupboards.
Kathy looked at her watch “Wow, is that the time? I'd better go. I think I've been out long enough to make my point to my husband.”
Jack hesitated, and then said “You could make him sweat a bit longer if you wanted to.”
Kathy gave him a piercing look. “And maybe you could just walk me to my car, and keep your thoughts to yourself”
Jack blushed. “I just meant we could carry on talking at a cafe or something. I don’t want you to get the wrong idea”. He got up and went to pay the bill. Kathy quickly followed him and dropped a ten-pound note on the counter.
“My half. I don't need looking after.”
“I can believe that” replied an exasperated Jack. “Let me walk you to your car, then. Mine is round the back. Where's yours?”
She looked at him for a second or two and her expression seemed to soften.
“I’m sorry Jack, I didn’t mean to be bitchy. I’m not used to getting so much attention, and I shouldn’t be so defensive. But as for my car, it's probably the only other one there at this time of night, don’t you think?”. They both smiled.
After saying goodnight to the bar steward they left through the sports club lobby, swiping their membership cards as they

went. The lights went off behind them, and as they went down the steps from the club the main doors were being locked behind them. They walked around the corner into pitch darkness which was immediately illuminated by a security light.

"Night, folks!" they heard from Sam as he hurried off in the opposite direction.

There was an awkward silence as they approached the back of the car park. The security light went off, its range being just to cover the main building. Kathy pressed her key fob and the car park was lit by flashing amber lights from her car, farthest away, but showing his car also, parked parallel about three spots away, and the only other vehicle there. She walked across to hers, opened the boot, dropped her sports bag inside and closed the lid. Then she turned and looked at him, her eyes darkening slightly and her breathing becoming heavier. She grasped the car keys harder in her hand, trying to fight a building desire. He had been standing there watching her, but now walked over to her, put his own bag down and started what seemed to have been a prepared speech.

"I just wanted to say, Kathy, that this was a very pleasant evening and that maybe we can meet up again sometime-"

Kathy couldn't wait any longer. She put her arms around his

neck and pulled his face towards hers, kissing him passionately. Jack's confusion at this dramatic change of mood lasted only seconds, being replaced by some pretty strong desires of his own. He mentally tore up his little speech and responded eagerly, wrapping his arms around her waist and pulling her gently towards him. They were leaning against her car, and Jack was being careful not to overplay his hand despite the passion he felt. He needn't have worried. Kathy was panting breathlessly, manoevered their interlocked bodies along the side of the car, opened the rear door and fell in on her back, pulling him down on top of her, their lips still engaged but her tongue doing most of the work. Jack was trying to tell himself that he was in control of the situation, but Kathy already had his belt undone and his trousers unzipped. "Pull that door closed", she whispered, "or the houses opposite will have a floodlit view". And as he complied she lifted one leg, shook off her shoe and rolled down one half of her jeans and pants to get her leg out of them. With the door closed, Jack settled back in place on top of her then slid himself easily inside her. She gasped at the sensation, then started moaning quietly in time with his rhythmical movement, getting louder as he kissed her neck and moved one hand around in her shirt, the other hand supporting his own weight, a difficult feat in the confines of the

back seat. He pushed and kissed, caressed and moaned himself in time with their movements, then Kathy suddenly seemed to need more urgency, tugging at first his shoulders then his waist and then buttocks to pull him deeper inside her. She gasped, "Come on, Yes, Yes , Yes!" and in seconds it was all over. They lay panting into each other's ears for some minutes, saying nothing until they felt their own sweat cooling their tired bodies. It was Jack who broke the silence, propping himself up on one arm.
"Wow. You really are something, you know that?".
Kathy smiled in the darkness, knowing he couldn't see her but feeling satisfied in several ways.. "You're not so bad yourself. But shut up for a while or we'll steam up the car even more".
They stayed coupled for a while longer before nature decided it was time to eject.
Jack started to say "Look, Kathy, -"
"You don't need to say a thing, Jack. Especially something like "I didn't intend this to happen" or "I've never done this kind of thing before". At least you can feel less guilty about it than I do. You didn't have any points to prove or frustration to let off like I did. Nor do I want you to feel you were being used. I think life is all about giving in to impulses. I certainly had one for you and I think you had the same. But I certainly wasn't

disappointed, and I hope you weren't either"

"God, no! Far from it, but..."

"But nothing. I needed to get something out of my system, and you helped me out. It doesn't hurt that you're a very attractive man, of course"

"Well, I hope it wasn't just sex" Jack replied, a little too primly.

"No, I had fun tonight, and chatting with you was much better than trying to finish that damn crossword, but it seemed natural to end it this way, don't you think?"

"I certainly can't argue with that. Sometimes things are just meant to happen, and the consequences are too distant to worry about in the heat of the moment. Sorry, am I getting heavy on you?"

"I assume you mean physically rather than philosophically" she said playfully. There was no reaction, she assumed because he wasn't quite on her wavelength. "No, you're fine, but I've left an incriminating bare footprint in the steam on that side window"

"Do you think it will suddenly appear again the next time the car steams up, like when you leave a message for someone on the bathroom mirror?" He didn't sound concerned about whether it did or not, it was just an observation.

"I don't think there's much risk of that. Mike is a lovely bloke

and he’s got some great qualities, but steamy windows is a long-forgotten phrase in our marriage”
Jack thought it prudent to gloss over that one, but the thought had triggered some concerns in his mind. “I hope I needn't worry about anyone else finding out about this”
“Well, I hope you can rely on me to be discreet. As it happens you've told me your life history, but not the name of your wife or your exact address, but it'll be easy enough to track you down”
Jack sat up quickly, cracking his head on the car roof in the process.
“Just kidding, honest! And I've never done this before either, so no-one else needs to know. But it won't happen again, you know that don't you?”
“Oh.” Jack couldn’t help but sound disappointed. “Well, as long as it's not my performance that's the problem”
“No, you were great, and in another world I’d have liked to test out your endurance a bit more. But right now it was exactly what I needed. I feel like someone finds me attractive and will take a few risks to give me what I want. Who knows, the last few minutes might be just the boost I needed to make things work with Mike. But to lighten things up a bit, I can give you marks out of ten, if you really want. For now though, just get

off so I can straighten myself out"
Jack backed himself out of the door and closed it. He stood for a few seconds with a smug grin on his face before he realised his trousers were around his ankles and the night was getting a little chilly. By the time he had rearranged his clothing Kathy had done the same and was out of the car, standing next to him and handing him his sports bag.
"So, if you see me in the club bar again, don't be so clever with your crossword-solving" Kathy smiled as she climbed into the driver's seat. As she reversed and then drove off, Jack could only stand and stare with the most self-satisfied grin on his face.

It took about ten minutes for Kathy to get home. As she approached the house she could see Mike's car in the driveway. She switched off the engine and coasted quietly to a stop on the street, then got out. She opened the boot and took her sports bag out, fished around inside it and took out a sweat-stained tee shirt. She glanced around at the other houses in the street. No lights on or any sign of movement. She used the Tee shirt to dry off between her thighs, then opened the rear door on the side where her feet had been. She thought for a moment about wiping off the marks, but didn't. As trophies go, not as good as notches on the headboard, she thought, but knowing her footprints were on that window might provide her with fond memories in an uncertain future. Instead she tossed the Tee shirt back in the bag, then closed the door and the boot lid, and walked up the path to the American-style bungalow. There were no lights on. She let herself in and glanced at the clock in the hallway. One o'clock in the morning. She went into the bathroom to check that she'd dressed properly. Her shirt was very ruffled, but she'd toss it straight into the laundry basket in the bedroom. She straightened her hair and tiptoed into the bedroom, then switched on the bedside light, closing the curtains out of habit. The bed was empty, and hadn't been slept in. There was no sign that Mike had been there. She checked the guest bedroom and study. Both empty and as tidy as they always were.

"Mike?" she called. And again. No answer.

She retraced her steps and switched on the lights in the living room. Everything tidy, nothing out of place. She went into the kitchen. Everything was exactly as she'd left it earlier that evening. Two completely untouched meals sat on plates on the red and white checked tablecloth. Both chairs had been pushed back from the table. On the stove, a frying pan and a saucepan. She paused, and could hear only the incessant ticking of the clock on the wall. There was no sign of him. If he’d left the car and taken a taxi maybe he’d called one from the land line? She checked the phone for the last number dialled. It was one she’d called herself earlier that afternoon. The only room left was the garage, through a door off the kitchen, although normally that's where Mike's car would have been. Normally. Hesitantly she opened the door and fumbled for the light switch. She shielded her eyes as the fluorescent light flashed several times and then illuminated her husband's body, hanging by the neck on a rope from the ceiling.

CHAPTER TWO

Gloria hadn't been sleeping too well. She seemed to have no problem dozing off almost as soon as she and Graham got into bed, but within an hour or two she was always wide awake. The same on Fridays, even though that was the night they had sex each week. She'd tried not eating too late, cutting down on spicy foods and she wasn't on any medication. No physical reason, and there seemed to be nothing on her mind – after all, she didn't seem to dream much. Perhaps it was some middle-age thing coming on, but whatever, it was really annoying to be lying there listening to Graham snoring peacefully. She'd tried drinking half a bottle of wine, she'd tried just having a cup of cocoa, she'd even tried eating a banana at bedtime like someone on the radio had suggested. She'd just have to count sheep or something equally stupid, if she could ignore the snoring. Maybe she would have to roll him onto his side again. It's a pity, she thought, that there's not much other noise to cover his contented sounds, this being a quiet cul-de-sac. The most disturbance they ever had was when the cats from the end house had a fight. Then, as if in answer to her thoughts, she heard a car door slam across the street. Funny, she hadn't heard the car pull up. There must have been a crowd of them - she heard at least three doors slam shut. Probably there's no quiet way of closing car doors, but as she looked at the clock she thought they might be a bit more considerate. She couldn't hear any voices, though, so perhaps they'd felt guilty and would be quieter now. Anyway, now for a concentrated effort to sleep, or feel like crap tomorrow at the breakfast table. Counting backwards from a hundred is supposed to do the trick, so.... one hundred, ninety-nine, ninety-eight, ...

She'd just counted sixty-seven when Gloria heard the most horrific scream from across the street. She sat bolt upright and a cold shiver ran down her back. She switched on her bedside lamp and saw that Graham was sitting upright next to her, staring wide-eyed at her.

"What in hell was that?" he gasped. She certainly hadn't imagined it then - there wasn't much that would wake him at night.

"I don't know, but there's something terribly wrong – it came from the Johnson's – and it sounded like a woman screaming. It must be Kathy!"

Graham was already up, putting his trousers on. "I'm going over there. You call the police". Even with the urgency of the situation Graham was careful to put on fresh underpants and socks. He was certainly a creature of habit. Gloria reached for

her dressing gown and wrapped it around her while she shuffled into her slippers, then quickly padded downstairs and picked up the phone. It was the first time in her life that she'd dialled nine, nine, nine so it felt a bit surreal, especially when it was answered in the same way they do on the telly.
"Emergency Services, which service do you require?"
"Police, please" she replied, then there was a pause and someone from the police came on the line, asking what the emergency was. "Hello, can you please send someone to Briar Crescent in Fareham? I think someone's in terrible trouble. Hold on, please" She put her hand over the mouthpiece as Graham rushed past her fully dressed.
"Don't you think we should wait till they get here Graham? What if it's a robber? What if he's armed?"
"I can't be worrying about my own safety" he replied almost self-righteously. "No, love, that scream sounded pretty urgent, so someone needs help over there. It might be Kathy, it might be someone else, but I have to see if I can help" and with that Graham was out the door and running across the street, as Gloria started explaining the situation to the police.
As Graham reached Kathy and Mike's front door, ringing the doorbell didn't seem the right thing to do, so he pummelled the door with his fist and shouted "Kathy! Mike! What's going on

in there?" All the lights were on, but it was a few moments before he saw any movement through the frosted glass. Kathy opened the door in tears.
"Graham, thank God! Quickly, come and help, it's Mike!" He followed her through the kitchen and out into the garage, where Mike's inert body was suspended.
"Oh, my God!" shouted Graham, and looked desperately around for something to help. There was a stepladder, still open, lying on the floor to one side. He grabbed it and stood it next to the hanging body, then ran to the tool rack where he could see a hacksaw. As he climbed the ladder with the hacksaw in his hand, Kathy screamed "What are doing Graham, he's dead! He must be dead – just look at him!"
Graham actually hadn't looked too closely. Now that he did so he could see Mike's bulging eyes in his grey, lifeless face. Graham would still need to do the right thing, though.
"Maybe not, he might still be breathing, or even if he isn't we might still be able to save him" he gasped, and with that he had reached the third step of the ladder and had his arm around Mike's waist, sawing frantically at the rope with the hacksaw.
"Hold that ladder steady, Kathy, and get ready to help me when the rope breaks".
At that exact moment the rope did break, sending Mike's full

weight onto Graham and sending them both and the ladder tumbling to the floor, with Mike on top of Graham, who grunted loudly as they hit the concrete. Kathy pulled the ladder to one side and grabbed Mike's arm, then pulled it until his weight was off Graham, who rather gingerly got up on his knees and felt for a pulse in Mike's neck. Nothing. Graham knew what to do next from those First Aid sessions he'd attended. He rolled Mike onto his back and started urgently pressing Mike's chest, repeating the chorus of Bee Gees "Staying Alive" song in his mind - at the same time thinking how ludicrous it was to be singing to himself at such a moment. He took a break every couple of minutes to feel for a pulse, but there was nothing.

Kathy had been sitting silently on the floor watching Graham's actions. She suddenly burst into life. "He's gone, Graham! My God, he's dead! Stop it now, it's no good, he's gone! You're pumping away at a dead body! My Mike is dead, can't you see?" She was getting hysterical.

"It's never too late, Kathy! I'll keep going till the ambulance gets here! Maybe I can still save him!"

A few minutes later they heard a siren and the paramedics arrived.

"OK, mate, we'll take over from here, you've done your best" said one as he unpacked breathing and resuscitation equipment. A young policeman who had arrived with them led Graham and Kathy into the living room, where Gloria was sitting, still in her dressing gown.

"Can you give me your name, please?" the policeman asked Kathy.

"Kathy Johnson, and that's my husband Mike" she nodded towards the door to the garage. She seemed to have recovered her composure a little. "My lovely but very dead husband Mike" she added numbly. They all sat and waited in silence until the paramedic joined them.

"Sorry, love, I'm afraid there was nothing we could do". Kathy put her head in her hands and sobbed quietly.

The policeman added his own condolences, and turned to Gloria. "Do you think you could look after Mrs Johnson till morning? I'll have to call this in and there will be a lot of people involved. "Why will there be other people involved?" Kathy blubbed. "It's pretty obvious what the daft sod has gone and done, isn't it?"

"That's not for me to say, I'm afraid" replied the policeman calmly, "but I'd suggest you're better off away from here for a couple of hours. I'd be obliged if you could leave everything as it is, don't even get anything from the bathroom or the bedroom, and go spend the night with your friends here. Maybe a cup of cocoa and a couple of aspirins would help" he continued, pointedly addressing Gloria.

"Yes, of course, come on love, let's go over to our place. We can just sit and chat if you like"

"Thanks Gloria, I suppose he's right. I really don't want to be here right now. And thanks, Graham, for doing what you could". Graham was close to tears himself.

"I just wish I could have been in time" was all he could say as the three of them shuffled out the front door.

As they crossed the street another car pulled up behind the ambulance. The driver watched them before getting out and walking up to Kathy's front door. He stopped, reached into his pocket and donned a pair of latex gloves, pushed the door and went straight in.

"Well, that was pretty quick, Pete", said the young policeman as he turned and saw who had walked in. Pete Thomas was a well-known figure in the Hampshire CID, best known for his direct manner and poor dress sense. He had been at Eastleigh for ten years now, having transferred out of Bristol after something that the rumour mill just couldn't define. He had been detective inspector since then, so obviously whatever it

was had ruined any higher promotion chances.
“My turn for On Call, I’m afraid. There’s a re-run of “A Touch of Frost” I was watching while the missus had gone to bed, so I was still dressed, and it’s only five minutes drive from here. I’ve been lucky really, you pull the On Call shift once a fortnight but this is the first time this year I’ve had to come out. What's the story so far?”
“Seems quite straightforward. Woman comes home and finds husband hanging from the ceiling, looking very dead. The only complication is that the neighbour is a “have-a-go hero” and has messed up the whole scene.”
“I suppose he thought he was helping”, grumbled Pete. “If he'd ever seen a dead body before he would have known that this was just another one, and leave well enough alone. Have you called SOC yet?” The Scene of Crimes team would take trace samples, dust for fingerprints and photograph everything, so that the scene was fully recorded, even if it turned out that there had been no crime committed.
“No, that's next on my list”
“I'll have a look around then” said Pete as the policeman started talking into his radio.
He walked through to the kitchen. On the kitchen table were two neatly set places. Knives, forks, wine glasses, an unopened

bottle of wine and two untouched meals – steak, chips and peas. Pete felt pangs in his stomach – he'd had Spag Bol at seven o'clock, but it looked like a nice couple of steaks gone to waste. Electric kettle, cold to the touch. Nothing on the drainer. He opened the dishwasher. Nothing inside. On the stove a dirty frying pan and a saucepan. There was a deep fat fryer on the worktop, again cold to the touch. He pressed with his shoe on the pedal bin and glanced inside. An empty can of tinned peas, a polystyrene tray from the meat counter of the supermarket, some onion peelings. The price on the meat wrapper gave it away as a quite cheap meal. He looked again at the table. Pepper and salt, but no ketchup. These are definitely a middle-class couple. The wine was an own-brand Merlot, mid-week plonk for those who drank every night. He went back through the living room into the main bedroom. Bed not slept in. Alarm clock on one side of the bed, with a John Grisham novel next to it. He pushed the alarm button on the clock. 7:45 it was set to go off. Pete had no idea if that was important information. He would just file it away in case. The bedside light on the other side of the bed was on. The curtains were closed. He looked into a second bedroom, but that didn't look as if it had ever been used. Tidy but dusty. A room for someone to stay over if they needed to, but no-one ever had. Certainly not a kid's bedroom. He walked back through to the door leading to the garage. It was closed. He pushed the door open slowly, As if expecting someone to jump out at him. No-one did, but that didn't stop him feeling a cold shiver.

The body was lying on its back in the middle of the room, a light sheet covering it. Pete looked around. There were two bicycles leaning against the wall, a washing machine and dryer, a chest freezer and a workbench with an array of tools neatly arranged on a board on the wall, an outline of each tool in black felt-tip to show where it should be returned. Only the hacksaw was missing, Pete could see it lying on the floor. On one of the wall supports was screwed a large metal ring, to which was attached a length of rope. The rope was about twelve feet long, the other end lying on the floor near the body with the end cut off roughly. Directly above the body was a wooden beam into which had been screwed another metal ring. The workbench had a series of drawers underneath the work surface, and Pete opened them one by one to check out the contents. The drawers were labelled and the contents reflected exactly the wording – screws, nails, fastenings... In the third drawer he found several large metal rings similar to those screwed into the wall and ceiling. The other drawers held

various washers, hinges and so on. Underneath the bench he could see several reels of electric cable and one of rope, looking like a good match for the piece still attached to the ring on the wall.
Pete slowly pulled the sheet off the top half of the body to reveal a typically blue-tinged puffy white face. The paramedic had closed Mike's eyes. Around his neck was tied the rest of the rope, in a kind of a slip knot, with about six inches left after the knot to where it had been cut off. Pete pulled the sheet right back, to reveal the body dressed in a shirt and tie, suit trousers and shoes. A quick check of the pockets revealed nothing of interest, certainly no suicide note. That would have been propped up against the wine bottle, if this was a "Frost" episode, Pete thought to himself. He covered the body again and went back into the lounge.
"SOC and the pathologist are on their way, guv" said the policeman.
"I suppose that was the bereaved wife going into the neighbours' house just then?" replied Pete.
"Yes, she was pretty upset. Well they all were"
"Did you ask them any questions?"
"No, I thought it could wait till morning. We were here within five minutes of the call, and I found the neighbour doing his

Gibb Brothers impersonation, so there's not much could have happened since he was found."

"No, I suppose we can ask the usual stuff about stress and financial situation, extra-marital affairs and the like tomorrow, over a nice cup of tea. I'll just have a quiet look around.

Pete walked back into the bedroom and checked the bedside table drawers. Nothing unusual. He opened the drawers of a chest on the side where the bedside light was on, Bras, pants, all kinds of female garb, all clean but just thrown into the drawer. The next drawer down had tee shirts and the next had skirts and jeans, neatly folded but certainly not ironed. He went across to the chest on the other side of the room. Underpants, tee-shirts, socks, all neatly arranged and even the socks ironed. He paused for a second to consider the differences in the two chests, and what inferences could be drawn. He'd probably need a bit more background before he could form an opinion. He went back to her side, and rummaged at the back of the underwear section, feeling around for anything that didn't seem to belong. His fingers felt a small box, which he drew out for closer inspection. It was a ring-box, which opened on a spring to reveal a wedding ring. He held the ring up in the light of the bedside lamp and read an inscription. "Kath and Mike,

forever”.
Pete replaced the ring box and walked around to the other side of the bed. The correspondingly intimate drawer on Mike's side of the bed contained just a pile of neatly folded boxer shorts. Pete felt carefully around the edges for anything unusual. Nothing. He thought about the different personalities on display, and went to the bottom drawer, pulling it out completely. Hidden beneath the drawer, lying on the base of the chest itself, was a sheet of paper. Pete unfolded it and saw that it was a printout on an online savings account. He sat on the bed and studied the account details. It was in Mike's name only and had been opened about three years earlier. There were regular monthly credits to the account starting at a thousand pounds and increasing each year by a thousand, with no withdrawals at all until about six months ago. The amounts withdrawn were significant. Exactly ten thousand pounds each time, in the first week of each month. The last one had been a month ago, and left only a hundred pounds in the account. Pete carefully replaced the book and the drawer, then stepped outside the bedroom just as the forensic team arrived.
“I'll leave you all to it and go home for a few hours shut-eye”, he announced. “Just drop your report on my desk before nine and I'll start up the investigation”

CHAPTER THREE

By half past nine Pete had already taken his "shut-eye", or at least as much as he could before being woken by the sound of slamming doors and school-run mums shouting for their kids to hurry up. He lived with his wife Jenny in a bustling part of suburban Portsmouth, a three-bedroom Victorian with red brick walls and bay windows. They'd had a lot more friends when they lived in Bristol, and it was a time in their lives when they could enjoy the Bristol night life, a mixture of student hang-outs and middle-class restaurants. They had lived in a town house just off the Clifton Downs, so if they needed a break from the lively city they had only to walk half a mile to the beautiful Avon Gorge and Brunel's famous Clifton Suspension bridge. That had all had to change when he'd had problems with the force there, and Portsmouth had seemed a reasonable second choice, near the coast and steeped in history. They had soon found out that the city itself was not one of the classiest places in England. He sometimes wondered why they'd chosen this particular neighbourhood, but knew it was really because he could get to the police station easily, and Jenny could drive to her school job in a few minutes. The only real criteria he'd had when they moved here was that the house should have a large vegetable plot and a double garage. As seemed to be the way with most of their joint decisions, this house had neither a vegetable plot nor a double garage, but it did have two spare bedrooms for when relatives came to stay, high on the list of Jenny's criteria.

After a light breakfast he was ready to face the day and was happy to have avoided most of the traffic on the way to work. Hampshire Police Divisional Headquarters is housed in an imposing brick building in the better half of Eastleigh, next to a pretty park. Being CID, there are no patrol cars parked outside, just the unmarked cars of the two dozen detectives and private vehicles belonging to the fifty or more administration staff. The building houses the investigative sections, including the Serious Crimes Unit. Any front line work such as interviews or "banging-up" suspects is taken care of at the local "nick" at Portswood, a couple of miles down the road.

Pete's desk in the Serious Crimes Unit was in a second floor office, where he now sat, wading just a little further into his backlog of uninteresting paperwork, all the while anticipating an interruption for the forensic results of the previous nights suicide. Dave Seddon, sitting opposite him, was already working on a threatening behaviour case involving a couple from the docklands, but apart from that it was a bit quiet in the serious crimes office. Dave had been Pete's second-in-command at the unit since Pete was transferred, and they got on well together. Dave's tendency to make a joke out of everything was sometimes a little tedious, but he was a dedicated investigator with an occasional spark of inspiration. He lived in a little cottage on the river Itchen, near Swaythling, with his long-term, and in Pete's view long-suffering girlfriend. Every chance Dave had he would go fishing nearby, although Pete would say he was crazy to eat anything coming out of a river with that name.

Dave looked up from his work as Pete spoke, not sure whether it was to him or himself.

“I might just give them a bell, can't think what's taking so long2.

As he picked up the phone in walked Jim Brunt, the head of forensics, with a couple of printed pages, which he dropped on Pete's desk.

“Hello, Jim” said Pete, “We don't see you in here very often”.

“It's not that often I get anything unusual to show you” Jim replied, smiling.

Pete looked up quizzically, then picked up the printout and started reading. There were a few moments silence while he read the opening paragraph, summarising the results of the tests

on Mike Johnson's blood.
"Holy shit, you can't be serious?"
"Oh, yes I can" replied Jim. "Your suicide had enough cocaine in his bloodstream to float a battleship"
"But still suicide?"
"Who the hell knows. It's plenty enough to get the inquest adjourned. I'll get on to the coroner straight away. What do you want to do next?"
"Well, I suppose I'd better get over to Fareham and do some detective work, starting with interviewing the poor widow. Is there a time of death somewhere in here?" he scanned the pages."Ah, sometime between six pm and midnight. Can't you be any more precise than that?"
"Well, that's the thing," Jim sounded apologetic. "The amount of drugs in his blood seems to have screwed up our normal estimates. Isn't that good enough for you lot, then?"
"I'm sure it'll do OK. I don't think there's much goes on in suburban Portsmouth that a few hours will make a difference. Right, then". He reached for his jacket. "I'll be off and make a start. Let me know if you find anything else. Give me a bell if you need me for anything, Dave" And with that Pete left the office and walked down to the car park. Before starting the car, he sat for a while and pondered the possibilities. Obviously

something a bit fishy here, but drugs aren't exactly rare these days, and suicides including drugs more common than you would think. But why hang himself? And why such an elaborate method to suspend himself? If he was that high, how could he have drilled in the hooks for his gallows? Maybe he'd set that up earlier, knowing what he was going to do. But if he had the cocaine, why not just overdo the drugs? And anyway where were the drugs now? - the house was clean. And where did he get them? Could he be a user without his wife knowing? " Pete started the car and headed towards the crime scene.

It was a grey day, but no rain, just the threat of it, which seemed enough to keep people indoors. Not much traffic, then, and Pete arrived at Briar Crescent after about ten minutes. The road was indistinguishable from a dozen others nearby, obviously part of a large development when a green-field site became available. The locals would probably remember when this was all grazing land, before a retiring farmer thought he would make a million or two by selling off. Briar lane was reached through Blackberry Way, naturally enough, but Pete couldn't see any "Stinging Nettle terrace" or "Deadly Nightshade avenue". Not very imaginative, these developers. Outside the Johnsons' house there was a white van with a little

"Hampshire Constabulary" emblem on the back, and signs of continued activity in the house itself. Pete parked and got out. He looked for a few minutes at the house to fix the image in his mind. A nineteen-eighties construction on a big plot, built along the lines of those split-level suburban homes you see in those American family sit-coms. Not much of a back garden – not even a vegetable plot – the property was all front, in both senses of the phrase. Maybe worth half a million at the current inflated house prices? He did a bit of mental arithmetic. If the Johnsons had a property to sell before buying this one, it would give them a profit of maybe two hundred thousand for the deposit, leaving a mortgage of about fifteen hundred a month. Definitely a bit of a stretch on a forty thousand salary without the wife working. Of course that wasn't including any expenditure od a drug habit. He looked up and down the road. A very quiet neighbourhood indeed, maybe he should live somewhere like this? One day. When I'm dead. He smiled to himself, turned and walked up the drive to the neighbours' house opposite, where he'd watched Mrs Johnson being taken the previous night.

Gloria came to the door in response to the bell.

"DI Peter Thomas, Portsmouth CID. Is Mrs Johnson up yet?"

Gloria was still as white as a sheet, but she nodded and said

“She’s in here” then led him into the hallway. Pete politely wiped his feet, it seemed appropriate in such an immaculately tidy house. He resisted a smile at the “Welcome” picked out in green on the doormat. He was shown into the front living room, where Kathy was sitting staring into space. “Would you like a cup of tea?” Gloria asked.

“Coffee, please – black one sugar, but can you leave it ten minutes or so, I need to ask a few questions in private” Gloria nodded, then realising what he meant she backed out through the door, closing it softly behind her.

Pete sat down opposite Kathy and spoke in a practiced formal but sympathetic way. “Mrs Johnson – can I call you Kathy? I’m afraid I have some questions I need to ask you”

Kathy looked up, her eyes blank. “Of course you have.” Then she stared down at the untouched cup of tea she was holding. “It was that job. I knew it would get to him eventually.”

Pete was prepared for some kind of outpouring. This often happened, the people touched by tragedy trying to find an simple explanation. Attaching some blame if possible, trying to share their hurt. It would happen a couple of times, he’d been trained to expect, before the victim could be level-headed. He waited for her to continue.

“ They had him working all hours of the day and night. Keep

promoting him, giving him more stuff to do and more pressure from above. Deadlines to meet, reports to write, presentations to prepare, just drop everything and work weekends or at home, just to get it done. And when he's not working on stuff, he's worrying about how his last project was rated or how soon his next one is going to jump the priority list. Waking up in the middle of the night and lying there going through figures, firing up his laptop in the kitchen to check his emails, sitting at the kitchen table when he does come home, a pile of paperwork in front of him. And what do they give you in return? A brass plate to put on your desk with "Vice President Money Transfer Department" under your name. And meanwhile, no pay rises for three years and we can't even afford a decent holiday. So it all comes down to this. Hanging himself in his own garage. The poor sod just can't take it and tops himself without even eating the nice dinner I've made him."

Pete had been quietly making a few notes, and looked up when Kathy paused.

"So when did you last see him alive?"

"About six o'clock the night before last. Monday night."

Pete looked quizzical.

"Yes, I know what you're thinking. Why so long? Well, we'd had a bit of a fight. He'd said he'd be coming home for dinner, which is quite unusual, so I did his favourite, steak and onions, and a nice bottle of wine. So he walked in just before six, looking like he'd won the lottery. Talking nineteen to the dozen, waving his arms everywhere and going on about how our lives are going to change and we'll never be short of money again. I thought he'd been drinking, but there was no smell on his breath – I'd never seen him like it, he's....I mean he was... such an ordinary bloke normally. So I got him to sit down and said let's eat, and he said No, there's no time to eat, he's got to go out again, back to work for a few hours and then everything's going to be all right. Well. I just lost it. I said you've been saying you're going to make it for years now and you never have. The last thing you told me was that they were threatening you with redundancy, that's why you were working all those hours, to try and keep your job, which barely pays enough to keep us afloat, and now you're suddenly their blue-eyed boy?"

Pete could sense her anger rising, as it must have the Monday evening. "And then what?"

"And then the row just got worse and worse. He was shouting about me not having faith in him. I was yelling that I needed more than just promises. And then suddenly he'd break into a fit of giggles and try to hug me – he said "Stick with me, babe, it's gonna be a blast!" as if he was in some kind of American teen movie. So I just walked out. I said "I'm going off to my sister's for a while. Maybe when I get back you'll have finished whatever you have to do, and either saved the planet or driven us into bankruptcy. And I went out."

Pete waited patiently for her calmness to return.

"So you went to your sister's, which is where?"

"Weymouth, Dorset." Kathy gave him the address. "I stayed there till late afternoon, then drove back. I still couldn't face going home, and I remembered I had my gym kit in the boot, so I went for some exercise to clear my head".

"The 999 call came in at 12:20 am. Where had you been till then?"

Kathy hesitated.

"Kathy?"

"I was at the gym." She could sense that wasn't enough. "But when I got there I realised I wasn't in the mood to work out, so I sat in the club bar till they closed. I just didn't want to go home, but there wasn't anywhere else to go. And then I drove around for half an hour or so. I didn't want to get back here before midnight. He's... He was ...always out working in the evening, but he usually came back between eleven and twelve. Now I think about it, that was probably just so that I wouldn't

be too deep asleep to get his leg over if he was in the mood."
Pete raised his eyebrows.
"We've been together a long time, you know. After a while, relationships – well, you know? We were kind of soul mates to start with, everything was fun. But he changed when he got that job. Maybe I changed too, but we still had more to our marriage than most people do. He provided for us – just about, and I supported him – just about. That's how it works. Or that's how it worked. Till he decided to throw in the towel." Her eyes started moistening. She looked towards the window, and through it to her own house. The rain had started.
"I think I'll have that coffee now" Pete murmured, leaving Kathy still lost in her thoughts and making his way to the kitchen. Gloria was standing by the sink and started making his coffee without being asked. There was a moments silence except for the incessant ticking of the kitchen wall clock.
"What time do you think Kathy got home last night?" he asked eventually.
"Well, I'm not sure", Gloria replied, "but it was only a couple of minutes before we heard her scream. And then I dialled 999 while Graham went to see what was going on".
"And where is your husband today?"
"He had to go into work. He's deputy head at Eastleigh comp,

and they've got exams today"
"OK. Well, I'll need to have a word with him later. What time can I find him at home? I'll call first"
"Any time after five – here's our number" Gloria handed him a visiting card she'd had at the ready. Probably out of one of those machines in the motorway services. "Graham Marshall MA, DipEd, Private Tuition to A-level". Someone else not quite making ends meet. "I'll bring your coffee in when it's done"
Pete returned to the living room and sat down opposite Kathy. "You said you were having trouble staying afloat financially. Can you tell me more?"
Kathy seemed to have composed herself, and the faraway look had gone from her eyes.
"Look, what I was saying earlier. I don't want you to think I hated Mike or anything. We had our ups and downs like everyone else, and he'd always held down a decent job. It's just that he was always dreaming of bigger things, but from what I could see he was never going to make the big-time. That made for a lot of pressure on him, and you can see where that led him, but also on our relationship, so yes, we had a few rows, but it was a good marriage and I'm sorry he's gone.
"OK, so back to money"

“Well, that place isn’t cheap”, she nodded through the window, “but it’s not exactly South Fork. Since I gave up my job I’ve had to depend on Mike, so in all I guess we spend, what, two grand a month, just surviving?”
“And how much does he earn?”
“Well, that’s where most of the problems have come from. Those tight sods at the bank where he works have kept him at 40k since he got promoted”
Pete wrote the numbers down without commenting. There was a knock at the door and Gloria came in with the coffee. Pete stood up. “I’m just going to make a quick call”, he said as he left the room. Gloria sat down next to Kathy. “Are you going to tell the policeman about those other people?” she whispered.
Kathy looked blank. “What other people?”
“When you came home last night. There were three door slams.”
Kathy looked at Gloria for a few seconds, completely bewildered.
“Gloria, I know you mean well, but those kind of helpful observations are just going to cause confusion for the real detectives.” Then she had a troubling thought, and an image of herself standing by her car wiping between her thighs with her tee shirt while Gloria watched from her window. “But I assume

you didn't actually see me or anyone else from your bedroom?"

"Well no, but I was awake and I heard the doors. I didn't hear anyone else, though"

"So I'm not going to tell the policeman there was a gang of us, because there wasn't. I was getting stuff out of the car, that's all."

A disappointed "Oh." Was all Gloria could manage, as Pete came back into the room.

"We'll continue here for a few more minutes, if you don't mind", he said, settling back into the chair and picking up his coffee cup, "Mrs Marshall?" he looked pointedly at Gloria.

"I'll be in the kitchen then". Gloria gently took the cold cup of tea from Kathy's lap. As the door shut behind her, Pete continued.

"So your husband didn't even eat the dinner you'd prepared?"

"No" Kathy replied. "He didn't look like he'd anything at all, unless it was more of that Hash Brownie or whatever it was making him act so weirdly"

Pete's phone beeped twice. It was still in his hand.

"Excuse me, please. I'm expecting this" He glanced down, clicked twice and read the text message. He tapped a quick response and put the phone back in his pocket, pausing a few seconds to prepare the next question.

"Mrs Johnson, would it surprise you to learn that your husband's annual salary was over 120,000 pounds?"

If Kathy had still been holding her coffee cup she would have dropped it. She stared at him open-mouthed.

"You have to be fucking kidding me."

CHAPTER FOUR

Pete had asked his assistant PC to find out Mike Johnson's salary at the bank, and text it to him. He wasn't to know that the response would come back while he was with Kathy Johnson, but when it did arrive it was too good an opportunity to miss. People's reactions to unexpected news are very good indicators, even if they aren't exactly firm evidence. Pete was not surprised that Kathy reacted the way she did – but if she really did know Mike's true salary then she was a very good actor. Kathy wanted to know more though.

"How could he have been earning that kind of money? He didn't dress well, hardly ever went out, drove the cheapest company car he was allowed. We never took holidays. As for his salary, I don't think I ever saw his pay check - his money went straight into the bank. He was a really meticulous person as well, so each month he'd check the statement and balance it back to the check book. He was always worried about going overdrawn, and it was a close-run thing some months, from what I could see. Would the bank have known anything about where his money was going?"

"You'll have to take that up with the bank, I'm afraid" replied Pete. "Which bank do you use, as a matter of interest?"

"Barclays Bank. We always have done, we closed our other accounts when we got married and opened up a joint account at Barclays. I've seen the statements, since I've been out of a job the only credit going in was about three thousand quid going in on the second of every month. It's been the same for at least two years. Where would all the other money be going? Did he have another life? Another family? I can't see how he could have. He was working all the time he wasn't at home with me. And anyway, how could he have kept it from me? We were really close – I thought. We weren't as passionate as when we started out, but we had a laugh together and I thought I knew him so well. And now he's gone and I can't ask him......" her anger and frustration were starting to rise.

"But how did you find out about this massive salary, when I didn't even know" she said accusingly.

"I asked the bank he works for. That's normal in this kind of investigation. They were very sorry to hear about Mike's death, and were quite keen to cooperate with us. I'm going over there now to meet with them. I hope we can clear up a few things and find out what was behind this tragedy"

Pete left as quickly as he could, leaving Gloria to console an even more shocked and confused Kathy Johnson.

The main task Pete had assigned to his assistant when contacting the bank was to relay the sad news of Mike's death. The question about his salary was to be masked amongst many others such as his job title, responsibilities, second-in-command and previous employment. The assistant was also to arrange an interview for Pete with Mike's boss, as soon as possible. The response to that was surprisingly quick – if he could make it there by eleven o'clock the same morning they would meet with him then. Pete drove the short distance to United Midwest Bank, which he had heard about but never seen. It was on the Winchester side of the town, as the urban sprawl started to give way to little villages with thatched cottages and the traffic became noticeably lighter. Rounding a bend with open fields on either side, he was greeted by a large glass and steel building, almost like a cathedral silhouetted against the grey morning sky. Pete seemed to remember the site as an army barracks back in the days when he used to come this way with his parents on holiday, but all that history had been bulldozed to make way for this 21st century goldfish bowl. He drove up the sapling-lined drive and followed the signs to visitors parking.

At reception his ID was checked and he was issued with a

visitor's pass "To be displayed at all times on site". He was asked to wait in the atrium, which resembled a three-storey greenhouse, and sat in a large waiting area, which was scattered with carefully manicured potted plants and stands full of glossy publicity material. He picked a few out to while away the few minutes before the meeting at eleven. "Our Mission" was the title of one, but it seemed to be filled with eager-looking models dressed in snazzy suits, both male and female, so not to appear sexist, he supposed. He was thumbing through a brochure entitled "Global Custodian of the Year", trying to understand what that meant, when a smartly-dressed man of about thirty strode up to him, hand outstretched.

"Inspector Thomas?" Pete nodded, stood up and shook the offered hand.

"Dan Mahoney. Pleased to meet you, although under such difficult circumstances. I'm head of IT security. Tom Baxter is our director of operations and has asked me to sit in on your meeting with him. Will you follow me, please?"

The easy confidence, eye contact and careful dress were an impressive opener. Maybe IT geeks were different in banks from those he knew back at police HQ, with their pale complexions and half their lunch on their cardigans. In contrast, Dan Mahoney looked like he took regular holidays on some Caribbean beach – that light tan certainly wasn't sprayed on.

"First of all" Dan continued, as he led the way into the office complex, "Let me say how appalled we all were to hear the news of Mike's death. He was a lovely chap and a great manager. He'll be a severe loss to the bank and his colleagues"

"Yes, I'm sure it must have been a shock to you – did you work closely with Mr Johnson?"

"Oh yes. As you might guess, Information Technology plays quite a central role these days, so Mike's department and mine worked closely together."

They had reached a set of vending machines, opposite yet another area of comfortable chairs, glass tables and potted plants. There was a slightly moist cool breeze everywhere, as if the air conditioning was designed to emulate the rain forest to make the plants feel at home. Pete thought instead that it might be to encourage the staff to keep their jackets on and look smarter.

"We have a few minutes before the meeting, would you like some coffee?"

"Black, one sugar, please" Pete said for the millionth time in his career. "You'll have to forgive me, Mr Mahoney, but I don't know much about banking except that they clobber me for interest if I don't pay off the credit card each month. Mike Johnson worked in Money Transfer, didn't he? What does that mean?"

Dan handed him a plastic cup with a stirrer, half full of strong-looking black liquid, and pushed another button marked "White No Sugar".

"Well, Money Transfer is one of the few departments we have which actually does what you might think they do".

Pete smiled encouragingly.

"If one of our customers wants some money from his account here sent to someone else's account, either here or abroad, we do it for him – and make some money by charging a fee for the service."

"But I don't suppose you're actually sending pound notes down a phone line?" returned Pete, playing his 'I'm just a dumb old policeman' role.

Dan laughed.

"No, it's a bit more complex than that. In the UK, there's an electronic clearing system, CHAPS. We send payment instructions to the paying bank, like an email message, through the CHAPS system, and so do all the other banks. At the end of the day the banks settle between them just the difference between what they've sent and what they've received. All the time it's just numbers held on accounts at the clearing banks. When the instruction gets to the beneficiary's bank – "

Pete looked confused.

" – the beneficiary is the person our customer wants to pay, so his bank tells him the money's arrived and he can do what he wants with it. If the money is going abroad, it's slightly different, there's a system called SWIFT which is a standardised message system dealing with all the world's currencies"

Pete didn't want to hear too much more detail.

"So what do you contribute to this operation?" he asked, as they sat in two of the comfy chairs with their coffees.

"Well, the computer systems we use have to be well locked down in terms of security. If the instructions come from the web through our secure banking software we need to authenticate the source of the instructions. If the instruction came through CHAPS or SWIFT it's already authenticated, so we move it through our systems and check that there's enough cash in the account before making the payment. That's the work of the Money Transfer department, and each one of the operators there is individually identified and logged as they work on each instruction. My department, IT security, sets up the operator Ids and passwords, authentication levels and so on, and ensures that the appropriate controls are in place. Basically these controls are programmed in and we respond to any flags that the system raises."

"So I couldn't send myself some money while your back is turned"

"It would be fun watching you try. You'd need a login ID, then access to the transfer functionality, then you'd have to have a friend in the same department who would have to have the authority to approve it. He or she could approve the transaction, then the transaction would have to escape a lot of "Flagging" reports that my department looks at. On top of that, you'd have to take the money from one of our customers' accounts, and they'd yell pretty quickly if money went missing. Our employees aren't allowed accounts here at the bank anyway, so there's no way they can top themselves up....." He stopped abruptly and flushed. 'Topping yourself' was well-known slang for suicide.

"I'm sorry, I got a bit carried away – that was an unfortunate turn of phrase in the circumstances." He stood and looked at his watch. "Shall we go up to the meeting?"

Pete smiled sensitively, and they both dropped their empty cups in the waste bin, then he let Dan lead the way to the first floor conference room. They passed through what appeared to be an aircraft hanger full of people sitting staring at computer terminals. All the screens seemed to show the same kind of information, but as keys were pressed and mouses clicked the details would disappear and be replaced with the next one in the queue. Fixed to the ceiling was an illuminated ticker-tape board showing queues, wait times and performance against targets. It felt like a large MacDonalds franchise, except there was hardly a murmur of conversation.

Halfway down the corridor between the banks of desk, Pete touched Dan's elbow and stopped to ask him a question.

"You said everyone has their own ID. Presumably all these people are human?" He made it sound like he had his doubts. "What happens when they go to the loo, or out for a fag break? What's to stop someone else doing the dirty with their computer screen, pretending to be them?"

"The terminals are set to time out if they are left without a key stroke for more than five minutes, then you have to key in the password again. We also have some floor-walkers around, looking for empty chairs and active screens. They can post a ticket on the screen if they think there's a security breach, and that can result in disciplinary action"

Pete raised his eyebrows. And he thought we had it bad in Portsmouth, avoiding traffic wardens, he thought.

They reached a large conference room at the end of the floor, all glass again. A middle-aged, balding man was seated next to a stunning young blonde woman. Both stood up and shook hands with Pete as Dan introduced him. Pete's first reaction was that the woman, about thirty years old and dressed in a tailored navy suit and cream silk blouse, must be one of the models from the glossy brochures in the entrance lobby.
"Tom Baxter, Director of Operations" said the balding man in a broad American accent. "And this is Amanda McCarthy, deputy head of the Money Transfer department. Such shocking news, we just can't understand it." He gestured to a chair and closed the door. "Please sit down Inspector Thomas. How may we help you?"
Pete cleared his throat. "I'm sure you're all very busy, so I'll get straight to the point of my visit. I'd like to get some idea of what Mr Johnson's job entailed"
"Well, it's fairly straightforward," began Baxter, "Mike headed up our Money Transfer department, supervising a total of some forty staff, managing a budget of around five million dollars. The department handles about two thousand transactions a day with an average value of two hundred thousand dollars. On top of that, various systems and operations improvement projects, compliancy with banking regulations, disaster contingency

planning, standards and procedures"
Pete decided to interrupt to avoid another list of corporate objectives.
"Sounds like a lot of responsibility. Would you say that Mr Johnson was under a lot of pressure?"
Baxter leaned back in his chair. "Well, you know, International Banking is a pressure environment, and we only hire or promote those we think are capable of handling it. The highest level executives, of course, are Americans, and quite frankly we're used to high stress levels."
Pete deliberately looked unimpressed by the 'big-Yank' approach.
"As you know, my assistant asked you for details of Mr Johnson's position, contacts and salary, so I don't have to ask you those questions. In summary, though, would you say that Mr Johnson was paid competitively?"
"Of course" replied Baxter glibly. "We are at the forefront of our business. Personnel and satisfaction levels are very high on our agenda. Mike Johnson was paid more than he would by most of our competitors, with a handsome profit-related bonus as well. I hope you're not implying that his remuneration had anything to do with his suicide?"
"No, No" said Pete, quickly. "In fact, the opposite. It may be

that the way he spent such a large salary contributed to his problems"

"If I may, Inspector" interrupted Amanda McCarthy, "That's one area we can't really do much about. We do, however, have counselling services available if employees need them. I'm pretty sure we would have seen signs in Mike if anything was amiss, though". She spoke in a voice as angelic as her looks. There was, however, a detectable accent, not the received pronunciation Pete would have expected in this seemingly all Rhodes-scholar environment. Her rounded vowels indicated South Coast, probably not too far from here.

"I'm afraid there must have been something, Ms McCarthy," Pete turned towards Mike's deputy and smiled condescendingly. "People simply don't commit suicide for no reason. Whatever pressures there were that led to Mr Johnson's demise, they must have started somewhere, and I have reason to believe he was under immense stress here. Mr Johnson was responsible for that floor-full of people out there, moving millions of pounds around in a tight timeframe. I'm told he had to compile reports and his performance was under close scrutiny. How stressful could all that have been for him, do you think?"

Amanda looked confused, then continued brightly. "Well, I

have to say, thanks to Mike Johnson since his arrival three years ago we've become a world-class, extremely smooth operating unit" she replied. Her eyes seemed to light up when she spoke. Pete wondered how the subject of banking could hold any interest for such a vivacious woman. "Obviously," she continued, "we have deadlines to meet, such as the three pm CHAPS cut-off, but we all work well together and there's never a lot of yelling and screaming going on. You should visit the Foreign Exchange dealers desk in London if you want to see a high-pressure environment."

"And as for his performance, the personnel department can give you copies of his annual appraisals, if you want" Baxter was exerting his authority. He was now the bank spokesperson and seemed to be getting protective. "You will see that his performance was in the top quartile, and indeed he received a twenty percent discretionary bonus just a few weeks ago. I know, because I gave him it"

Pete was getting frustrated now. "OK, so he's a great performer. His job isn't under threat. But he's still working all hours that God sends to meet his deadlines. That must be stressful. If it's such a cosy environment and Johnson is so good at it, why did he spend all his evenings and weekends working?".

McCarthy and Baxter looked at each other and frowned.
“He didn’t”, offered McCarthy. “We have a policy of encouraging substantial quality time away from the office, so most managers work a staggered eight-hour day. Mike was always the last to leave his department, but he was always out by six pm”.

CHAPTER FIVE

Pete went home for lunch. He often did, rather than grab a sandwich at his desk or a salad or bowl of soup at the police cafe. He's seen plenty of TV programmes where the tired old detective would live on his own because his wife had left him, eating beans and chips at the canteen or living on takeaways. These days detective work was like most other jobs – you were expected to be available when you were needed, but you had some flexibility in the hours you spent at your desk. Pete sometimes worked quite late into the evening at the office, but would then make up for it by spending the afternoon at home dozing in front of an old movie in his comfy chair. The exception to this flexibility was the "On-call" status, where he had to be available when required, so he would spend the time on his new hobby, geocaching. He'd invested in a GPS device recently, and every chance he had he would be wandering around the countryside with it, looking for plastic boxes hidden by other devotees of the game. All the information he needed for this hobby was on the internet, so he spent many hours in front of the screen in their spare room, which gave his wife Jenny plenty of her own time to watch the soaps and quiz shows that were her relaxation. She had been to college, and got her degree in fine arts, then went on to a teaching degree and was a teacher for a few years until the kids came along. When the kids had grown up and left home, she thought about going back to teaching, but realised that such a thankless devotion of her soul in trying to get teenagers to absorb knowledge was really for a younger woman. She simply didn't have the energy to face kids who didn't want to learn anything, so she never went back. She spent a few years getting a law degree at Southampton University, and now she was a trainee solicitor. She worked nine till six in nearby Portswood and loved it. She was at home for lunch as often as Pete was.

The two of them sat at the breakfast bar with a toasted cheese sandwich each and orange juice. Jenny was wearing one of several dark business suits she kept for work, a light-coloured blouse and 'sensible' shoes. Pete thought the business attire actually made her look very sexy, and he'd lost count of the number of times he'd tried to drag her into the bedroom on these lunch breaks, usually (but not always) without success. He reflected with a smug grin that it's not easy to go back to work in the afternoon looking like he'd been wrestling fully clothed, and hiding the fact that, yes, that was exactly what he had been doing.

Jenny had her hair up, as she did for work 'to make her look serious', even though Pete preferred it down. She was describing a client she'd met that morning.

"So she's sitting right opposite me wearing an old jumper and jogging bottoms, obviously hadn't washed her hair for days and stinking of stale fags, wittering on about how she wants to take her husband to the cleaners. I'm surprised she knows where the cleaners is. Honestly, I couldn't tell whether she had dandruff or it was cigarette ash all down her front. Of course, it's his fault the marriage broke up, he was always on the lookout for a bit on the side, hardly surprising, and now he's found some. Some slapper works behind the bar down the social club, all make-up and no drawers – probably puts out for every bloke who walks in. But this client's telling me she's been clever, you see, she's got pictures of them both together, after she's staked out the bedsit where they sneak off to do it before he comes home after work. Now she wants to divorce him, keep the house and take his car plus half his pension! So I have to try and explain how all this "Who did what to Whom" stuff is irrelevant these days, despite how rich she wants to be. It's sometimes difficult to get people to see the real world, isn't it?"

Jenny could see that Pete was just nodding in the right places,

so she asked about his day instead.
“What are you working on, then?”
Pete had no problem discussing his cases with Jenny, any more than any other couple would discuss happenings at work. He’d try to avoid names, as Jenny had done, but they both knew that what they discussed would remain between them. She knew already that he’d been called out the previous evening, she’d felt him creep back into bed in the early hours and had sleepily rolled over to cuddle into him.
“Apparently it’s an open and shut case - suicide. It was a bit of a nasty one, not the usual handful of pills. This couple over at Eastleigh didn’t seem to get on very well, and last night she came home and found him hanging from the garage ceiling. We can’t pin down the motive just yet. He was drugged up to the eyeballs, and it looks like he’s been shunting half his pay packet off to someone else”
Pete took another bite of toast. Remembering the image of the dead man lying on the floor, he took a gulp of tea to wash it down.
“Must be another woman” Jenny smiled “Paying the rent for her, maintaining the kid she’s had by him maybe. Jewellery, holidays, posh dinners, clothes, all the little spoiling things we married women can only dream of?”

"It's different when you're having a bit on the side. You dish out all kind of sexy presents and stuff because it's still a novelty. And you don't mind paying through the nose either, as long as you're getting what you want in return. When she stops obliging, you stop paying – easy as that. It's not like being married, after all" Pete observed dryly.
Jenny almost rose to the bait, opened her mouth to object, then, seeing the telltale half smile on his face, contented herself with a sardonic "Yes, dear, of course"
"Although I must say, if it is a woman then there's already a frontrunner at the bank where he works. I was over there earlier – tall, blonde, pretty, clever. Mmm, I wouldn't mind if I did...." He felt her piercing glare and realised he might be winding her up too tightly. "But certainly not in your league, sweetheart"
Jenny forced a smile and continued eating.
"But I can't see her having anything to do with the money side of it." he went on "She's obviously not short of a few bob herself, so I don't think the payments are to her. Anyway, an affair isn't big news these days, even royalty have those and nobody bats an eyelid"
"So it must be blackmail" offered Jenny "He must have a guilty secret and he's paying someone off. Then they've asked for more than he could give and he's topped himself. I don't

suppose this bloke was ever a priest, was he? Maybe someone confided something to him, and now he's been tortured and killed after he's been made to reveal the secret?"
"No he wasn't a priest", chuckled Pete, "and there is no dastardly plot against society, and this isn't a Dan Brown book. And if he's kept some secret from his wife for three years, we haven't got much chance of finding it ourselves"
"But why does it matter? The poor bloke's gone and won't be back any time soon. And it doesn't matter if he was insured, as most policies exclude suicide. I learnt that in one of my courses". She smiled professionally. Pete could feel some familiar stirrings, but thought better than act on them.
"We have to get to the bottom of it all, just to tie up loose ends really, he continued, "We need to be sure there's no foul play involved, and then you're right, it doesn't really matter what pushed him into doing it. I don't know. I always think it's a shame when people are driven to suicide, it's such an admission of hopelessness. There surely must be a better way out, always. Of course, the people left behind are the ones to suffer in the end. His wife was in a real state when I saw her this morning. Poor woman doesn't seem to know what day it is. Anyway, I've got to go back to work in a minute. I'll be a bit late tonight, I'm going round to see the bloke who lives

opposite the Suicide Man, to see if he was party to any of those secrets"
"Well, if you're really off to see your fancy woman from the bank, tell her you can't afford any more jewellery, because you're saving up for my surprise birthday present"
"That gives me till December, at least"
"But my birthday's in Novemb – " Jenny stopped mid-word, well aware that Pete was grinning broadly even as he walked out the front door.

The office was quiet when Pete got back, not much urgency in the air, and Dave Seddon was at his desk reading from a folder in front of him. Dave looked up.
"Hope you don't mind Pete – SOC sent up their draft report and I didn't have much else to do, so I've had a quick look. That domestic thing hasn't been moving much, and nothing new has come in since your Suicide Man"
"No sweat Dave" replied Pete. "Saves me ploughing through all the jargon, plus a second pair of eyes welcome, and all that stuff. I tell you what, though, that glass cathedral they call a bank was a bit of an eye opener. It's no wonder people get up in arms about all the money they get. I didn't see one suit that wasn't Versacci or Armani. Made my hundred quid Burton

look right out of place. And the skirt!" He looked around in case there was any female eavesdropper hearing his rather non-PC language. "I tell you, there's not a bird in there who's over thirty five. Beats the hell out of this place for scenery. I might have to go back and question a few of them again. Anyway, on to our Suicide Man's report. What have we got?"

Dave grinned good-naturedly at Pete's assessment of the banking staff. From his days not so long ago as a single man he knew too well the difference between talent on show and actually available.

"Scenes of Crime went over the house and garage. They couldn't find anything out of the ordinary apart from the two unfinished meals in the kitchen and the bank statement in the bedroom that you tipped them off about"

"And of course the dead body on the floor with a noose around it's neck"

"O.K., wise guy, plus the dead body. In the garage, there were traces of sawdust on the floor under the body and on the bench under the hook in the wall. Under the microscope the sawdust matched the beam and the wall. The electric drill had been tidied away, but one of the drill bits still had traces of wood, which matched the sawdust from the wall, so he drilled that one last, if that is in any way significant. In a drawer of the workbench there were more hooks the same size as those in the wall and ceiling. There was no blood on the floor, just traces of the usual body fluids."

Pete made a face. Bodies do horrible things when they're left hanging. He interrupted Dave.

"So, no blood means only that he didn't cut himself. The drop onto the noose would have stopped his heart anyway, so he wouldn't have bled after that"

"Yes, but the complication is that 'Have-a-go-Harry' cutting him down resulted in a pile of bones and innards hitting the floor like a pavement pizza"

Pete wished he hadn't had that last mouthful of cheese on toast.

"I assume you're paraphrasing the more technical detail in Ted's report?"

"Of course." Dave continued.

"The team had a look at Johnson's car. Again, nothing out of the ordinary. The car was immaculately clean, which is probably the way he always kept it, given the neatness of his side of the bedroom. No shopping or petrol receipts, no flyers from under the wipers, no sweet wrappers, no old shopping lists, post-it notes or parking tickets, but in the boot, in the spare wheel compartment, they found a couple of things – a copy of yesterday's "Sun" newspaper and a mobile phone.

"Seems an odd place to keep your mobile" observed Pete.
"Was there anything in the calls list?"
"I thought you might ask that, Sherlock" Dave continued, "Just one contact, named "Spike", and loads of calls to him, going back several months, the last one being a week ago. No incoming calls at all."
"Maybe our Mr. Johnson was doing some heavy breathing calls instead of coming home for his tea. Have our boys tracked down an address to go with Spike's number?"
Dave looked down and checked the report.
"No, it says here that it's a pay-as-you-go phone, no address registered."
"Hmm." Pete sounded intrigued. "That doesn't gel with a cosy domestic suburban life, does it? It does fit in with someone who's got his share of secrets, though. Did they dial the number?"
"Of course. Got a 'No longer in service' message".
Pete picked up his desk phone and dialled an internal number.
"Ted, it's Pete Thomas. It's about the Johnson case. Thanks for your report. Some interesting stuff there. Did you bring everything from his car back to the station?" He paused, listening to the answer. "Great, I'll pop down now and have a look at it." Pete replaced the receiver and reached over to take

the report from Dave.

Dave looked quizzical. "Something not right?"

"Well, unless it's to look at some tart with her tits out on page three, I don't really see Johnson being the type to buy the Sun. I would doubt the security folk would let that rag through the hallowed portals of their precious bank. Maybe there was something special in yesterday's edition".

Pete left the room and headed downstairs to where Ted and the Scenes Of Crime team were based.

Ted was on the phone to someone, but on his desk were two clear plastic evidence bags. One contained the phone, the other the newspaper. Ted indicated "Help yourself" and carried on talking. Pete pulled up a chair and sat down, put on his latex gloves and took the newspaper out. As he flipped through, he noticed that Miss Page Three was indeed, noteworthy, but probably not relevant. There seemed to be nothing significant in the newspaper at all, which was exactly how he remembered The Sun, so not too surprising. Then he reached the sports page, racing section. There were pen markings next to the runners in seven different races at three different racecourses. Pete took out his notebook and made a quick note of the races and runners, then carefully replaced the newspaper in its plastic bag.

Ted interrupted his call, with a "Can you hold on a few seconds please?", put his hand over the mouthpiece and whispered to Pete. "Something I didn't put in the report yet, didn't know if it was relevant. We did both the Johnsons' cars as a matter of procedure. When we went over Mrs Johnson's car we found a very distinctive triangular damp patch on the back seat. Still quite fresh, like the previous night. A bit of a giveaway, if you know what I mean"

Pete didn't often look surprised, but this was one of those moments.

"I'll be a few more minutes on this call" Ted continued. "Need anything else?"

"I need a copy of today's paper, one with the racing results in it, like the Mirror or the Sun" Pete whispered back.

Ted pointed to an unoccupied desk in a corner, with a copy of the Daily Mirror in the In-tray, and continued with his phone call.

Pete sat at the desk and opened the Mirror to the sports page, looking for the previous days sports results. He checked the notes he'd just made against each race shown on the Daily Mirror results page. Taking them in chronological order of when the race was run, he added to his notes the position and starting price of the horses Johnson had picked out. Each one of the first six horses had won, at good odds. The seventh horse had come second.

CHAPTER SIX

The huge car park was screened from public view by some tasteful landscaping. The publicity following the successful planning application included an announcement that the developers would be building a special tunnel under the car park so that the resident badgers would not be disturbed. Some, of course, would have seen this as a sop to the conservationists who had fought so long to prevent any building in this beautiful part of the Dorset countryside. At this hour, early in the morning, the car park was less than a quarter full, with the management section having the fewest empty spaces. That section was distinctive, though, in consisting mainly of Audis, BMWs and other high-spec new cars. There was room here for the eccentric, however – the parked cars included a Ford Thunderbird and a Hummer. The management section was, of course, full of company cars, while the rest of the car park was for those who had to provide their own transport. Kathy had been sitting behind the wheel of her own car in the visitors section for the last half an hour, watching the car park slowly fill up and the people in suits scurrying off to the relative warmth of the Mid Western bank offices. A sleek white convertible pulled up and stopped in its allotted space. Kathy opened her car door, got out and walked over to intercept the driver. Amanda McCarthy had just turned away from locking her car door when she saw Kathy barring her way. Amanda blanched, recovered and addressed Kathy in a soft, sympathetic tone.

"Oh, Kathy. Kathy. I'm so, so sorry." She stepped forward to embrace Kathy.

Kathy held her ground but let Amanda embrace her and hold her a few seconds. She stood back and tearfully looked for answers in Amanda's eyes.

"What's it all about, Amanda? Why did he do it? I just don't understand anything anymore"

"Look, Kathy. It's early days yet. You're still in shock. You shouldn't be wandering the streets on your own. Don't you have someone you can stay with, a friend or something?"

"No, I'm fine. I stayed with my neighbour Gloria last night. I just can't figure out why he did it. We weren't blissfully happy but we were OK, and we've always been the best of friends, so how could he keep any secrets from me? I thought the answer must be here, at the bank. Maybe you can help me fill in some of the gaps?"

"Kathy, I really have to get in and start work. Do you want to meet up for a coffee later? I'll make some time so we can talk,

but we can't just stand here in the Car Park"
"No, I'm fine" Kathy repeated. "I just need to work out what he was up to. You worked closely with him, Amanda – he must have said something to you. What was he spending all our money on?" Kathy started to get a little tearful. "That was our money, not just his. That was our future. That's why he needed to get on so well at work, that's why he was always working late, he said. It was so we could buy somewhere and spend some time together. What happened to all that?"
"Kathy, Mike was a good man and a hard worker." Amanda paused as she considered telling Kathy about Mike always leaving work on time, but thought better of it. "But I don't think it was the pressure of work that drove him to it. We worked together every day, and I can't see – " Amanda broke off as she saw a change in Kathy's eyes. "What? What are you thinking, Kathy?"
"So you worked closely together, eh? How closely, Amanda? Were you just as close together outside of work? Is there anything you want to confess to me? Like you know where half of our money was going, because it was going to you?"
Amanda pulled back with a horrified look on her face.
"Can you be serious, Kathy? Can you hear what you're saying? Your poor husband's been driven to suicide and you think I

might have something to do with it? Mike was a lovely bloke and a great colleague. We'll all miss him terribly, but believe me, I'm as much in the dark as you are about why he might have done what he did. Please, Kathy, go home, or go to Gloria's and take a few sedatives. Like I said, you're still in shock. You don't know what you're saying" Amanda put her arms around Kathy's shoulder. "Look, you know damn well that there has never been anything between Mike and me, and you know why. And I have to say, I don't think Mike was the kind to be messing with anyone else either" She kissed the top of Kathy's head. "Now please go home and rest. I'm going in to work and see if I can't get through the day as if it was normal. God knows, we all loved Mike and it's just a terrible, terrible thing that's happened"

"You're right, of course, Amanda" Kathy sobbed. "I just don't know what to do. I need to find some sense in all this, though".

"Hang on a minute, did you say half his money was going somewhere else? Wouldn't his salary all be paid into the one account?" Amanda looked confused. "If it's a joint account you would have noticed the payments going out each month, wouldn't you?"

"That's just it" Kathy whimpered, "I've checked our bank account at the Halifax and it shows the pay going in every

month, but the amount is what Mike told me he was earning, not what that detective told me he was really getting".
Amanda fished around in her bag for her phone, and dialled a number. "At least we can clear up that one quite quickly" she said as she waited for an answer.
"Hi, Rowena? It's Mandy. I'm with Mrs Johnson. Yes, I know I shouldn't be involved in this, and yes, I'll refer any future questions to Human Resources so they can rely on behalf of the bank, blah, blah, blah. But I need you to confirm something to me. I hope we can skip a few formalities? Good. Now, can you tell me which bank Mike's salary was paid into each month? Yes, I'll hold on"
Kathy started drying her eyes. Maybe something was going to become clearer.
"OK, Rowena, thanks a lot. See you at lunch time". Amanda hung up and looked at Kathy. "Apparently Mike's salary, all of it, was paid into an online account with Co-operative Bank".
"Oh" was all that Kathy could utter. Then without a word of thanks she turned abruptly and walked back to her car.

She didn't really have much idea where she was driving, only that the centre of Portsmouth seemed like a good idea. The traffic was quite heavy now as it was both rush hour and school-run hour. It seemed to her that twenty years ago, when she went to school, she walked everywhere, she wasn't driven a half mile in a people-carrier to double-park outside the school to be dropped off. Indeed, she remembered her mother telling her than in her day she would have not only walked to and from school at start and end of the day, but would have to walk home at lunchtime as well, as she wasn't allowed to have school lunches. In those post-war days they also gave out free school milk in the mornings and had outside toilets, not to mention the lice inspections, so at least some things had changed. This little daydream of a safer, more innocent past seemed quite a comfort to Kathy, so she let herself stay there a while. She was brought back to modern reality by a honking from the cars behind as she lingered a few seconds to long at a changing traffic light. She thought it best to park as soon as she could, surely there would be a Co-op bank in the centre of Portsmouth? She pulled over and stopped next to a parking meter, put in enough coins for an hour, and started walking up from the Bargate, which is a beautifully preserved section of the old city wall, but today was simply a landmark for her to find her car later. She remembered someone showing her Smartphone app that would remember where your car was parked and guise you back to it with a GPS map. Certainly different from her sixties dream environment. She passed a McDonalds and a Wimpy without a thought that she hadn't eaten for almost twenty-four hours. Finally she reached a crossroads where a lot of banking premises seemed to be clustered together. There was Halifax, of course, Nationwide, Barclays, then she saw just a little further down the one she wanted, the Cooperative Bank. She marched up to the door and through into the lobby, where she could see they had just opened for business. There were three cashiers behind the glass partitions, all waiting to serve her, dressed in identical uniforms and armed with identical smiles. She chose the girl on the far left and walked up to address her, keeping her voice low.

"I'd like some information about an account, please?"

"And in whose name is the account?" smiled the cashier.

"Johnson, 14 Briar Crescent, Eastleigh. Here's my passport"

Kathy took her passport from her handbag and slid it under the glass wall.

The cashier tapped a few keys and studied her computer monitor.

"Yes, we have an online account in that name, and registered at that address, but it's in the name of a Mr Michael Johnson" The cashier pushed Kathy's passport back to her. "I'm afraid we can't give out any details except to the account holder."

“But I’m his wife”
“I’m afraid that makes no difference, madam, unless it’s a joint account with your name on it, which it isn’t”
“Well, what if I told you that Mr Johnson is dead? He died last night”
The cashier swallowed, but training kicked in and she didn’t bat an eyelid.
“I’m very sorry to hear that, Mrs Johnson, really I am. But the rules are very strict. I would need written authority from his estate. I’m afraid that until you have that I can’t do anything”
“But I’m his bloody widow!” Kathy was getting a little heated.
“Please don’t get abusive with me, or I’ll have to call security. I’m afraid I can’t discuss the account with you”
“Can you at least tell me if the account in his name only, or was a joint account with someone else?”
The cashier could see exactly where this was leading, but held her nerve.
“I’m afraid I can’t madam. You have my every sympathy, and I can have a more senior advisor discuss the procedure with you if you like, in one of our private conference rooms?”
“No, don’t bother. I don’t need your fucking sympathy. It’ll all get clearer soon enough” and Kathy stormed out.

The Cricketers Pub in Eastleigh is a large, “Olde Worlde” kind of establishment that still prides itself in good food and carefully kept real ales. It has a large beer garden and is on a main road, so it’s popular with families. On weekdays, though, it can be quiet, as Kathy found when she walked in just after lunch. Cheri, the landlord’s wife, was polishing glasses behind the bar, and there were no diners or drinkers. These were the hours that most publicans hated, with a busy lunchtime and early evening service either side, so all they really wanted to do was have a few hours sleep rather than serve a few people who would stroll in and sit in a corner for the afternoon over one drink.

“Well, well, well, if it isn’t young Kathy! How you doing, love?” A typically hospitable welcome, but with meaning, as Kathy had often been here with Mike.

“Bloody awful, Cheri. Give us a double G and T, will you?”

Cheri poured the drink and went back to polishing glasses. She kept up what she thought was the normal “hell of a day” banter.

“So what’s he gone and done now?”

“Topped himself”

There was a split second where Cheri thought Kathy must be joking. Then she realised she wasn’t. Then Cheri dropped the glass she’d been polishing. The very loud crash brought her

husband Tom running through from the kitchen. He stopped before saying anything because he'd seen the look on Cheri's face. She hadn't moved, still polishing the imaginary glass, the real one being in pieces on the floor. Kathy broke the silence.
"Yes, bloody Mike killed himself on Tuesday night. I've got no idea why" she continued matter-of-factly.
Cheri and Tom looked at each other. Tom, being the landlord, took control and was first to speak.
"Wow, I'm so sorry love. Here, have this on us" He took Kathy's untouched drink and added another shot of gin.
"I was on my way back from Southampton, so I thought I'd just drop in and say hi. I really don't know what to do, so I thought I'd drink enough to go straight to bed when I get home."
"Sensible idea, apart from having to drive home" commented Tom.
"Can't say as I care much about that" replied Kathy, and drank the triple G&T straight down.
"Look," she continued. "There's something I need to ask you, Cheri, and I want the truth. I'll know if you're lying, believe me"
Tom looked at Cheri a little nervously. What was going on here? Cheri felt her heckles rising, but tried not to sound

defensive.

"You can ask anything you like sweetheart, you'll get the truth from me"

"OK. Were you screwing Mike?"

Cheri paused, gave Tom a "Whatever next?" look, turned to Kathy and smiled sympathetically.

"That's easy, love. He would have liked nothing better, but so would most of the blokes who drink here. And Mike would have been near the top of the list if I was that type, but I'm not. No, Mike was lovely but he was a customer. Nothing more. Now, you need to get yourself home to bed before you're too pissed to walk to your car".

CHAPTER SEVEN

Pete hadn't been inside a betting shop for years. He hadn't really thought about it, but as he was driving through the Eastleigh suburbs he had time to reflect that it had been a big thing in the sixties, his Dad had told him, when gambling had become legal. Up till then, any betting on horses and dogs had to be conducted at the actual racetrack. There was, of course, betting on football results, but this was arranged through a system of agents who would collect "the pools coupons" from the punters' homes. The coupons listed all the football games to be played that Saturday, and all you had to do was to mark a 1, 2 or X next to eight different games. The strange thing was the scoring system, one point if you'd correctly predicted a win for the home team, two points if you'd picked a win for the away team, but three points if you'd guessed correctly that it would be a drawn game by marking an X. Pete remembered even now the poor "Pools Man" who would stand at his parents' doorstep while Dad went off to find his completed coupon and the two bob stake money. Pete smiled as he remembered – it was always £75,000 pounds for the jackpot. He remembered his Dad promising them all a share of that figure every Saturday as he watched the teleprinter on the "Grandstand" sports program on their black and white television. They would, as a family, check the coupon as the results came in, and cheer each time points were scored on Dad's coupon. He wondered whether seventy-five grand was a legal limit for the payout back then? It would hardly buy a decent car nowadays.

As for gambling now, Pete's experience was minimal. Whenever there was a sweepstake at work, for a big race like the Grand National or the Derby, he would cough up a pound for the name of a randomly chosen horse, but it usually turned out to be an outsider with no hope, a bit like the lottery syndicate he'd been persuaded to join. He considered the mentality behind gambling. Could it become a habit so bad that you got in deeper and deeper and the stress could become strong enough for suicide? He thought back again to his childhood. He had a distant memory of a smoke-filled shop with blacked-out windows where once his mum had sent him to fetch his dad, late home on a Saturday lunch time. His Dad, embarrassed, had ushered him out of the place as soon as he'd wandered in, as if he'd stumbled into some satanic ritual. All Pete could remember was a lot of blokes sitting around in silence as a radio loudspeaker swawked out what must have been a race commentary, the words coming faster and increasing in pitch as the horses approached the finish line, and as they crossed it there was a collective moan from almost everyone there, and a confetti of torn up race tickets dropped to the floor.

His dad would not have recognised the establishment Pete walked into that afternoon. Carpeted floor, drink and snack vending machines, not an ashtray in sight, although he'd passed a smoking area outside. Even the multiple TV screens on the wall seemed clean, and you could actually see through the windows to the real world, although he had noticed before entering that the public could not see in. He'd chosen this bookie at random, assuming they were all more or less the same, by looking in the Yellow Pages under "Betting Shops". There were seventeen in the Eastleigh area, which surprised him, as he thought that online betting must have driven many out of business, as online retail seemed to have done to many neighbourhood shops. Strangely, most of the betting shops in Yellow Pages seemed to be called "BetFred", which he assumed must be a franchise, like MacDonald's, so instead he chose one which had its own identity, and he hoped would give him a more candid view of the business. Pate walked up to the counter, behind which sat a rather bored-looking middle-age woman. She was filling in a Sudoku grid from a book full of them, her concentration being so intense that it was a full minute before she noticed Pete standing in front of her. He flashed his warrant card discretely, and asked her if he could speak to the manager. She pressed a button under the desk without uttering a word, and pointed to some comfortable chairs not unlike those Pete had relaxed in earlier at the bank. Pete sat and looked around. There were two quite young men playing on slot machines, but no-one else in the "shop". The TVs played continually different sports from different countries and parts of the UK. It seemed like there was a ball being kicked or batted , a horse leaping over a fence or a greyhound chasing a rabbit somewhere at all times around the globe. A few minutes later a man in a long-sleeved casual shirt, smart trousers and trainers emerged from the back room, spoke briefly with the woman and came over to meet him.

"My name's Johnny Smith, officer", the man shook Pete's hand "I hope we're not in trouble for anything?"

"No, I just need some help understanding some gambling procedure, and yours was the first Turf Accountant I came across" Pete smiled. He had actually used that old-fashioned phrase to search Yellow Pages, and was surprised when the results were all financial advisors and landscape gardeners.

"I think we're allowed to call ourselves Betting Shops these days", said Smith, visibly relieved that there was no suspicion of a crime. "So how can I help you?"
"I'm working on a case that's possibly gambling-related, and I can't go into any details, but I'd like your advice on a hypothetical horse racing scenario."
"Let's take a seat" offered Johnny, and they went to a corner away from the cashier, although she had already gone back to her book. "So let's hear your scenario" he continued as they sat.
"The problem I have," Pete began, "is that this scenario caused someone a huge problem, with catastrophic results, and I can't see why it got so intense. Anyway, here goes. Let's say I'm going to bet on seven horses. If I pick out the seven horses, and six of them come in winners, that should make me quite happy, shouldn't it? Even if the seventh doesn't win?"
"Yes, you should be happy," Johnny replied, "unless you gambled more on the last race than you'd won in the previous six. As far as how happy it makes you, that would depend on the SP, which are the Starting Prices, and by that I mean the odds given for a win when the bet was placed. In each race where your horse wins, you'll make a profit even if your horse was an odds-on favourite, for example odds of five to four on,

because you get your stake money back, so if your stake was five pounds you'd win four pounds plus you'd get your five pounds back making a total of nine pounds. But if the odds were good, say you put a tenner on each horse and the odds were three to one, you'd get forty pounds back for your tenner. If that was the same for each of seven races and you got six winners out of seven you'll get a total of two hundred and forty pounds back for your seventy quid investment. Not bad for a day's work, but us bookies would soon be out of business if you found a way of doing that every day!"

Pete appreciated the speed at which Smith had calculated the winnings, but wasn't too impressed by the rate of return in this "hypothesis".

"No, I wouldn't be doing it every day, just once, I think. So if I wanted to win thousands I'd have to put a heck of a lot of money down – forty thousand to win a quarter of a million. In my scenario, I know already that tens of thousands of pounds are being spent somewhere on a regular basis"

"Well, you wouldn't get me or any high street bookie to take thousands in stake money. It would ruin us if the bet came good, however unlikely it might be. Of course, you could use an accumulator"

"Which is?"

“It’s a bet where the proceeds of each win rolls forward as the stake in the next bet. The forty pounds you won on race one is the stake in race two. The hundred and sixty winnings from that goes on to race three, and so on. If your seventh horse wins you’ve just won a hundred and sixty thousand pounds”

“And if it loses?”

“You’ve just lost forty thousand”.

Pete thought for a moment. “That puts things a little bit in perspective. Thank you. Just one more thing – how many betting shops, say, within twenty miles of Portsmouth would take a bet like that?”

“There must be at least fifty, and they’d all take the bet because it hardly ever pays out”

“And would you keep a record of bets that didn’t pay out?”

“There are some shops that keep computer records, but mostly it’s still paper. And even on the computer records we don’t identify the punter, the customer, that is.”

“But I suppose most gambling is done online these days?”

“You’d be surprised. Quite the opposite of most other shops, online alternatives haven’t hit betting shops much at all. In fact there’s been no noticeable decline in business over the last five years, when online gambling has become so commonplace”

“So that would mean more people are getting sucked into it?”

Pete immediately regretted the implied judgement.
“It’s a common fallacy that gambling is run by the mafia to screw the working man for every hard-earned penny. In fact, the rate of return to the punter is over ninety percent, and most of our customers can afford to lose”
Pete looked at the two men on the slot machines, well dressed and relaxed.
“I suppose it’s different when you’re just on the penny arcade machines, though”
“No, it feeds the same need, the thrill of winning, but to get any return you have to invest something. Those machines can take up to a hundred pounds stake at a time” He waited for Pete’s reaction. Pete gulped, then smiled as he conceded that his view of gambling was a little outdated.
“OK, thanks very much for your explanation Mr Smith, it’s all a lot clearer now”
“Will you be staying for the Kleeneasy Stakes? It’s a big race and worth a flutter”
“Not for me thanks, driving on the roads around here is enough of a gamble for me”

Back at his desk Pete decided it was time for a bit of research. Some background information was always useful, and these days you don't have to dig through library archives or old issues of newspapers on microfilm. All you need is a keyboard. Who was Mike Johnson? Key the name into LinkedIn and you get over twenty-four thousand hits. Use a filter to find those connected with United Midwest Bank and you end up with four. The LinkedIn site is all about keeping in touch with people who can be useful, and making sure that you and your talents are known to a wide audience, so most of its members keep their photo up to date as well as their CV. It was easy to identify Suicide Man, Mike Johnson. Three years at the bank, preceded by five years at another bank in Bournemouth, Dorset and a similar stint at a bank in France. Before that, an insurance company in London and various other jobs since leaving Manchester University with a 2.2 in Economics. People he was "linked" to included the three Pete had met that morning and another half-dozen from United Midwest, plus a handful from each of his previous workplaces. That left ten non-"work-related" contacts. These were probably people he'd met at conferences or on business trips, all part of the "networking" that modern business people use to make sales, gain competitive information and promote their own career goals. Pete made careful notes of each name, as if he was building up a family tree, which in a way he was. Nothing stood out from the list of names, so on to Facebook. Many more Mike Johnsons here, of course, but filter by location this time and less than a dozen results. No helpful photo in the profile picture this time, mainly cartoon characters and holiday scenes, but most people inadvertently leave enough access to see who they're friends with, and sure enough he found Suicide Man quite quickly again – he was the one who had Kathy Johnson as one of his friends. Only a few photos were available, and none of interest. Pete bookmarked the page and jotted down the names of a few "friends" who didn't appear as "colleagues" on LinkedIn. He was disappointed, but not entirely surprised, that there was no-one on either site connected with Mike Johnson who went by the name of "Spike", as found on Johnson's mobile phone. On a whim, Pete typed "Spike" into the Facebook search box and found hundreds of people with that name. Then he noticed that there were also some "groups" in the search results. One was called "R.I.P. Spike". He clicked on it and read the description, about a "Spike" who was a hero of the local music scene in Bournemouth, around thirty miles away. He seemed to be connected with some high profile club names in the area, and played in his own band. Pete clicked on a link to one of the band's videos and the office was filled with loud noise masquerading as some kind of punk/rap fusion. Pete quickly hit the mute key and looked around sheepishly, where several of his colleagues smiled good-naturedly. Back to Spike's timeline. Having no time for conventional lifestyle, he seemed to travel a lot, mainly to attend rock festivals and night-club launches, drove fast cars and engaging in dangerous sports – bungee jumping in New Zealand just being an example. As for the "R.I.P Spike" group, there were twenty or so members, all having contributed a sentence or two in praise of Spike and his love for living "on the edge". One of the entries began "The best brother a bloke could have" and was in the name of Des Palmer. Pete read through all the entries and noted the names. This Spike seemed a popular chap and would be missed. Then something caught his eye which he thought couldn't be coincidence. The group "R.I.P Spike" had been formed only a week ago.

Pete flicked over to a new Google tab and accessed the local news website. In response to his query for "Spike Palmer" he found an article from the Bournemouth Evening Echo entitled "Local music figure dies of cocaine overdose". After bookmarking this for later reading, he took a break and wandered over to the snack machine. It was time for a bar of chocolate and his hourly cup of black coffee. Taking both back to his desk, Pete phoned Gloria Marshall, the Johnsons' neighbour, to say that he'd be round at about six to speak to Graham. He then logged into the National Crime Database to check up on Spike. No form. The same couldn't be said for his "friends" though. As he checked through the group members he found four counts of possession, one of threatening behaviour and two of Grievous Bodily Harm. He noted the names of these last three: Graham Danes, Phil Davies and Terry Walton. Although there was no prosecution, Spike's brother Des also featured in an assault investigation.

When he got to the Marshalls' house, it was evident that the evening meal had already been served and they were ready for a cosy evening. Instead of the formal living room where he had met Kathy Johnson, he was shown into the lounge at the back of the house next to the kitchen, where Graham stood to welcome him.

"Terrible business" began Graham

"It certainly is, Sir" replied Pete, deciding to defer to Graham's "position" in the hope that he might be more forthcoming. "I don't want to take up much of your time. Your wife has given us most of the details about last night, but I had some follow-up questions. I know you were woken by the scream around

midnight, but did you hear any noises outside before you went to bed?"
"Well, we wouldn't really, we spend the evening at the back here. Our bedroom is at the front, upstairs, otherwise we probably wouldn't have even heard poor Kathy scream"
"So you wouldn't know what time Mike normally comes home, Mr Marshall, or if they have any evening visitors?"
"Can't help you really, officer. We keep ourselves to ourselves. It's quite a shock to have this suddenly happen We know Kathy and Mike quite well – went to dinner there, and them to us, and so on, but not much more than that"
"Apart from your Spanish evening classes", interrupted Gloria. "You used to give Kathy a lift"
"But that was last year" continued Graham, "And we - I mean several of us from the class – would sometimes stop for a beer on the way home. At the cricketers, that's our local pub. Anway, we didn't do the evening classes for long. We only did one term, we were both rubbish at Spanish. Maybe we should have done pottery."
"So to summarise", Pete was writing in his notebook "You were here all of yesterday evening, then went to bed and were woken by the scream just after midnight."
"Not quite" corrected Graham. "I often go to the pub, that same

one, for last orders. I did last night, got back about eleven thirty"

Pete stopped writing. He looked up and spoke directly to Graham.

"So you were out last night? And was Mr Johnson's car in the road when you came home?"

"Yes it was. Funny, I should have thought about it then, it's unusual for him not to use the garage. I suppose he had other plans". Then realising how callous that might have sounded, he added "I mean he must have had other things on his mind, to drive him to what he did to himself".

"Well, we really don't know what state his mind was in yet" replied Pete, then returned to his previous train of thought.

"Tell me, Mr Marshall, did you always do the driving when you and Mrs Johnson went to evening classes?"

"Oh no, we took turns. Her car one week, mine the next"

"And have you ever been in the back seat of Mrs Johnson's car?" Pete tried to make the question sound unloaded.

"Er, no. I mean I don't think so" stammered Graham, reddening a little. "Why the question?"

"Oh, no particular reason" Pete lied. "I'm just tying up loose ends."

He got up to leave. "I don't expect I'll need to speak to you again. We're aware of certain pressures in Mr Johnson's life and at the moment there's no reason to suspect foul play. Thank you for your time, and have a good evening"

Pete had been looking at Gloria after he asked the question about Mrs Johnson's car, and saw the black look in her eyes. He could sense that the Marshalls would carry on with this discussion for some time after he'd left.

CHAPTER EIGHT

Pete had keyed in a draft version of his report and had read it back to himself several times before he was satisfied. Before submitting the final version, he was reading the draft to Dave. This "peer review" was part of the standard procedure, and they found it useful as a way of checking that all avenues had been explored.

"OK", Pete began "The facts known are that Mike Johnson was found by his wife Kathy, hanging in his own garage by the neck at 12:07 yesterday morning. They live at 14 Briar Crescent, Eastleigh, Hampshire." Pete paused. "Should I have said 'lived' there, Dave?"

"Doesn't matter" replied Dave. "Go on".

"The paramedics were called by Mr. Graham Marshall, who lives across the road at number 17 and Mr Johnson was pronounced dead at the scene at 12:39. The body was fully clothed, with a noose around his neck." Pete paused again. "Should it be 'with a noose around its neck, it being a body?"

"You really don't like doing these, do you?" Dave sighed.

"No, I bloody don't. Anyway, where was I? A stepladder was lying on the floor. Above the body was a firmly attached rope which Mr Marshall cut in an attempt to save Mr. Johnson's life.

The body fell to the floor and Mr Marshall attempted to revive the victim until the emergency services arrived. Initial interviews with Mr Johnson's widow revealed that they had argued that night and that Mrs Johnson had stormed out. She reported that Mr Johnson seemed to have been in an intoxicated state, and she returned to the house around midnight. I met the following morning with Mr Johnson's work colleagues and they were of the opinion that he was not under abnormal work pressures. A discrepancy in working hours between their account and his wife's suggests that perhaps there was some other stress on him, possibly connected to gambling."

"Don't forget what your missus suggested"

"What, about the other woman? Well, I haven't put anything to Kathy Johnson about it, and in my view there's no need to. If he was getting his leg over somewhere else, good luck to him I say, but it's not against the law. It looks like Kathy Johnson did her share of playing away, so it was love-all, so to speak. If some strange bird turns up at the funeral we'll ask a few questions, but till then I think that's leading down a blind alley." He looked down at the report to pick up where he'd left off, returning to his more formal style.

"Mr Johnson had a significant amount of cocaine in his body,

source of which is unknown but possible associates of his include someone who moved in drug-related circles. This person is recently deceased so unable to corroborate. We continue to investigate how Mr Johnson obtained the illegal substance, but in the absence of contradictory evidence we believe that the drug was self-administered. In summary, there are a number of possible contributing factors in Mr Johnson's death, but none of a suspicious nature. While we view the death as unusual, we feel that nothing would be gained from exploring the circumstances further unless firm evidence comes to light, so we recommend a verdict of death by suicide"
"Very eloquent Pete, but total crap."
It wasn't Dave who spoke, but an older man in a cardigan and corduroy trousers, who had slipped quietly into the office. Jim Brunt was head scientist in the forensics lab. Pete put down his report and sighed.
"OK, Jim, what have we missed?"
"Your right about him taking the cocaine himself, there are pinch traces on his fingers and a fair amount around his nostrils. But there's something else I should have seen on the body the first time I looked at it, but it's only clear when you look at the photos"
Jim took some large coloured photos from a folder he was

carrying and placed them on Pete's desk. Pete and Dave stood either side of Jim and studied them. There were four. One had been taken on the night of Johnson's death, and was a close-up of his discoloured head, as he was lying on the floor of the garage with the noose still around his neck. The other three were of Johnson's head as he lay on the autopsy table. The noose had been removed and the photos were from the left, right and front.

"What are we looking for?" asked Pete.

"OK, you can see where the rope was, in the first picture" Jim pointed to it. "On the autopsy pictures you can see the rope burns here, here and here". He pointed to the neck in each of the three other pictures. "But if you look closely you can also see it here." He pointed to the front view photo again, and you could make out a fainter line a couple of inches below the distinctive rope burn.

"You mean he hanged himself twice?" offered Dave.

"Hardly", replied Jim, "Although if he had it would be the best example of gallows humour I've ever come across" The others didn't seem to get his little joke, so he continued. "It looks to me like his weight had been supported by the rope in the fainter position, before the drop that caused his death, when the rope was in the more distinctive position"

“So how do you think that could have happened” asked Pete.
“Well, if he did it himself, he stood on the top of the ladder and sagged forward onto the rope. The he jumped off the ladder”
“Seems an odd thing to do, unless he was testing his weight on the hook in the ceiling” suggested Pete.
“A possibility, but he would have to have been very composed to do that. I’m afraid a more likely scenario is that someone carried Johnson up the ladder and put the victim’s head in the noose, then left him leaning against it while he climbed down the ladder. The he kicked the ladder away and left our “Suicide Man” hanging there”
“Holy shit” breathed Pete. He crumpled up his draft report and tossed it into the wastebasket.

His boss was not too sympathetic when Pete gave him the news.
“So you had this one down as an open-and-shut suicide, now you think there’s some doubt?”
“Well”, offered Pete from the other end of the phone, “It’s only just come to light, and it still seems a bit far-fetched, someone humping Suicide Man up to the top of a stepladder then letting him swing free. It would call for some strength if it was just one person, to say nothing of cold-blooded determination. I’m

thinking it might be a professional hit".
"Who could he possibly have been involved with who could have arranged that?" demanded Superintendant Mazari.
"As you know, sir, there are quite a few gangs out there with hit-men in their pay. Some are Eastern European, some are home-grown, but all of them have that cold-blooded view of murder that lets them make a living out of doing their paymasters' dirty work. Johnson didn't have any obvious links to such gangs, but his drug supplier, whoever that was, probably did. As I said when we thought it was suicide, he's been spending a lot of his income away from home, but it's all in cash, so there's no trace. That money was going regularly to someone, but then suddenly stopped, which means that someone was out of pocket. We thought maybe the pressure of having to repay the money led to him take his own life. His final attempt at getting the money back, by trying a huge gamble on horses, seems to have backfired when he lost the lot in the last race. Somewhere in the middle of it he seems to have blown his mind on cocaine, just to confuse things. Anyway, as we're pretty sure now it wasn't suicide we're convinced that he was into something too deep and someone got tired of waiting to be paid"
"So what's your next move?"

“I’ll speak to his wife again. I can’t believe she wouldn’t have noticed anything suspicious. On the other hand she seems to have been up to some extra-curricular activity herself –“

“Meaning what?” Mazari interrupted.

“I mean she may have had a boyfriend, we don’t know yet, so maybe there’s a connection on that side. Either way, we’re going to have to go take another look at the house. Can you let me have the SOC team back in there?”

“I’ll get them down there first thing in the morning. I assume there’s no risk of the scene being contaminated before then?”

“No, the widow is staying with neighbours”

“OK, but now that it’s a suspicious death, you’ll need some help. Tell Dave Seddon to drop whatever he’s working on, and get a couple of D.C.s if you need them. Will you get Mrs Johnson to move out when you talk to her?”

“I’ll have to. I’ll get the boys to take in both of the Johnsons’ cars as well”.

“OK, give me an update before midday tomorrow. The press will be snooping around soon”.

Pete hung up and looked over at Dave, who had been listening to their end of the conversation.

“Sounds like it’s all getting interesting” said Dave.

“Oh yes” Pete replied “And you’ll be part of it, you lucky man.

Come on, you can help me break the news to the grieving widow"

It was mid-afternoon by the time they pulled up at the Marshalls' house in Briar Crescent. Gloria answered the door and looked surprised.

"Do you have any more questions, Inspector? Or is it my husband you're after, checking if he's where he should be?"

Pete ignored the sarcastic tone. "No, it's Kathy we're looking for. Is she there?"

"No, she's across the road at her own place. She said she'd rather sleep there".

"Oops", thought Pete.

He thanked Gloria and led the way across to the Johnsons. The house looked deserted, but both their cars were still parked outside. Pete rang the doorbell and they waited patiently for a couple of minutes. He rang again, this time for a lot longer. A pause, then they could hear movement from upstairs, and through the frosted glass door they could see Mrs Johnson approaching. She opened the door. She had obviously been asleep, and she was still wearing her dressing gown, but she also looked twenty years older than when Pete had last spoken to her.

“I’m sorry”, she began “I seem to have been asleep most of the day. You’d better come in while I pull myself together”. She left the door open for them and went back upstairs. Dave looked at Pete, who returned his resigned look and the two of them went into the lounge and sat down. It was a few minutes before Kathy Johnson returned, now dressed and looking fresher, having regained a few of the apparent lost years.
“I didn’t get much sleep last night” she volunteered before they could say anything. “After you’d spoken to her, Gloria seemed to think it best that I spend the night here, and not with them, for some reason” Pete shifted uncomfortably. “But I couldn’t bear to sleep in our bedroom, so I was on the couch tossing and turning all night, then I took a few sleeping tablets and lay down in the spare room in the attic. It’s all started to take its toll, I suppose”
“Quite understandable” replied Pete, although he was already taking mental note of the fact that there was a room in the attic to be included in the search later. “And we’re sorry to have to disturb you again”
“I suppose you’ve come to tell me about the money?”
“What money?”
“The rest of Mike’s pay packet, that he was keeping hidden from me. You told me he was actually earning a hell of a lot

more than he was bringing home" Kathy began to talk faster as her mind kicked into gear. "Where did it go? Another woman? A family? Just because I didn't want kids, has he got a house full of them living over in Gosport or Hayling Island? Well, I'm telling you, if that's what this is all about, she can go to hell if she thinks she's getting anything else. This house is half mine and so are the cars, unless...." She paused for breath and a panicked look took over her face. "Oh my God! He's written me out of his will, hasn't he? The bastard! I know we weren't getting on too well, but how the hell could anyone do that? Well, you can tell her from me that I'll fight her all the way. I mean....."

She stopped abruptly at the two impassive faces watching her. "What?"

"There have been some developments we need to talk to you about" Pete offered, "But first of all, a few more questions I'm afraid. We haven't had time to look into the background events, and we're hoping that you'll be able to fill in some details. For example, did Mike ever take drugs?"

Kathy looked shocked. "Absolutely not! " She retorted. "Even something like pot would mean he would have to relax, maybe even lose control. That's not the kind of man Mike was. It was difficult enough getting him to take a second glass of wine"

She took a breath, and seemed to be reliving previous events.
"Do you mean that's why he went all crazy last night? He was doped up on something? He never as much as smoked a joint as far as I knew"
Pete cleared his throat. "Look Kathy", he said softly. "We've been doing some digging around, to see what kind of stress Mike might have been under, and what could have led to him taking his own life. Drugs, gambling, even another woman – they're all possibilities. I have to tell you, though, that something has come to light that means we'll have to change our whole approach."
"What are you talking about?" Kathy looked fearful.
"I can't be specific about what we've discovered, but I'm here to tell you officially that we are now treating Mr Johnson's death as suspicious". Pete paused and watched her face for a reaction. There was none. She just looked at him. Then her eyes flickered as if her brain had just received and processed the information. It took a few more seconds for her face to redden and her eyes took on a watery sheen. Her mouth opened slowly but no sound came out at first. When it finally did she seemed lost for words.
"You mean.....someone else did that to him? ......but how?..... why would anyone?........" she stammered.

“Look Kathy, it might be that we’re mistaken and there’s a more innocent explanation, but as it stands now we’ll have to look into everything Mike was involved with, and who he knew, to try and find a motive for any foul play”

“OK” was Kathy’s only response. Her eyes had left Pete’s and were frantically scanning the room and beyond, seemingly searching for an explanation of this latest blow.

“I’ll need to be able to go through all of your husband’s paperwork and his computer, to build up a picture of his recent activity. And did he have a mobile phone?” asked Pete, knowing at least one answer to that question.

“Yes, it’s right there where he left it, on the charger” She pointed towards a table in the hallway.

“Just one mobile was there?” continued Pete

“No, there were two”

Pete looked at her enquiringly. Maybe she knew more than he’d thought.

“We had one each” She went on “Mine is in my handbag”

Pete hid his disappointment by consulting his notebook. “Just one more question for now” he continued. “Does the name Spike Palmer mean anything to you?”

“Who was that, Mike’s fancy woman?” said Kathy bitterly.

“No, it was a man. Someone who your husband might have

known” continued Pete. “How about Des Palmer?”

“Never heard of him. Do these people have something to do with this ‘Foul Play’ idea of yours?”

“It’s too early to say, we’re just trying to form a picture, as I said”.

There had been no hint of recognition to the two names. Pete continued. “We’ll need to collect much more detailed forensic evidence now from the house, especially the garage. I’m going to have to ask you to move out for a while. It’s probably best that you don’t stay with anyone that both you and Mike knew. Maybe a local hotel or a B & B would be OK?”

“Well, I can’t say that I know anywhere” she began, and then seemed to form an idea. “No, wait a minute, I do. I’ll go and stay at the Travel Lodge.”

CHAPTER NINE

It had been a bit of a day already. The board meeting at ten was everything he'd expected it to be. All those highly-paid people who didn't really have a clue about the business, but were sitting in judgement over his project. Most of them had been on his side when he'd made his initial pitch, but he should have realised they'd jump like rats from a sinking ship at the first sign of trouble. They'd made it to the dizzy heights of Board Member by knowing the right people. All that entailed was sitting around this boardroom and half a dozen just like it for a few hours each week, nodding wisely and asking the occasional question, but mainly looking forward to their wine-soaked lunch at the club and the pleasure of claiming it on expenses, then waiting for their OBEs or knighthoods for services to the finance industry. Well, he'd laid it on the line to those fat cats. The software was late, he told them, because of changes to the specification. The operations managers wouldn't sign off in time because they each wanted their own empire-building requirements included, so it was hardly his fault. He'd shown them his original plan as a reminder of the agreed schedule – the dependency diagrams, the PERT charts, all in vivid colour in the images projected on the boardroom screen.

It was a pretty picture to paint a not very pretty picture, and it looked professional so they would have to believe the message. He'd spelled it all out in the presentation, talking through each point and answering any questions smoothly. If this deadline slips, was the message, then the whole schedule collapses like a line of dominoes. He'd been asked to wait outside for a few minutes, then was called back in for their reaction. They wouldn't buy a delay to the delivery date. He'd have to get his team to work harder to catch up with the lost time. Work later and at weekends. And to be told this by people who worked six hours a week! He'd stayed calm and tried to reason with them, there was simply no slack in the schedule. He'd even tried to lighten the atmosphere with his favourite project planning joke: The first 90% of a project takes 90% of the time, the last 10% takes the other 90% of the time. It had fallen on deaf ears. So had his offer to quit if they weren't happy with him as project manager. No, they knew they could beat some more shit out of him at the next meeting, why spoil their fun by bringing in a replacement, who they'd have to give a fair chance? He'd spent the rest of the day rescheduling some of the critical tasks on his charts and bringing his team up to date. Then he'd decided he was going to leave work on time at six. He wasn't going to let them push him into burning the midnight oil. Not yet, anyway.

He was mentally recalculating the remaining float on that phase two delivery date as he walked into the Travel Lodge lobby. He was sufficiently preoccupied not to notice the person sitting in the lobby lounge area next to reception as he walked up to the desk.

"Hi Sarah", he said wearily to the receptionist "And how are you tonight?"

Before she could answer he'd turned his head instinctively to the woman sitting, who was now looking at him and smiling. He stopped dead. All thoughts of schedules and budgets evaporated. Instead, his mind was filled with the image of a steamed-up car and some very intense activity.

"Hello Jack" said Kathy Johnson.

"Kathy? What are you doing here?" His voice was faltering despite his best efforts. He took his room key from Sarah, who discretely started busying herself with paperwork.

"We're neighbours. Or more accurately, we're cohabitants. I'm staying here for a couple of days"

"On your own?"

"Yes. My husband is....." she hesitated. "Elsewhere. I'll explain later. I knew you'd get back here sooner or later, so I thought I'd sit and wait. Lucky you didn't go straight to the gym"

"No, not tonight. I've had my physical workout at the office. It's been a hell of a day."

He looked over at Sarah, still intently studying her files, then back to Kathy. "Can I get you a drink at the bar?"

"Good idea. She stood and walked towards the bar, which was full of after-work business people winding down. He followed her. She went up to the barman and said "Two double vodkas and orange, with ice, please". Jack looked enquiringly at her. "And a pint of bitter for Jack. Put it on room 26" And walked over to a quiet corner and sat in an armchair. A few minutes later Jack arrived with the drinks on a tray. She downed the first vodka before he raised his pint glass to his lips.

He paused, then closed his eyes as he took his first, deep, satisfying mouthful of the lukewarm brown liquid. The troubles of the day melted away with the froth of his beer. He took another long draught, opened his eyes and let them slowly focus of her face. She was smiling too. He was more than curious. "So are you trying to tell me that this is a coincidence?"

"Of course not" she replied. "You wouldn't believe me if I did." She looked at him and held his gaze. He'd spent the day fighting his corner against some pretty determined opposition. He wasn't going to flinch in a staring competition with an attractive woman. As it happened, she was the one to relax first, as she took a drink from her second glass.

"Don't worry Jack, sweetheart. I'm not here to boil any pet rabbits or to tell you I've got some dreaded disease. Something's happened at home, and I didn't want you involved in it, but I need someone to lean on for a day or two"

Jack breathed a sigh of relief. So we're both agreed that the other night wasn't the start of anything complicated?"

Kathy smiled at the irony. " No. No complications. Not between us, anyway. Just friends, OK?"

Jack smiled back and took another drink "So, what are you up to?"

"I've been here all afternoon on the phone. I've been trying to find out something about two men connected with my husband. They're brothers. Spike and Des Palmer."

"Never heard of them" said Jack. "Should I have heard of them?"

"I'd be surprised if you had. Spike was apparently a bit of a low-life. Drove fast cars, always had plenty of money to flash around, did a bit of dope peddling to the Chelsea Set in Southampton. He died of an overdose a couple of weeks ago"

"Wow!" exclaimed an impressed Jack. "How do you find out stuff like that?"

"Well, the phone calls were to someone I know at the Evening Echo, a reporter called Ben Walters. I helped him with a piece he was writing a few months back about corruption in the banking world. He got a lot of praise for his story, some of it even ended up in the national press, so he owed me a favour. Anyway, through him I found out a bit more about Spike's brother Des. Have you ever heard of the Monte Carlo?"

"I think I told you I'm from Bath. That's a long way from Monaco"

"But not so far from Southampton. The Monte Carlo is a big casino there, built on some of the reclaimed docklands and doing very well"

"Somehow I don't see Southampton as a Mecca for the high-rollers" observed Jack dryly

"You'd be surprised. Southampton is the point of departure for a lot of cruise liners, and the oil tankers all offload nearby at Fawley. It has an international airport and it's just across the Solent from the Isle of Wight, where a lot of private yachts are moored at Cowes marina"

"OK, so this chap Des Palmer works in a casino?"

"No. He owns one."

Jack paused, taking it all in. "So he owns a casino and his brother was a drugs dealer till he popped too many pills. They

know your husband. What has any of this got to do with me?"
"I was just getting to that", continued Kathy, at the same time signalling to the barman that he should bring them two more drinks. Jack looked at his glass, which was still three-quarters full. Hers was empty, and he realised that the two drinks being ordered were just for her. Kathy noticed his glance.
"I'm summoning up some Dutch courage" she explained. "I need to talk to this man Palmer. Tonight. He knows something about my husband, and I'm determined to find out what"
"But you're not driving to Southampton after four double vodkas?"
"No, of course not. You're driving me there, when you've finished your pint. I'm not really brave enough to face this chap on my own, and you agreed just now that we're going to be friends"
She certainly had a way about her, he thought. Smart, sexy, pushy, manipulative – with just a hint of vulnerability. Maybe just what he needed to counteract the pressure he'd felt at work today from all those pompous bastards. And no strings attached? What could possibly go wrong? Suddenly, Bath seemed a long way from where he was sitting.

Kathy didn't talk much in the car. Jack chatted away, almost to

himself, a mixture of nervousness and excitement.
"I suppose this little adventure is no different to starting a new project for me, if that doesn't sound too IT-Geeky. I love the thrill of something new, with people I've never met. There's always something to learn new experiences, both good and bad, lo look back on later. I don't tyhink I'll ever want to work too long in the same place, I get restless – so I volunteer for a lot of oddball projects just for the challenge. Maybe I like to take a few risks every now and then, and you're certainly one for coming up with a new challenge – look at us, haring off down the motorway into the night."
He looked at her and she seemed to be lost in her own thoughts, hardly listening to his ramblings. His own mind drifted back to the night in the sports club car park. Would there be a repeat performance later tonight after their trip to Southampton? Her room, or his? Certainly not the car park. Maybe he'd play a little adventurous himself and suggest a stop on the way home. There are a lot of parking spots in the forests of Hampshire for picnickers and ramblers – although he'd stumbled across a TV program recently about "dogging". People driving to remote car parks to watch couples having sex, with the couples knowing full well they were being watched, and the whole thing turning into a mass orgy at the

end. Maybe they were just doing it for the cameras. He'd read about the Hawthorne effect, where people modify their behaviour when they know they're being observed. Maybe, he thought, there simply isn't a reality any more. And maybe this whole thing with Kathy has been dreamed up by a TV production team, and he was part of some secretly-filmed experiment.

He broke out of his daydream as they approached Southampton at about eight, and drove straight to the address Kathy had given him. It was in a rather dingy part of Southampton, the still-working part of the docks area being brightly illuminated nearby, but the buildings neighbouring the casino were mainly new office blocks. The entrance was a wide staircase covered in all-weather red carpet with a purple canopy sheltering it, with hidden spotlights picking out the marble statues on either side of the main door, the whole effect looking as tacky as the Oscar ceremony. They had been able to park right opposite the entrance. Although the sign read "24/7" it was clear that the evening proper hadn't yet begun. They walked the red carpet, Jack held the door open for her and Kathy walked boldly into the reception area as if she owned the place. The girl behind the reception desk seemed interchangeable with the one at the

Travel Lodge, and smiled sweetly as they approached.
"Good evening Madam. And Sir" she added as Jack followed Kathy a little reluctantly through the door. "Are you both members?"
"No, we're not" replied Kathy. "We'd like to speak to Mr. Des Palmer"
The girl hesitated. "Do you have an appointment?"
"No, we don't, but I think he'll want to meet with us"
"Can you tell me what it's about?"
"No I can't. I know through a contact that he's here tonight. Will you please call him and tell him that Mike Johnson's wife would like to talk to him"
The girl paused, her mind weighing up the options. The couple were both well dressed, he wore a smart suit and a tie. They didn't look like trouble-makers. She said "Just one moment" and disappeared behind a partition, then could be heard speaking to someone on the phone, paused for an answer and came back to the reception desk.
"Mr Palmer will be down in a few minutes. Would you wait in the conference room, please?" She indicated a door opposite.
Kathy and Jack walked through and found a small room with a long table and four chairs on either side. They sat opposite each other and Jack turned to Kathy in a stage whisper. "So you

already know this bloke, then?"
Kathy looked amused. "I'm glad you got that impression. No, I've never met him before, but I guessed that curiosity would get the better of him"
"So what's he got to do with your husband?"
"That's what we're here to find out"
Jack was certainly uncomfortable. He didn't know why she was here, and even less did he know why he'd agreed to come with her. He was just wondering whether he could make a run for it when the door opened and in walked a tall, elegant middle-aged man in an open-necked shirt and tailored jeans. He was followed by a shorter, younger but much broader man in a suit and tie, who's hair was long and greasy, giving him a rather unpleasant demeanour. The shorter man stopped in the doorway, blocking it completely.
"Mrs Johnson?" The older man offered his hand and Kathy shook it, remaining seated. "I'm Des Palmer, and this is my assistant Terry Walton" indicating the man in the doorway. "How can I help you?"
"My friend Jack and I have some questions to ask you" replied Kathy. Jack swallowed hard. Did he have to think up some questions now?
"First of all", interrupted Palmer "I need you to tell me who the

hell Mike Johnson is"
Kathy didn't miss a beat. "Don't you pretend you don't know him. You agreed to meet us when I said I was his wife."
"No, it wasn't because I know him, it's because I don't. I was intrigued. Someone I don't know comes into my club and wants to see me, I would normally tell my staff to send them on their way. But you seem to think I know your husband , so I'm giving you a few minutes to explain how I know him"
Kathy's face reddened, and Jack's uneasiness increased.
"Don't give me that shit" she fumed menacingly. "You can protest your innocence all you like, but I know you and your thugs had something to do with this, and I wanted you to look me in the eye and deny it. The police have already got your name – and your brother's"
"What do you know about my brother?" Palmers face was getting more threatening.
"I know he was a dealer and my husband was one of his mugs"
"You don't know anything missus" Palmer sneered. "My poor brother died last month so he's paid the price for anything he was mixed up in, God rest his soul. Your husband must be even more stupid than you if he thinks he can lay anything on me. Why don't you take your pet monkey and piss off out of my club before I lose my temper"

Jack wasn't offended by the insult aimed at him. He was ready to drag Kathy outside himself if he got a chance.
"You know as well as I do that Mike is dead. Made out to look like suicide and I know you've got something to do with it!" Kathy shouted and jumped to her feet. Jack was so astounded by what she'd said that her next move left him flat-footed. With a scream she launched herself towards Palmer, landing on him at chest height and they both fell to the floor behind the chairs, with Kathy on top of him and her hands around his neck. She lifted herself up and sat astride him, yelling into his terrified face.
"You bastard! You've got all the power and the money and the tough guys to do your dirty work! You did this! I know you did! You're not getting away with this!"
Palmer's aide seemed as shocked as Jack and was rooted to the spot.
"Terry! Terry! Get this fucking woman off me! Don't just bloody stand there! Terry!"
Hearing his name broke Terry's inability to move. He climbed on top of Kathy and pulled at her hands, slowly prising them free of Palmer's neck. Suddenly Kathy let go and went for Walton, grabbing his long hair in both hands and pushing him backwards till she had him pinned against the wall.

"And you're the tough guy who does all his dirty work for him!" she screamed, holding him against the wall with surprising strength. "Well how does it feel to be on the receiving end for a change?"

"Boss, get her off me!" Walton shouted, almost in a whine "She's got handfuls of my fucking hair!"

This was getting totally out of hand, thought Jack, and reached forward with both Arms to grab Kathy in a "full-nelson" Walton screamed as her hands were forced away from his head, as some of his hair came away with them. Jack spun Kathy around to face a "neutral" corner, where she stood sobbing uncontrollably into some tissues tissue she'd pulled from her jacket pocket. Palmer was on his feet now, staring daggers at her back, and started towards her. Jack didn't want this to get any uglier, so he turned in front of Kathy, facing Palmer with his palms outwards in a calming gesture.

"Look, mate, I don't know what's going on here any more than you do. I'm just acting as a taxi driver. I'll get her out of here and back home. There's no need to get the police involved, is there?"

Palmer had regained his composure a little. "Calling the police was never an option, pal. If you don't get her out of here right now, the only police involvement will be them dragging the

both of you out of the Solent tomorrow morning"
Jack got the message and grabbed Kathy's shoulders, almost frog-marching her through the lobby and down the steps. She was still sobbing as he buckled her into the passenger seat.
"I'm not sure I want to hear what his is all about Kathy" he said as they drove away. "I'll take you back to the hotel and then I think it's better that we go our separate ways."

CHAPTER TEN

Kathy was sitting in a quiet corner of the Travel Lodge restaurant, slowly stirring her coffee and staring into an untouched bowl of cereal. She hadn't slept much the previous night after the fiasco at the casino, so she'd showered and dressed early be in a position visible from the lobby. She looked up occasionally to the doorway, hoping to see Jack, but she knew he wouldn't be stopping for breakfast today. She doubted if he ever did, more likely he'd have a coffee and a roll from some vending machine at the office. Anyway, as it was Friday he had probably checked out already and would be heading back to Bath tonight. They'd continued their silence all the way back from Southampton, with just a curt "goodnight" as they parted in the lobby. At least all the stress was good for her diet. She hadn't eaten last night, and today's buffet breakfast wasn't tempting her either. She took a sip of her lukewarm coffee and stirred it yet again. She looked up as a figure approached her table.

"Morning Kathy." Pete Thomas took a chair and sat down. "Mind if I join you?"

"Be my guest, Inspector" Kathy replied languidly.

"As you know," Pete began, "Our forensic people will be going through your house today in much more detail. You won't be able to go back till maybe the end of next week. Meanwhile, I'll need you to come down to the station sometime so we can take some fingerprints and DNA swabs from you. That way we can eliminate you from anything our search picks up. That goes for anyone else who might be regular visitors. Can you give me some names, please?" He flipped open his notebook and took his pen from his jacket pocket.

"That's easy. There isn't anybody. Just me and Mike. And you've got as much DNA of his as he'll ever have." She looked glum.

"What about Gloria from across the street?"

"Yes, I suppose she's been in a few times. She tends to pop round some evenings if Graham's gone off to the pub"

Pete paused. "And Graham?"

"Yes, he must have been there as well, I guess. They've both been there for dinner, hung their coats up, all that stuff" She seemed distracted. Pete decided not to pursue the Graham connection this time. He supposed that the shock was starting to catch up with her.

"OK, I'll get them both down to the station. Of course, we'll also need to go over both cars again."

"Both?" Kathy looked troubled.

"Just to get a complete picture. Any problem with that?"
Involuntarily, Kathy looked again towards the doorway.
"No, of course not, but – ". She sighed. "But what's the point of all that, Inspector, when we both know who's involved in this?"
"And that would be?"
"This Spike Palmer and his brother Des. You told me Mike knew them"
"No, I asked if you knew them. That's different. Can you let me do the detective work, please? If you start jumping to conclusions it will only get in the way of what we professionals are trying to do. Look, I know it's difficult and you're just coming to terms with what's happened, but you'll have to be patient while we follow through all the possibilities here. To be honest, there's a lot of information we don't have that you could help us with. To start with, why didn't you tell me about Mike and his gambling?"
"What gambling?"
"Horses, mainly, although if it was a habit it could have been anything"
"Well, I certainly didn't know about it. He used to get involved in some big poker games down at the Cricket club in Bournemouth, but I don't think he's played since we moved up

here."
"It may be that he's not a regular gambler, but there's evidence to suggest he owed someone some big money on the day he died. Maybe if his bet had come in he wouldn't have ended up the way he did. We think maybe he was desperate to make this final payoff and it failed"
"But that's ridiculous. Mike was the last person on earth to risk money unless he was sure he could win. That's why he played poker. Even with a poor hand he could bluff his way to a win. Of course I can't say I really knew him, now you're telling me he was regularly siphoning off our money to pay someone else, but he could never have been a compulsive gambler. He was just too conservative, bless his heart."
"Well, I'm afraid the Sun sports section we found in his car contradicts that."
For the first time in days Kathy laughed out loud. Pete was shocked.
"That really takes the biscuit, Inspector!" she took a few seconds before she could speak again.
"Mike was not only conservative, he was a complete snob. He would have given the rest of his salary away, rather than be caught with a copy of the Sun!" She stopped laughing paused to reflect then looked at him quizically. She shook her head.

“You don’t get it, do you? That paper was so obviously planted, by whoever wanted us to think it was suicide.”
“Well, of course, that’s what we were thinking too” Pete replied, rather too quickly. “I’ll just grab a quick coffee from the buffet. I’ve got an appointment at ten”

Jack had phoned ahead and asked to meet with Amanda McCarthy, Mike Johnson’s second-in-command at the bank. He thought it wouldn’t hurt to have at the top of his list those lines of enquiry involving the prettiest witnesses. After all, this job had to have some perks. He was unprepared for the pleasant surprise as he was met in the bank’s lobby.
“Inspector Thomas? I’m Rowena Saunders. From Human Resources. Amanda has asked me to sit in on your meeting with her. I have Mike Johnson’s personnel file with me”.
Rowena was the exact opposite of Amanda in everything but the impact of her looks. Petite, short dark hair, wide green eyes and the kind of lips you didn’t need much imagination to get into trouble with.
Pete straightened his tie, flushed at the implication of doing so, stood up and shook her outstretched hand.
“Pleased to meet you, Ms Saunders”
Amanda McCarthy was already seated in one of the conference

rooms off the reception area The three of them exchanged pleasantries, sipped the obligatory machine-vended coffee, then got down to business.
"Since you're here Ms Saunders" Pete began, jotting her name in his notebook. "I'd like to start with Mr Johnson's personnel record. I'll be direct, if I may. Perhaps you can tell me whether there's anything to suggest that he might have had a gambling or a drugs problem?"
Rowena and Amanda both sat up straight.
"Good grief, no" replied Rowena. "Mike Johnson was meticulously tidy and was always coherent and well-presented. There were certainly no outward signs of behavioural problems. Medically, there's absolutely nothing unusual in his file. We insist on our senior staff attending a "Well-Person" health check-up when they're hired and every two years while they're employed. The summary results are right here from both check-ups, and Mike was in very good shape indeed. He didn't smoke and didn't drink to excess. Certainly any long-term drug problem would have shown up. What would lead you to suspect that he had such a problem?"
"Well I can't be too specific, you'll understand, but there are certain dates when Mr Johnson was spending large sums of money. It might have been to fuel a drug problem, may have

been a gambling habit or some other pressure that led to his demise. In any event, we're trying to find out who this money was paid to"

"Can you give me the dates?"

"For the last six months it seems to have been the second Tuesday of each month"

Rowena looked at her file.

"That ties in exactly with days he took off work during that period"

"Yes" added Amanda, "He would always insist on nothing being scheduled for the second Tuesday of each month. I did ask him once what the significance was, and he just said that he was a creature of habit"

"But hang on a minute" interrupted Pete, "The day was found dead was only this Tuesday, which was the second Tuesday of this month"

"That's right, and he didn't come to work, as usual. I thought you would have known that he wasn't at work the day he died. Sorry, Inspector"

Pete was annoyed at himself for not finding that out already. He pressed on valiantly.

"So is there anything else in his file that might be relevant?"

Rowena scanned the file quickly. "No, nothing unusual here.

Apart from his monthly day off, he would take a few days at Christmas and the rest in June. We insist that everyone who has twenty-five days or more vacation has to have at least ten consecutive days off"
Pete tried not to squirm at the use of the American term for holidays.
"Oh, and why is ten days in a row significant?"
"It's an audit requirement. If there's any funny business going on, a full weekly cycle without the perpetrator at his desk would normally show it up"
"So fraud is a common problem?"
"No, of course it isn't" Rowena smiled sweetly "But we can't be too careful"
"And of course, if you found any "Funny Business" you'd report it to the police" Pete countered, "Rather than dealing with it internally to avoid adverse publicity"
Rowena just smiled again. Amanda took the cue to move the discussion on.
"The two weeks in June, that was always Mike and Kathy's Bournemouth trip. They used to go back to visit friends. She comes from there and that's where Mike met her. At the bank he worked at before moving here"
"And which bank is that?"

“Banque Bordelaise. It’s a French bank with a big FX operation in Bournemouth”
“FX?”
“Foreign Exchange. You know, buying and selling foreign currencies. Mike was quite a Francophile, and worked for them in Bordeaux for a couple of years. He always talked about retiring over there” She stopped and looked a bit sad. “I guess he won’t be doing that now”
“Sadly, no” agreed Pete. Then, to Rowena again, “Is there anything else in his attendance record I should know?”
“Nothing here” she confirmed “Just a day or two a year, with colds or bugs. We don’t have much of a problem with sickness. Anything more than three days we follow up and make sure it’s genuine. If there’s any doubt we don’t shirk from moving people on to more suitable employers. We have far less absenteeism than the public sector”
She smiled again, but her pointed comment wasn’t lost on Pete. He would have guessed that in Rowena’s case the “H” in HR stood for “Hatchet”.
“But there is one item I should point out in Mike’s file, Inspector. He was the subject of a sexual discrimination hearing just after joining us”
Pete looked interested “And?”

Rowena continued. "It was brought by a chap called Nigel Broome. Nigel maintained that he was the best candidate for a junior management role, but he was passed over in favour of a woman less qualified, Karen Peterson. Mike was the one who made the appointment, and Nigel told the hearing that he thought Karen was having an affair with Mike and that's how she got the promotion"

"And what was the outcome?"

"The hearing found in favour of Mike, there being no evidence of an affair. Just sour grapes, I suppose, and Nigel's still working here. He got promotion in another department a year later."

"What about Karen Peterson?"

"Well, that's the strange thing. Although she got the promotion, the hearing seemed to have left a bad taste for her. She quit a few weeks later."

"Do you know where she is now?"

"She's still in the area, I believe. We'll have a forwarding address for her annual pension statement. I can email it to you"

"Thanks for that" said Pete, taking one of his business cards from his wallet and handing it to Rowena. "And if there's anything else I need, I'll call you"

Amanda needed to know more. "Can I ask you, Inspector, why

you’re looking into Mike’s death so thoroughly?”

Pete paused. “I’d like you to keep this to yourselves for the moment, but we think there may have been someone else involved in Mr Johnson’s death”

They both looked stunned. Amanda was the first to react.

“But that’s terrible. Why on earth would anyone else be involved? Mike was such a lovely man”

Pete seized the moment. “Did you see much of Mike outside of work, Amanda?”

If there was an implication in his question, she either didn’t pick it up or chose to ignore it.

“No, definitely not. We’ve been on the same courses together, and I’ve been to dinner at theirs once, with other people. We just don’t mix in the same circles, really”

“So did you think there might be something in this ‘affair’ accusation? Was Mr Johnson the kind of man who would, for example, harass female employees?”

“Far from it. As I said, we didn’t associate much outside of work, but the department he managed is predominantly female, and I never saw him act inappropriately”

“Hey, don’t forget the incident with Brenda Howard” interrupted Rowena.

Amanda gave her a dark look. “OK, let’s mention that, just for completeness. Someone phoned HR to say that Mike was in the conference room with his arm around Brenda. Rowena here called me and asked me to check everything was OK. As it turns out, Brenda had just heard that her Mum had died, and Mike, being a caring kind of person, had taken her aside to comfort her. I hardly think they'd have had sex on the conference room table with a hundred people watching through the glass wall."

"I just thought we'd better mention it before anyone else does, as it's not on his record" mumbled Rowena glumly.

Pete, seeming satisfied, closed his notebook. "Thank you, ladies, I think that's enough for now. I'll be on my way then". He checked his watch. He was meeting Dave Seddon up at the Hamble sailing club in half an hour.

The gorgeous Rowena escorted him out of the building, and as he signed out he wondered why banking and not the police force should benefit from the best-looking women. Probably something to do with money, he decided.

He and Dave weren't meeting up for lunch, that was much too expensive, so he'd go home afterwards instead. The sailing club was in a nice setting, very quiet and the staff were extremely discreet. Neither Pete nor Dave were members.

Neither were they sailors, but the club served a nice coffee and it didn't hurt to have a couple of policemen as regulars. Dave was at their usual table on the terrace overlooking the marina, nursing his coffee, when Pete walked up with one of his own and sat opposite him. Dave had volunteered to supervise the forensic team at the Johnsons' house that morning.
"Ok, Dave? began Pete, flipping open his notebook, "What's new at the house of Suicide Man?"
"Certainly not enough to make any notes on" replied Dave. "No sign of any suspicious behaviour, no forced entry, no violent struggle. The SOC boys have gone over the whole place with their tweezers and vacuum cleaners and have bagged everything up from the garage floor, and the main house – including the attic room. They'll do the same in Johnson's car then look at it all back in the lab."
"Don't forget Mrs Johnson's car. I want to put a name to that stain, even if it's irrelevant. When will we get the results?"
"In a couple of days. We've photographed everything and checked dustbins, cupboards, under chairs, all the usual places. The Johnsons seem to have kept their house and cars a lot cleaner than mine or yours. The boys did come across one thing though. Fallen down between the driver's seat and the handbrake was a car park ticket from Southampton Parkway,

dated February 9th of this year”

“Don’t tell me” smiled Pete. “I bet you’ve already checked. That date was on the list of withdrawals on the statement we found. And I know already it was the second Tuesday of the month”

CHAPTER ELEVEN

Pete studied the parking receipt for a minute, then put down his coffee. He poke to Dave, but all the time he was gazing through the window at the peaceful scene outside. A few people were busying themselves at the quayside, or standing and watching a handful of boats slowly wend their way into and out of the tiny harbour. The sun reflecting on the gently lapping waters contrasted starkly with the dark clouds gathering behind the tall trees on the opposite bank.

"Like most people," he began, "I only take a train when I really have to. They always seem to be going to not quite the right places or at not quite at the right times. On top of that they're bloomin' expensive and have a habit of getting cancelled or delayed. You can drive to most places faster and cheaper, and you don't have to take a taxi or a bus when you get there. The only exception is going into the big cities, like London or Birmingham, where it's impossible to park unless you have an "on police business" card you can stick in your windscreen. I suppose there are thousands of poor sods who don't have a choice, and who spend hours every day travelling to work, but even the thought of having to cram into a sardine can while dressed in a sweaty suit makes me go cold. You'd never get me

commuting into town – I'd rather go on the dole."
He looked at the ticket again, and continued.
"OK, Dave, so where can you go by train from Southampton Parkway?"
"I'm so glad you asked me that" Dave said smugly, having waited patiently through Pete's meanderings. "There's a station here in Hamble, so I picked up a route map on my way here".
He pulled the map out of his inside pocket and unfolded it on the bar table in front of them. "Parkway is just off the M3/M27 junction, so it's easy to drive to from almost anywhere in the Southampton/Portsmouth conurbation. There are two main railway lines passing through the station. One runs from Weymouth in the West Country up to London, and Parkway is about half way. The other line runs from Southampton City Centre along the south coast to Portsmouth and Brighton. From Parkway the train takes about ten minutes to get to Southampton and an hour to Brighton" Dave pointed to each line in turn on the map, with its start and end points, as he spoke.
"London is about forty minutes from Parkway, into Waterloo station. Johnson used to work in the city, so he may have had some good contacts there, but there's no way we could trace his movements in the hundreds of thousands going through that

route every day. If he took the London Underground from Waterloo, he might have used an Oyster Travel Card registered in his name, and that would give us the time he went into the underground system at Waterloo and the name of the tube station he left it. Most stations have cctv now, so we could start tracking him through the city. I've got Sanjay working on that back at the office. Looking in the opposite direction, on the London to Weymouth line we've got Bournemouth only an hour away, where the Johnsons used to live. That's my best bet at the moment"

"Makes sense to me" agreed Pete, "Besides, if he was heading for London he'd have been driving in the wrong direction when he left the car at Parkway" He traced his finger from the Johnson's home town, Eastleigh, back to Parkway then up to London. He paused, then traced the line left from Parkway to Bournemouth. "But look here", he continued. "The first main stop in the Weymouth direction is Southampton Central. Very convenient if he was visiting Spike's brother Des".

"So you're still thinking along the gambling lines, Pete?"

"I know the horse racing seems unlikely now, replied Pete, "but there are not many pursuits that can make money disappear that quickly, and one of them is gambling"

"OK, so what about the other direction, towards Brighton or

Portsmouth?"
"Mmm", Pete mused. "Well, sorry if I'm stereotyping a whole town, but I can't see Johnson having a gay lover, so Brighton's a long ride if he's just out for the day. Portsmouth's a lot closer, so more likely, I reckon. If it had been a Saturday and not a Tuesday he might have got off at Fratton Park to watch Portsmouth play. But then he would have used his blue and white scarf to hang himself, the way they've been playing football lately"
"No, he'd have been a Saints supporter," countered Dave, using the Southampton football team's nickname. "Portsmouth are too down-market for him to have been a Pompey fan"
"You'd be surprised. A lot of the biggest thugs there are middle-income office workers by day. Just a few lines of coke and they're back to the tribal warfare of the seventies" Pete stopped abruptly and looked up at Dave. "Which reminds me – we need to find out how Johnson got his fix that day"
Dave nodded. "So where do we go first?"
Pete looked at his watch. Half past ten. "Give the office a call and have one of the gophers drop by Parkway train station. See if there's any cc tv for the time of the ticket and if he can spot Johnson on the platform. At least knowing which platform will tell us which direction he went. As for us, we'll take a drive

down to Bournemouth. Kathy Johnson said that Mike had been a regular poker player at the cricket club there. Bournemouth also seems to be where this Spike Palmer character hung out, which may or may not be a coincidence. I'll phone ahead and touch base with Andy Withers, he's the liaison between Dorset and us in Hampshire, and he's based at the Bournemouth CID office. I'll tell him we'll go to the cricket club first, then call in on him to find out about this Spike character"

"And what about Des, Spike's brother? You told me over the phone earlier that he was Kathy Johnson's favourite to be the hit man".

"And I wish I hadn't told you that now." retorted Pete. "I'm not going to be dictated to by some amateur Miss Marple. She can suspect who she wants to. I'll get to Des Palmer in my own good time, and anyway I've got plans this weekend. Mike Johnson's not going to get any deader by Monday, so I'll pop down and see Des Palmer then"

The drive through the New Forest was pleasant, as always. The stretch from the end of the motorway to the Ringwood roundabout could have been Dartmoor or the Scottish lowlands. Long, curving dual carriageway with empty moorland on both sides and rarely a building in sight. Dorset is still the only county in Britain without a single mile of motorway, and it would attract huge opposition if one was proposed. Thirty miles to the North, a similar East-West route passes by the historic site of Stonehenge, and is just as unlikely to ever become a modern road capable of handling the traffic it carries. Indeed, anyone trying to get from London to the Southwest counties of Devon and Cornwall in a hurry would have to take a detour via Bristol and add miles to their journey.

Pete was glad they hadn't left this trip any later in the day. There could be miles of queues on this road once the weekend caravanners started their lemming-like trek in the summer months. As it was, the rolling moors and sparse forest land passed by at an agreeable rate, and Dave dozed peacefully.

At Ringwood, a fast drive down the spur road brought them to the busy seaside town of Bournemouth, and the cricket club just outside its centre. There was a game in progress. A dozen or so spectators were sitting outside the clubhouse, although none of them seemed to be watching the game, instead they were involved in amicable conversation like any other English drinking club. A few had opted out of both the match and the conversation, dozing off in the afternoon sunshine. Pete and Dave went into the bar, flashed their warrant cards and asked to speak to the manager.

“That’s me. Ken Rawlings, how can I help you?” he offered, as he took them to a quiet corner.
“We’re investigating the death of Mike Johnson in Eastleigh, and we understand he used to be a regular here” replied Pete.
“Mike? Oh yes, he certainly was, a while back. We heard a couple of days ago about what happened to him. Terrible business. They were a very nice couple, the Johnsons. Though I must say, we haven’t seen him in here for a couple of years, since he and Kathy left the area,”
“So you knew them both?” Pete had been jotting down notes.
“Yes, there was a big crowd of them would come in on a Friday afternoon – well, some of them still do” he nodded towards a corner where a half-dozen business-suited young men and women were engaged in a noisy banter. “It seems to be the thing with the banking crowd. They used to knock off early and hit the champagne bars when their offices were in London. Then they were all relocated down here, given huge incentive bonuses which pushed up the house prices and made it impossible for the locals to buy anything. Now they take over places like this or country pubs in the New Forest, before going home to their wives and their Aga cookers, in their thatched cottages with security cameras and electric gates”
Dave smiled at the bitterness in the local man’s tale. “Probably

does your business no harm" he commented, looking at the older regulars outside, dozing off over their half-pints of ale.
"No, of course it doesn't" continued Rawlings "It gave us and the town a new lease of life. Before they came you could roll up the roads at seven in the evening, as soon as the Senior Citizens special had finished serving."
"So what do you know about Mike Johnson's crowd, especially with regard to gambling and drugs?" Pete took a deliberately direct tack to gain a reaction.
Rawlings' demeanour changed immediately. "There was never, I repeat, never any trouble like that here. They would get tanked up on their clever cocktails, trying to outdo each other on how much they could spend on a round, then it would eventually get on to a game of poker. They'd sit there for an hour or two playing for matchsticks."
It sounded to Pete like a well-rehearsed monologue, as Rawlings continued.
"As you know it's illegal to play for money in premises licensed only for drinking, but everyone knew that each matchstick was worth a lot more when it came time to settle up outside in the car park, maybe a hundred quid each from what I've heard. It sometimes got a bit noisy, and if somebody was losing a lot there could be some pushing and shoving, but that's

when I would step in and send them on their way. Where they went after that I never knew or cared, and no cash ever changed hands in this club, I can assure you of that."

"So are any of that lot over there part of Mike Johnson's old crowd?" Pete nodded towards the smartly-dressed group.

"No, they're all too young. The original lot have either moved away or settled down to retirement as gentlemen farmers" laughed Rawlings "You don't need to be in that banking business for more than a couple of years to make a comfortable fortune. When the three of them moved up to Portsmouth the gang disappeared and a new crowd of rich layabouts took over"

"The three of them?" queried Dave

"Well, yes" Rawlings continued "Kathy, Mike and Dan Mahoney."

Pete and Dave looked at each other. At that moment one of the bankers got up and walked to the bar, wallet in hand.

"And if you've finished with me, I've got another expensive round to serve up". With that, Rawlings smiled at the customer and went back behind the bar.

It was past four o'clock when they met Andy Withers in the cafeteria of Bournemouth police station. After introductions, Pete got straight down to business.

“We need to know about Spike Palmer, Andy. We know he died from an overdose a few weeks ago, but we want to know if he had any connection with that after-work banking crowd from the cricket club.”

“Not sure I can help you much Pete” Andy replied. “Spike was a real character here, everyone seemed to know him. He had his own band for a while, played a couple of times in the Kiss FM concerts on the beach. Then he was a DJ and a record producer with his own studio. Made quite a bit from managing a couple of indie bands, but would spend it all on some pretty wild living. He was a regular at the discos, the hotel bars, the clubs, just about anywhere people had money to spend, but he was a real clever bugger and never got into any bother. We always suspected he bought and sold some hard stuff, but every time we found an excuse to pull him in there wasn’t even an ounce of pot on him or at his pad over on Sandbanks”. Andy referred to the exclusive residential area of neighbouring Poole, where the mansions overlook the sea and you could pay fifty thousand to buy a beach hut. “He would usually hang out late with the clubbers over at Tower Park, on the way to Poole, or here in Bournemouth at the Artful Dodger Pub, where all the foreign students get their sample of British culture. There was a bit of activity with the ‘early doors’ crowd at the ‘Moon in the

Square' pub, right in the centre of town here, but that was mainly the students again, trying to score a joint or two for smoking back at their digs. If there's any connection with the cricket club scene, that's where it would be".
Pete couldn't hide his disappointment. "Never mind, I didn't expect there to be an obvious link between Suicide Man and a dead drug dealer. Maybe you could do a bit of trawling around for us Andy? Show the staff and regulars some pictures of Johnson and Spike Palmer, see if anything clicks?"
Andy nodded. "You get the photos e-mailed over and I'll get someone down there, plugging away at the early crowd. I'll e-mail you with any results by Monday morning".
"Thanks mate" Pete turned to Dave. "Let's hit the road before the holidaymakers start clogging up the roads. I want to stop in at Kathy Johnson's sports club to check a few things"

Pete dropped Dave off at the police station at Eastleigh and went on to the sports club. He was surprised that there were not many cars in the car park, but then realised that on Fridays there were a lot more interesting things to do than working out. Those who didn't live in the area would be well on their way home. Those who did live here would be getting dressed up for their Friday night out. He walked through the main door and up to the reception desk, showing his ID to a young receptionist who rcacted to it by immediately looked guilty.

"Do you have a computerised attendance system here?" he asked.

"Yes we do", she replied, turning her computer screen towards him so that he could read it. "I hope we're not in trouble for anything. Do you want me to call the manager?"

"No, that's fine. Can you explain how the entry system works?"

"Of course" She started to relax. Maybe the police weren't interested in the little cash backhanders she took instead of issuing temporary membership cards. "Each of the club members is set up on our database and has their own membership card. They swipe it at the desk here". She pointed to a card reader. "And that operates the turnstile into the changing area. They're supposed to swipe it again when they leave, but a lot of them don't bother. It's supposed to help if there's a fire and we have to take a role call out in the car park, but we've never even had a practice - " She stopped suddenly as if she'd said something that might get her into trouble.

"It's alright, I'm not really interested in Health and Safety right now. This is about the death earlier in the week of Mike Johnson. Can you bring up the records for Tuesday night?"

Pete interrupted, trying to put her mind at rest.
"Oh, yes, I heard about that. Such a shame, wasn't it?"
Pete didn't bother responding but waited for her to comply with his request. She got the message after a few seconds and tapped the keyboard a couple of times, then turned the screen a bit more towards him so he could see it. "This is from six o'clock to midnight, although we usually close at eleven. What are you looking for?"
Again Pete didn't reply. He'd already seen Kathy Johnson's name on the first page, signing in at eighteen twenty.
"Can you page through slowly up to the last entries that day, please?"
She did so, watching his face as he nodded for her to continue with each new page. On the last page for that day, he saw Kathy's name again, last-but-one member to leave, at twenty-three ten. He made a note of the last member to leave, also timed at twenty-three ten. Jack Martin."

CHAPTER TWELVE

The business about DNA and fingerprinting seemed quite straightforward to Kathy. She'd had nothing better to do that Saturday morning, so she dropped in to Eastleigh police station, told the desk sergeant what she'd come for, and waited patiently till a nice-looking young policeman showed her into a room which looked a bit like a doctor's surgery. Kathy didn't particularly like surgeries, doctor or dental. Too many times those visits involved pain and discomfort, even if the end result was worth it.

"I need to take a swab of the inside of your mouth, Mrs Johnson" said the young PC. Putting on latex gloves he made some polite conversation about the weather and Christmas coming, before using a test kit to scrape her mouth and put a sample into the waiting test tube.

"That's fine, now I just need some fingerprints" he continued, leading her across to a small table where there was a very complicated-looking machine.

"So where's the inkpad?" She asked, bemused.

"Ah, it's a lot more sophisticated nowadays" he replied. "Our good friends at the FNI have come up with a new system, where we just scan your fingers and your prints get digitised.

They automatically get sent to the States and are available to any other law enforcement agency”

As he carefully positioned each hand and scanned her fingers, she was amused by his non-stop patter about the local news, sport and holidays. She felt like asking him if he’d ever been a hairdresser or a dentist. She didn’t remember her gynaecologist chatting away like this during his probing, but maybe that would have made her giggle too much. The young policeman was probably waffling like that to make the work more interesting. She guessed that all trainee policemen had to go through this menial and boring work before they were allowed out to beat up criminals.

It was quickly done. Kathy walked back through the lobby and was politely saying her goodbye to the PC when she stopped mid-sentence, as she saw Graham and Gloria sitting there, waiting their turn.

“Hello you two, long time no see!” she said brightly before they could pretend they hadn’t seen her. She turned to the policeman. “I suppose they’re next? Make sure you use a different swab, I don’t want them catching any STDs. Or do you think they’ve they come to confess?” The policeman actually blushed.

“Hello Kathy”, Gloria replied, noticeably coldly. “Still seeing

the funny side of everything then?"
"Sorry Gloria, you know me well enough by now. I've had a couple of days of feeling sorry for myself, but now I reckon there's not a lot I can do about the situation, so I may as well make the most of it. I'm not quite in the mood yet to throw a party, but staying at a hotel turned out to be a good idea. I'm still a bit hurt, though, that you didn't want me sleeping at your place".
"It's not that I didn't want you, I just didn't want Mr Horny here to get any ideas" She nodded in Graham's direction.
The policeman turned redder and quickly went into another office.
Gloria stood up to face Kathy. "That detective seems to think that you and my husband got up to some mischief the day Mike died, and not for the first time, either"
Kathy couldn't contain herself. She burst out laughing.
"Oh my God, is that what he thought? You must be crazy to think anything like that would happen. You live right on top of us, for Christ's sake! And besides, who in their right mind could imagine me having it off with dear old Graham? It's laughable! Hey, Graham, don't tell me you ever had the hots for me? Or did you?"
Graham shifted uncomfortably. "Well, actually, there was a

time when I – "He saw the look in both women's eyes and realised that silence was his best course of action.
Kathy continued. "That copper is just looking for connections that aren't there, and I for one am not going to be bothered by him. He can picture me swinging from Graham's chandelier as much as he likes, it never happened. Sorry Graham, but you can keep the image if you need it to get to sleep at night. As it happens, I've got another idea I'm following up, so I'll be busy the rest of the day. But how about we get together tomorrow, down at the Cricketers? My treat, and we can get rid of any lingering discomfort".
"Of course" replied Graham, who had recovered enough to speak for them both. "But obviously there was never any doubt. Look," he nodded as the policeman came back in "The constable is ready for us now. We'll see you around one o'clock?"

Kathy's next stop was the library, where she made herself comfortable in the reference section at a desk with a microfiche reader. Although most recent records are now computerised, the local newspapers were still diligently filmed and indexed to make the content more accessible to people without basic computer skills. She started first with the Portsmouth Evening

News, going back to four years previously and working forward twelve months. Progress was slow, but the process was quite simple, as she was only interested in the birth announcements column for each day. She had been prepared for a long session, maybe expanding her search to include the Southampton Evening Echo and the Hampshire Gazette, but after an hour or so she found what she was looking for: "Karen and Matthew Peterson are proud to announce the birth of their son Alfie Oliver Peterson at Portsmouth General". Kathy hadn't even know whether Karen had been married at the time she left the bank after the discrimination case, but she remembered Mike telling her that he was pregnant at the time. Now Kathy scanned the British Telecom Portsmouth white pages for the name Peterson. If Karen had been living alone, it would have been Peterson, K, so no-one would know her sex, but of course a man would be listed with his full name, which left those with just an initial being female anyway. There was no Matthew Peterson listed, but there was a K. Peterson, at an address in Fratton Park.

Sunday lunchtime at the "Cricketers" pub saw the bar packed as usual. It was famous for its carvery, and the queue for the roast beef and Yorkshire pudding was a long one. Kathy was always surprised that the British continued to enjoy a mountain of tasteless food smothered in lumpy gravy, in preference to the more subtle pleasures provided by lightly cooked and smaller portions of food that wasn't available to their mothers. The "Pile it High and Sell it Cheap" mentality was still very entrenched though, and Kathy just needed one breath of the smell of boiled cabbage before she decided that lasagne might be a wiser choice. She cast a glance over the heads in the public bar but couldn't see her neighbours anywhere. It was a warm dry day, so she continued into the beer garden and found them sitting next to each other at a table for four, she with a port and lemonade, he with a pint of dark, flat English ale.

"Hi folks!" she beamed. "Sorry I'm a bit late. I needed a long shower after that workout at the gym. Still training your arm muscles for that pint-lifting marathon, are you Graham?"

Graham took a long, slow, sip before he replied. "I suppose I should be used to your ways by now Kathy" he sighed, "But it seems to me that we should have buried poor Mike before we get too light-hearted"

"I'm sure you're right" she answered contritely, "It's just my way of dealing with it I suppose. You know as well as I do there wasn't a lot of fire left in our relationship, but I do miss him, you know that."

"So what made that copper think we were having a fling? Can't I even go to the pub at night without them thinking I'm up to no good?"
"It must be those devilish good looks of yours" she flirted, then noticed Gloria's glare. "Sorry, Gloria, I just can't help myself, can I? No, the truth of it is that I was late back from the gym that night. Mike and I had had a bit of a Barney, not for the first time, and I stormed out. That copper's innuendo about the back seat was just to wind you up, just to get a reaction. And I must say you responded brilliantly for him by getting all snotty towards me. But bloody hell, how long have we known each other now? I think I can just about keep my hands out of your trousers if I try hard enough. Although from what Gloria says there's not a lot to find in there."
Gloria finally smiled. "You can say that again, love!"
They were interrupted by the landlord walking by. "Hello Graham, Gloria. And Kathy, can I say again how sorry I was to hear your bad news, about Mike. Anyway, life must go on, I suppose, so if you're thinking of eating you'd better get a move on. Last orders in twenty minutes."
"No problem, Tom" Kathy was quick to answer for them all. "Just one thing though. I don't know if the police have asked you this yet, but they will. Can you remember if Graham here

was on his own last Tuesday night?"
"Tuesday night - are you kidding?" replied Tom. That was darts night. He was at the bar with Pat Murphy, arguing over how much you're allowed to shuffle over the oche before it's a foul throw. It was past eleven thirty when I finally got rid of them both"
"There you are Gloria" smiled Kathy, "Even I couldn't be that quick!"
Tom the landlord looked puzzled.
"I never doubted either of you" replied Gloria, Now let's eat, I'm famished. I quite fancy the carvery, don't you?"

Fratton Park is a sprawling suburb of Portsmouth, built mainly for navy personnel so not far from the docks, but mostly known to the outside world for its football ground. Kathy found Bramble road thanks to her Sat Nav, which guided her down the main thoroughfare, past the Cooperative Funeral Service and the tattoo parlour into an intricate maze of pre-war housing, some neatly kept, some severely neglected, but all of which had seen better days. Number sixteen still had its original brick facade, but for some reason had been painted pink. Kathy parked as near as she could, but as it was Sunday and anybody who worked was now at home, it was still a good fifty yards walk back to the house. She looked around as she locked the car door, hoping it would still have its wheels when she got back, and walked to the house. She rang the bell and waited a few moments, saw movement behind the frosted glass front door, which then was opened by a young woman, with a child of about two holding on to her leg.

“Mrs Peterson?” Kathy began.

“If your preaching, selling or scrounging for votes you’re out of luck here” the woman interrupted.

“No, none of the above” Kathy continued, “I’m Mike Johnson’s wife”

A look of panic flooded across Karen Peterson’s face. She bent down and picked up the child, then pulled the door gently to behind her as she stepped into the street. She pushed her face directly into Kathy’s and spoke in a snarling whisper.

“What the fuck do you want? I thought I’d seen the last of you lot when I walked out of the bank. My old man’s round at the legion club getting tanked up on cider, and he won’t be best pleased if he comes home and finds you here”

“I just came to tell you, if you didn’t know already, that Mike’s dead”

Shock registered in Karen’s face. Then it was replaced by a worried look, and back again to her defensive demeanour.

“Well, I’m sorry to hear that, but it’s none of my business any more. Now piss off.”

“But what about the money he’s been giving you? How are you going to manage now?”

Karen didn’t miss a beat. “Do you think I’d be living in this shit hole if he’d been giving me money? Or living with a deadbeat like the one I’ve got coming home soon?” She looked nervously down the road.

Kathy took the hint. “Look, I know you know something, even if you’re frightened to speak to me here. I’m staying at the Travel Lodge in Eastleigh. Call me or come and see me. I think we should talk.”

“And I think you should get your head examined” replied Karen, and with that she pulled the child inside and slammed the door.

It was dark by the time Kathy got back to the Travel Lodge. Even though she’d eaten at lunchtime she’d only picked at her lasagne while Graham and Gloria had waded through the all-you-can-eat special, so she thought she’d kill some time before bed, with a dessert and coffee in the restaurant. She was deep in thought when she heard a voice she recognised.

“So the Times crossword got too hard for you?”

Jack Martin pulled up a chair opposite her and sat down.
"Are you talking to me now?" she smiled, not even trying to hide her relief. "Jack, I'm sorry I got you involved in that mess at the Casino. I just needed an ally. It all went too far. Can you forgive me?"
"Of course I can Kathy. You seem OK to me, a bit weird, but that's not a bad thing, and you seem to have been through a bad few days, so nothing to forgive. I've had the weekend to think about it, and I've decided I want to hear the whole story. If you're up to it, that is"
She smiled. "You'd better order something. It's not a short story"
"I've already ordered, they'll bring it when it's ready."
She began filling in the details of the night she'd found Mike's body, about the row she'd had with him when he seemed to be high. His wild claims about having the answer to their financial woes, her storming out, and then coming home after the sports club and finding his body. She'd reached the part about the police sending her over to Gloria's for the night, when a shadow was cast over the table. Kathy looked up, expecting to see the waiter with Jack's meal, and saw a giant of a man swaying over them.
"Mrs Johnson" The voice was slurred and the smell of cider

unpleasant.
“I’m Carl Swann. Karen Peterson’s bloke. Iwant to talk to you. Let’s go outside”.
Kathy and Jack exchanged glances.
“She’s going nowhere with you” replied Jack “unless I come too”
“There’s no need to be gallant, Jack” smiled Kathy. “He’s twice your size but he wouldn’t dare lay a finger on me. Anyway, you’ve seen me in action in Southampton, I can give as good as I get”
“No argument Kathy. I want to hear what the gorilla wants, anyway.”
“Suits me” said Swann, and led the way out to the car park.
The car park was floodlit but there were plenty of darker areas. Swann walked over to one and turned to face them. They followed him and stopped a safe distance from him.
“My missus tells me that you’ve been pestering her” Swann began.
“You know that’s crap” replied Kathy. “Did you know she’d been receiving money from my husband?”
“She told me that’s what you said” he replied. “And she told me she hadn’t been given anything. The trouble is, I believe her. If I didn’t she knows I’d tear her apart as soon as spit on

her"

"Well it's up to you what you believe. Now if we're finished here, I'll get back inside."

"No you won't, you cow" he walked menacingly towards them "because I know you've got plenty of money. I think your old man did give her money, and she's clever enough to hide it from me. And I don't think we should stop that, it's just that now you'll be giving me money instead of her getting it from him"

"Don't be ridiculous. Why would I do that?"

"Because the secret he was paying her to keep is the same one you'll pay me to keep"

"I don't think so. Whatever secret he may have had has died with him. I don't give a rat's ass what you think you know or what you can get from your wife. You won't get a penny from me"

"Well, maybe there's something else you can donate to the poor of Fratton Park" and with that he rumbled forward and grabbed her shoulders. She momentarily lost balance and was about to fall when she felt Jack's arm supporting her. His other arm, however was moving in a blur towards Swann, a curled fist ready at the end of it. The blow hit Swann square on the jaw and moved him back a pace. He let go of Kathy and smiled at

Jack.

“Now you’re going to regret that, you – “ but was interrupted by a left fist into his kidney from the hand that had now released Kathy. He doubled up immediately and was rewarded with a fast combination to the solar plexus that made his gasp for breath. He raised his eyes to Jack just in time to see the fist heading once more for his face, and was able only to turn slightly so that it smashed into his nose instead of his cheekbone. He ended up on all fours breathing heavily but awkwardly.

“I’ve left you conscious so you can drive back where you came from. But don’t ever come near this lady or me ever again”.

Jack held Kathy’s arm and they went back into the Travel Lodge. At the entrance to the restaurant they paused.

“That was mighty impressive for an IT geek” commented Kathy.

“I was in IT working for the military before I went into consultancy” he smiled. “They teach you a lot more than programming if you want to learn”

“Well, I’m grateful. Although of course I could have handled it myself. Now I think you were about to eat dinner.” She smiled. “How about you get room service to deliver it to my room?”

Jack smiled back. “That’s where I told them to bring it”

CHAPTER THIRTEEN

Jack was up and showered, whistling to himself as he shaved, sneaking a glance in the bathroom mirror at the half-covered form of Kathy sleeping contentedly in an admittedly very ruffled-looking bed. He actually hadn't done this kind of thing before. He hadn't even been tempted. All the times he'd stayed in hotels during the week, there had been a mix of male and female business people in exactly the same situation, and behaving themselves just as he had done. He'd gone to dinner with colleagues of both sexes, taken part in team-building exercises involving both sexes and struck up conversations with equally lonely people, again of both sexes, in hotel bars and pubs. None of these encounters had led anywhere else, and he had never wanted them to. He thought it might be because the 'work-ethic' continued on into the corporate hotel life, where often you would continue with meetings, phone calls and e-mails, and you'd often be running into people you'd known from previous assignments. Sharing a hotel bed with someone you worked with seemed no different to him than having a quickie in the company filing room – it would only end in trouble. This time things seemed different. Sort of natural. Maybe it was because Kathy was so easy-going, despite the nightmare story she'd revealed the previous night. The horror she'd gone through discovering her husband's body made her desperate for some comfort, and he'd been only too happy to oblige. Was he taking advantage of her? Perhaps, but they were both grown-ups. This casual affair, he knew, would end very soon. But while it continued, it was a very pleasant experience indeed, and a great boost to his confidence, continually dented at work right now. He asked himself what the housekeeping staff would make of it. Very little, he decided, other than some rich gossip – they would be used to such goings-on, and he knew that it wouldn't get back to anyone he knew or cared about. The last thing he wanted was this rather flattering experience to end up hurting anyone. He looked closely at himself in the mirror and smiled. Not bad, he thought. You're wearing quite well, you know. No wonder he'd struck so lucky. About time someone appreciated you more. Then he felt a pang of guilt and thought briefly about home life in Bath. No, to paraphrase a well-worn saying, what happens in Eastleigh stays in Eastleigh. He would worry about his conscience when this was over.

He finished dressing and went into the bedroom, picked up his briefcase then stooped to the bed and kissed Kathy lightly on the shoulder.

“I’ll be down at breakfast. Will you be joining me or have I exhausted you?”
She replied in a purr, but without opening her eyes.
“Mmm, I think I need some calories after last night’s workout, but don’t get carried away, you haven’t seen me reach second gear yet!”
He smiled again. She rolled over and opened her eyes.
“But you’re not leaving this hotel till we’ve got the kitchen staff talking about us as much as the housekeeping staff, so yes, I will have some breakfast, thank you. I’ll sneak back first to my own room to shower and change. Wearing the same clothes two days running is a dead giveaway, even if no-one knows me here. I’ll see you in the restaurant in ten minutes”.

Jack took his usual seat and pored himself some coffee. He glanced around the room at the other diners, nodding at a few he’d met. He wondered if they could detect anything different about him this morning. A bigger smile? A twinkle in his eyes? A bouncier walk as he entered the restaurant? He realised he might be getting carried away. No-one else knew or cared about what he’d been up to. And he needed to snap out of it and carry on as normal. He did, though, now have a bit of fire in his belly. Those old codgers criticising his project had better watch out. He was ready to take them on now! He'd seen Kathy take on some powerful people last night, it was refreshing to be so unafraid and he was going to follow her example. He was going through notes for that morning's meetings when he noticed Kathy arrive. The sheaves of paper he was holding seemed to dissolve in his hands in the same way as his stomach did. Get a grip on yourself, he thought, and went back to his reading, now with one eye only. She stopped at the buffet and poured an orange juice, then walked over to his table.

"Excuse me, do you mind if I join you?" she enquired politely.

"Why of course not – Mrs Johnson, isn't it?" he replied, louder than really necessary.

"Please, call me Kathy. I hoped you'd remember. We met at the gym the other night." Equally loud. No-one seemed to notice, but everyone heard. She sat and calmly sipped her juice. He was sweating profusely, looking down at his papers and pretending to read them. Eventually he looked up and realised that Kathy was trying to suppress a giggling fit.

"Jack, you are so no good at this!" she whispered. "I'm sorry if I'm making you uncomfortable. I'll be off in a minute." She drank her juice and watched him squirm. Then she slowly put down her glass and cleared her throat, seeming to take on a comparatively serious air. “But there’s something a bit strange I need to talk to you about first”

He looked up, concerned, and put his papers down. “What is it?”

“The thing is” she hesitated. “I’ve got a feeling someone’s been in my room”

Jack responded immediately, smiling. “Of course they have. While we were diving from the top of the wardrobe last night the rest of the hotel had an orgy in your room, trying to compete!” He stopped. She hadn’t changed her serious expression. “Oh. This isn’t a wind-up.”

“No, it’s not Jack. I wish it was. I don’t want to spoil our fun, but it scared me. I mean, the room’s not messed up or anything. The door hasn’t been forced and the window’s still locked. There’s nothing missing, but I can just tell that someone’s gone through my stuff”

“Wow. I’ll get the manager to call the police – “ Jack started. His natural protective nature had kicked in again, boosted by his performance against Carl the previous night.

“That would be pointless Jack. It’s just a feeling, after all. Anyway, I’m not hanging around here today, but I’m not planning any more vigilante activity either. I’ve decided that I’m going to behave myself and leave it to the professionals. In fact, I'm going to pay that detective man, that Pete Thomas, a visit and find out if they're getting anywhere. And, of course, how soon I can move back into my own house and get on with picking up the pieces of my life."

Jack could feel the beginning of a quick end to their relationship, but remained gallant. "I know it sounds selfish, but I'll be sorry to see you leave here"

"Oh, I think we'll probably run into each other at the sports club, don't you think?" She smiled. Maybe this wasn't over yet.

"You can bet on it." He smiled back. Then he looked at his watch. "But now I have to run, I've got a meeting at – "He stopped as he noticed she was staring wide-eyed through the restaurant window behind him. He turned and followed her gaze but could see nothing unusual.

"What is it?" he spoke urgently.

She seemed to be in shock, and for a few seconds was silent. "Nothing. I think it was nothing. I mean I thought I saw someone. You know? Looking in? Someone like, well like that bodyguard bloke from the casino. That Terry, or whatever his name was. But it couldn't be, could it?"

"Stay here, I'll be right back" Jack got up and moved towards the exit, but Kathy grabbed his arm.

“Don’t do anything rash, Jack! You were a hero last night, but that bloke’s as strong as an ox. He’s not a bodyguard for nothing”

“I’ll take my chances” replied Jack smoothly and disappeared through the exit door. His expression changed gradually from super-confident to ‘what in hell am I doing?’ as he disappeared from Kathy’s view.

She waited nervously, and kept looking out the window in case anything kicked off, but all she saw was Jack walking briskly first one way across the car park then the other. He was back within minutes.

“Nobody.” He was breathless. He’d had a good walk around the building. “If it was him, he disappeared pretty quickly. Are you going to be OK?”

“I’ll be fine. I’m not going to let them intimidate me. I know him and his boss are up to no good, but I don’t think they’d try anything. I just don’t know how Mike got himself mixed up in it”

“Let the police take care of all that, will you? Look, here’s my mobile number”, he handed her a business card from his briefcase. “If you need me, just give me a call”

“Thanks, Jack. I appreciate all your support. And I thought you were just a good fuck”

Jack stopped dead in his tracks and slowly reddened. He wasn't used to such directness, even as he realised it was a joke to lighten the atmosphere.
"I'll see you later" he managed, and left the restaurant, straightening his tie and trying to look business-like.

Gloria was on her third cup of tea of the morning, but still in her dressing gown. Getting dressed was one of her afternoon activities. She'd sat through "Jeremy Kyle" and ranted at the screen as a parade of no-hopers from Birmingham had slagged each other off in an argument over some poor kid's parentage. She was now in the middle of the "Coronation Street Omnibus", recorded on Sunday afternoon while they were at the pub, and now being used as a stop-gap till it was time for "Loose Women". Gloria wondered what people watched before there was daytime television. Maybe they just recorded stuff or downloaded it? That couldn't be it. There must have been daytime television always, it was just that she hadn't watched much of it before she got laid off from the Call Centre. Funny, though – she simply wouldn't have time for a job now, with so much on TV. Suddenly there was a frantic banging on the door and at the same time her doorbell was being rung repeatedly. Gloria jumped up and held her dressing gown tighter around her. She heard shouting and peered around the lounge door to see the letter box in her front door held open and familiar eyes staring at her.

“Gloria! Will you open this bloody door? Come on, I need you to let me in, NOW!”

She’d never seen Kathy so agitated. She froze momentarily then warily approached the front door.

“Kathy, is that really you? What’s the matter?” Gloria shouted at the letter box.

“Of course it’s me, you dumb fuck!” Open the sodding door!”

Gloria complied, trying to pull the door open just a little bit, in case it was some kind of con trick, but Kathy shoved it open all the way and tumbled in. She turned and pushed the door shut, with Gloria’s hand still around the doorknob. She pulled Gloria’s hand away and leant against the door, breathing heavily.

Gloria could only stare at her. Eventually she ventured “What on earth is wrong, Kathy?”

Kathy had calmed slightly. She took Gloria by the elbow and led her into the lounge.

“Take a look outside, Gloria” she asked, pushing her forward and pulling the lace curtain back so that Gloria could see across the road. “Can you see anything?”

“I think it’s starting to rain. Is that it?”
“This isn’t a bloody weather forecast – can you see a car?”
“Only yours”
“No behind it, further down the road. There’s a silver BMW”
“Well, I’m not sure what a BMW look like really” whispered Gloria apologetically, “Ours is a Mondeo and they all look the same to me”. She could see that Kathy needed her to try harder.
“But I can’t see any silver car at all”
Kathy moved Gloria out of the way and looked down the road.
“He must have stopped at the end of the road”
“Who must have?”
“That bloke from the casino. I was on my way to the police station. I pulled out of the hotel car park and noticed a silver BMW pull out behind me. I didn’t think much about it till about halfway to the police station, but he was still there, so I turned into a side street, and then took a few more turns to get back on the main road. When I looked in the mirror he was still there. I got panicky, he wasn’t getting any closer but he was still there, as if he was warning me. I thought, I can’t go to the police now, so I came here”
“But what would he want, and why can’t you just go to the police?”
“You don’t think he’d let me get there, do you? Whatever Mike

was involved in, they must think I've got something on them. They mean to keep me quiet somehow"
"Really Kathy, I think you're being a bit over-dramatic, aren't you? This is Hampshire, not the Bronx"
"Well someone strung poor Mike up in our garage right across the street from you, and I'll be damned if I'm going to be their next victim. No, I've been over to Southampton, to that casino where this bloke works. His boss is a nasty piece of work, I wouldn't put anything past him. I reckon there's a lot more going on with them than meets the eye, and Mike, the silly sod, was in it up to his neck." She paused as she realised the irony of that last phrase.
"So what are you going to do?" asked Gloria, her face uncomprehending.
"I'm still going to the police, as I planned. But you need to do me a favour."
"What's that?"
"As soon as I go, get on the phone to that Inspector Thomas. Here's the card he gave me with his number on it. Tell him I'm on my way there, but I think I'm being followed"
"And what do you expect him to do about it?"
"Well, if he's got any sense he'll have someone watch out for me, and they'll be able to grab that bloke if he's on my tail"

"But wouldn't it be better if you called the police from here and then they could catch the bloke at the end of the road, if that's where he is?"
"No, I think he'll be too clever for that, he'd be gone. But if I can keep ahead of him while he's following me, and I'm near the police station when he tries to do something, they can nab him."
"Sounds pretty far-fetched to me," grumbled Gloria. "I think you've been watching too much TV. That and all the stress you're under, maybe you should just lie down for a bit?" She saw the pleading in Kathy's eyes. "But of course I'll do it. You can rely on me"

Pete Thomas was on a break at the coffee machine when Dave came up to him with the message, scrawled on a post-it note. "What the hell is that woman playing at?" was his first reaction. He read it again. "She thinks someone's following her, someone involved in her husband's murder, and I'm supposed to ambush him?"
"Well, that's about the gist of the message" observed Dave dryly. "Should I get a few squad cars together and set up a road block like on telly?"
Pete just looked at him. "I'm on my break, and I'm fed up with

that woman's cops and robbers stories. I don't even know why she's coming here, she doesn't know anything that might help the case, just keeps getting in the way."

"So what are you going to do?"

"Absolutely nothing. If we hear about some woman being gunned down in the streets of Eastleigh by some thug driving a BMW then you can tell me I was wrong and I'll hand in my badge. But in the meantime, I've got work to do. I got an email from Johnson's bank just now. They've found an address for that woman in Johnson's discrimination case. It's in Fratton Park".

He paused for effect.

Dave whistled softly. "So that was the train ride?"

"Looks like" smiled Pete. "I'm off down there when I've finished my sandwich".

"You can sure leap into action when it's called for, I'll give you that. So what should I do when Mrs Johnson gets here?"

"Give her a nice cup of tea and tell her we're following up some more serious leads"

CHAPTER FOURTEEN

Pete pulled up right opposite Karen Peterson's front door. There was enough room for traffic to pass, so he just put his "police business" notice on the dashboard and got out. He studied the front yard, not as unkempt as some of its neighbours, but certainly wouldn't win any landscaping prizes. There were a few token rose bushes along one wall, but the rest of the front "garden" had been concreted over, with the front wall removed so that some "off road" parking could be provided. There was a 10-year-old VW Golf standing on the concrete, with a few dents and an out-of-date road tax disc. A wheelie bin stood on the path up to the front door. Pete edged around it and a couple of kiddies's ride-on toys before he could reach the front door, then pushed the bell. There was no corresponding bell sound from inside, so assumed it must be broken and knocked hard on the door instead. After about thirty seconds Karen Peterson opened the door an inch, a chain preventing the door from opening further. Pete could see a bruise on her cheek.

"What do you want?"

"Karen Peterson?"

"Might be. Might not. I might never have heard of her. You're not a debt collector ‘cos you didn’t shout abuse through the letterbox. So you must be the police. Just as bad. What do you want?”

“I want to talk to you and I’m not going to do it through this gap. Now open up or I’ll get the heavy mob in!”

Karen paused a second then closed the door, removed the chain and let him. Then she re-chained the door and led him into the lounge, which was covered in played-with toys and yet-to-be-washed baby clothes. She sat in a chair facing the TV without turning it off or even adjusting the volume. Some mindless game show where all you could hear was canned laughter, whooping and applause. Pete searched around for a gap in the debris to sit down, then picked up some toddler clothes to make a space. He held up the handful of the grubby clothes inquisitively.

“How old is the little ’un?”

“Three. What’s that got to do with anything? This is about Carl, isn’t it?”

“It might be. Might not. I might never have heard of him”

“Ha Ha. Very funny. I know it’s him again. I told him not to go up there. He gave me a whack for my trouble”. She touched her cheek gingerly.

Pete paused. He hadn’t expected the visit to provide him with

much of a lead, but Karen looked ready to talk.
"And by 'up there' I suppose you mean Eastleigh?"
"Maybe"
"So where is he now?"
"He's not back. But then he's not here much anyway. He's probably gone off on another bender"
"Who did he go to see in Eastleigh?"
"That woman. Mike Johnson's missus, of course. Who else?" She hesitated. "You knew that already, though, didn't you?" fingering her bruise again.
"Of course", replied Pete, more than a little confused. "So let me get this straight. He goes up to Eastleigh to see Mrs Johnson. What did he tell you about that? Did he say anything about Mr. Johnson? Did he say there was any kind of a confrontation?"
"Well, of course there was a confrontation. If Carl's involved there has to be. I don't know what Carl thought he could get out of it. Anyway, he came off worst in the end."
"Worst? What could be worse that getting killed?"
"What do you mean? Carl didn't get to even hit the bloke who was with Kathy Johnson, before he got dumped in the Travel Lodge car park"
"Hang on a minute" it was slowly dawning on Pete that they

were talking a cross-purposes. “You’re not talking about last Tuesday night, are you?”

“Course not. Last Tuesday was when Mike Johnson topped himself. I’m talking about last night. Carl went after Kathy Johnson after he got me to tell him where she was staying”

Pete adjusted his train of thought away from the night of the murder. “And what was he planning to do with her?”

“He thought I was making money out of him, and maybe he could do the same out of her”

Pete was back to his original thought about Johnson and the discrimination case. Had there really been an affair after all?

“And were you taking money from him?” He picked up one of the discarded toys pointedly.

“Of course I bloody wasn’t. I told that Johnson lot I’d never see them again, and I was serious”

She seemed to have missed the inference.

“So tell me about the kid” he asked directly.

“Nothing to tell. It’s a private matter” She’d obviously rehearsed the reply and had used it before.

“So what’s to be gained by pestering Kathy Johnson?”

“Carl seems to think there’s something there for him, and I let him get on with it. At least it gets him out of my hair for a while”

Pete breathed a long sigh.
"OK Karen, I'm going to need to find Carl and get his side of it. What's his full name, what does he look like, and what was he wearing last time you saw him?" He flipped open his notepad and wrote while she described her partner Carl Swann.
"Now look Karen" he said as she finished, "I'm going to ask you a question, and you know I can check your answer easily with just a phone call, but you can save me some time. Does Carl have any form?"
She looked resigned. "Oh, the usual stuff. He beat up a few people when they wouldn't pay their dues to the loan shark he worked for. But he's a reformed bloke now. He only knocks me about, not other people. And he's not really a bad bloke. He took me and the kid on, no complaints. One day, he's going to get a job and it'll all change. And whatever job he does get, at least it'll be an honest living, not organised thieving like those pratts at the bank"
"You sound bitter. You sure there's nothing you want to tell me?"
"Nope"
Pete closed his notebook and stood up. "This is getting me nowhere Karen, so I'll be off. But if I find out you've been hiding something, there'll be big trouble"

“You won’t” she replied confidently, and with that Pete went back to the car.

It was late afternoon by the time he returned to the police station car park. He couldn’t help but notice Dave Seddon leaning against a wall just up the road from the car park, so he walked back to speak to him.
“Bit of a long way from the office for a smoking break” he started, then stopped. “Bloody hell, don’t tell me you’ve been standing here waiting for Kathy Johnson and her mystery stalker since I left?”
Dave looked embarrassed. “Well actually, apart from a couple of loo breaks and checking on e-mails and such, I guess I’ve been here about two hours all told”
“More fool you, then. But you’re still here. What time did she turn up?”
“She didn’t”
“What did I tell you?” beamed Pete. “The woman must have realised she was dreaming it up and has gone to sleep it off, or maybe off to the mall for a bit of retail therapy. I’ll call the Travel Lodge first thing in the morning and ask if she’s still seeing shadows. Let’s go back to the office and see if Andy has any leads in Bournemouth.”

They walked back up the road and into the office. Sure enough, there was an email from Andy, short but to the point. “I’ve got a couple of names you might find interesting in connection with Mike Johnson: Dan Mahoney and Dizzie James. Can we meet at the Artful Dodger at eight tonight?”
“Just what I need”, sighed Pete. “Another evening shift. All these young coppers like Andy think it has to be like Miami bloody Vice, working twenty-four hours a day and rushing around with sirens blaring.”
“Oh, yes, I forgot” smiled Dave. “Monday night is University Challenge on the box, isn’t it? I still don’t see why it’s your favourite TV program, you hardly ever get any answers right”
“I’ll have you know, I got six right last week. You’d be surprised how much I know about Austrian philosophers. Anyway, I’ll just have to record it and watch it later. I suppose if there’s a connection with Bournemouth nightlife I won’t find much happening at lunchtime”.

But Pete needn’t have worried. Bournemouth at eight pm, like most UK towns, was pretty much deserted. Those who went out for an after-work drink had now gone home, those looking forward to a night out were still getting ready. The pub scene on a Monday night was even quieter than most lunchtimes. As

Pete peered into the Artful Dodger pub he wasn't even sure it was open. The lights were dim and there was no-one behind the bar. One side of the room had a set of wide stairs leading down to the "Basement Jaxx" nightclub, which kicked off at 11pm on weekends, but wouldn't be open tonight. Thursday would be packed with students, as the beer was cheaper that night to entice them in, but Monday through Wednesday would be as quiet as everywhere else in the town. Pete had always thought of Bournemouth as a retirement town, with its bowling greens and floral displays, but had heard that it changed character completely at weekend, with the streets filled from early evening with lads-night-out and hen parties, all pre-fuelled with cheap booze back at their B&Bs then on to that vacuous quest for exhibitionism and drunken oblivion that seemed to be the only goal of today's youngsters.

He walked towards the bar, expecting to see someone appear from nowhere in case he was going to help himself from the till, but instead heard a shout from the other side of the room.

"Pete! Over here, mate!"

Pete turned and saw Andy waiting for him at a table. He walked over and sat opposite.

"I won't get you a drink, 'cos I know you don't on the job"

Andy was halfway through a bottled beer – no glass.

"Just as well" returned Pete. "I don't think they'd know how to keep a good beer. My favourite down this way is Fortyniner, from the Ringwood brewery – I bet the closest you could get in this place would be something from Norway with a slice of lemon stuck in it"

"Yeh, you wouldn't get much real ale around here, Pete – the locals will go out to the country pubs for that, but I think you have to show your Zimmer frame before they'll serve it to you. Most of the town pubs are geared up for the foreign students, and if the beer's dark and warm they think it's the soup course. Anyway, I'm just clocking off so I thought I'd grab one. The espresso here is pretty good, if you want one"

"No thanks, I don't trust any coffee that hasn't come out of a vending machine. Who would serve it, anyway?" He looked back at the bar.

"Don't worry, Maurizio will be watching as usual through the mirrors from the back room". He pointed to the glass wall behind the shelves of designer beer bottles. "We just have to wave if we need anything"

"I don't want to hang around too long. I asked Jenny to keep dinner for me – it's shepherd's pie tonight, as it's Monday. Now what's this about the names you were checking out?"

"OK, so your Mike Johnson, as you told me, was one of the

cricket club set, along with Dan Mahoney and a couple of the other big-earners. Well, one of the people I showed the photos to recognised Dan Mahoney because he used to work with him."

"At United Midwest you mean?"

"No, before that. It seems that his previous job was over at Royal Bank of Canada, in Poole, where he was a junior IT project Manager".

"Hang on a minute. I'm not too good with corporate titles, but that's quite a promotion, from junior manager to head of IT security, isn't it?"

"Yes it is. The guy I talked to admitted that Mahoney had the qualifications and some experience, but had been surprised when Mahoney got the job, as there were plenty of other people applying who seemed to have much better CVs. More interestingly, he said that the application would have gone straight in the bin if United Midwest had heard the rumour about Mahoney that was going around at the time"

"Which was?" Pete got attentive. He hadn't taken much to Mahoney when they'd met.

"According to the rumour mill, Mahoney was a member of a betting syndicate, under investigation for fixing horse racing results"

Pete drew a deep breath. “Well I never. That’s an subject that’s already come up in this case, Andy”
“Of course, it might be just a coincidence” said Andy. “Nothing was ever proven. But I understand that RBC were quite happy to give Mahoney a glowing reference when he applied for the United Midwest job”
“Doesn’t surprise me somehow that the banks would big someone up just to get rid of them” replied Pete, remembering Rowena the Hatchet. “What is it about those banking types that makes my skin creep? Sounds like I need to talk to Mahoney again. I’ll do it first thing tomorrow. You mentioned another name – Dizzie James.”
“Yes, he might be the connection for the cocaine. No convictions, but used to hang around with Spike Palmer and his crowd. He’s a bit of a loner, sleeps under the pier a lot and plays Bob Dylan to the local teenage girls. He’s been around and he’s got some contacts, although no obvious connection with the Johnsons, but I wouldn’t be surprised if he could score some lines if he was paid enough”
“What is it with the naming conventions for kids of a certain age? Spike? Dizzie? Am I going to end up interviewing the modern equivalent of the seven dwarfs?”
“Well, I don’t know about Dizzie, but I heard that Spike

Palmer's dad was a fan of the Goons, whoever they were"
"I won't embarrass myself by admitting I remember them, then. OK Andy, thanks. I'll do some of my own digging on this Dizzie chap"
"So how is the rest of the case looking? " Andy asked.
"There are a couple of suspicious-looking characters around, but we're still a bit sort of motives. The victim's wife is stirring things up a bit, keeps thinking she's being stalked by some thug from Portsmouth. I can't see it myself, although I'm sure there's a connection between the thug's missus and the victim."
"Does the thug have a name?"
"Carl Swann." Pete saw Andy react. "Sound familiar?"
"You bet it does" smiled Andy. "Does more than his fair share of threatening behaviour in Bournemouth and Poole, so I'm not surprised he's known in Portsmouth. I haven't seen him down here for a while though"
The pub was beginning to fill up now. Maurizio had come out from the back and had served a dozen or so customers, most of whom were still standing near the bar. Andy looked around, and noticed a familiar face.
"I suppose you've already got a description of Carl Swann?" said Andy, in a lowered tone of voice.
Pete started reciting the description given by Karen Peterson.

“Blond, thick set, twenty-seven years old.... “
“Don’t bother” smiled Andy. “I was just kidding. That’s him over there” He nodded towards the bar.
Pete glanced up just as Carl Swann turned his head towards them. It took a couple of seconds to recognise Andy, and he didn’t know who Pete was, but he quickly put down the pint of cider he’d been drinking and walked briskly to the main door. Andy and Pete rose as one and hurried after him through the exit. As they came out they saw Swann sprinting down the main shopping precinct. Pete was first to run after him, and quickly reached the corner that Swann had just turned, leading down to the sea front. Andy overtook Pete on the corner and started down the underpass beneath the busy road, but Swann was already coming out the other side, heading towards the pier. Bournemouth, like any traditional British seaside resort, prides itself on its lovingly-maintained Victorian pier, a structure some forty feet high sticking out into the bay, for people to stroll along and enjoy the view, with an amusement arcade, ballroom or theatre at the end as the culmination of their old-fashioned entertainment.
“Andy! Andy!” shouted Pete, already a bit breathless. “Come on back, it’s not worth it!”
“No, I’ll get him!” Andy yelled back. Pete felt honour-bound to

try to keep up with them, and eventually found Andy waiting at the pier entrance.

"I saw him go in, so it'll need two of us – there's a central seating area all the way along, and he could be either side."

They advanced slowly either side of the seating area.

They were two-thirds of the way along when Andy heard Pete shout.

"Bugger!"

Pete was looking back at the entrance. Carl had been hiding in one of the souvenir shops, and was now running back to the town centre. Andy ran a few paces and was on the verge of chasing Swann just for pride's sake, but reluctantly stopped, turned and rejoined Pete

"Like I said to someone earlier", Pete said with an ironic smile, "This isn't Miami Vice. I'm going home to watch telly."

CHAPTER FIFTEEN

The next morning Pete was waiting in the glass-walled atrium of the United Midwest Bank just before 10 a.m., having called earlier to make an appointment with Dan Mahoney. The IT security man himself came out to meet him.
"I hope it's not too early for you, Mr Mahoney," Pete began, "I know you banking types like a nine-to-five life"
Mahoney smiled indulgently. "You really must read some more modern background material, Inspector. Maybe in Dickens' day we were all sitting behind legers with our quill pens listening to the clock ticking, but it's different in the twenty-first century. I've been here since seven and won't be leaving till the same time tonight. Would you like some coffee?"
"That would be very nice" replied Pete as Mahoney led him into yet another coffee/relaxation area, "Black, no sugar".
Mahoney pressed the requisite buttons and they sat in a quiet corner. Pete was wondering why there was no money needed for the coffee machines, but supposed that free coffee would hardly make a dent in a global bank's profits. He'd thought about how he would approach this particular discussion, and had decided to let Mahoney's ego do the driving. He sipped his coffee slowly while Mahoney waited patiently, a polite smile

unfaltering on his face.

"So tell me how you came to leave Royal Bank of Canada in Poole" Pete said pleasantly, as if they were talking about his latest holiday. He took another sip and waited for a reaction. There was none. This guy is pretty smooth if he is hiding something, thought Pete. Mahoney drank some of his own coffee, placed the plastic cup down and calmly replied.

"I was wondering what you'd meant by 'some supplementary questions' when you call earlier. I knew it wasn't go get even more details of our money transfer procedures, with my previous description having almost sent you to sleep, so it must be to look at me personally, my relation to Mike Johnson and whether I have any skeletons hiding in my closet. Assuming it's relevant, the RBC move happened this way. Senior management and I had a disagreement over operating practices, I decided that it was time to look for a position elsewhere, I got headhunted and ended up here at United Midwest."

"And did those operating practices have something to do with your outside work connections to a large betting syndicate?"

Mahoney looked slighted. He sighed, took another drink and tried a smile, but his whole demeanour had changed. He was no longer a friend having a quiet chat over coffee, but a corporate officer answering impertinent questions and defending his position in the language of his well-documented standards and procedures.

"You will find that the matter was thoroughly investigated by RBC's ethics committee and that I was exonerated of any wrongdoing. There were people I associated with outside office hours, who had no relationship with this bank or any of its competitors, but who it seems were being investigated for irregularities in syndicate betting. It turned out, as I'm sure you must have read, that they were the subject of some scandalous rumours, but in fact they have never been charged with any offence."

"Yes, you're right, I did do some background reading before I came out, so I know about the syndicate, and that you were involved with them in Bournemouth. I haven't seen Mike Johnson's name in anything I've read. Was he involved?"

"I'm sure you have the means to find out who those people associated with, without my help"

"Look, all I'm trying to do is see if there's a connection between Mike's gambling and his death. Do you know if Mike continued in the syndicate after he moved to Eastleigh?"

"Mike and I really only had a business relationship once he'd moved here, apart from occasionally having dinner with each other. There was no involvement with any of those people in

Bournemouth, and I resent the implication that I was somehow involved in anything inappropriate, either before or after being appointed head of IT security here. I'm in a highly sensitive position here, and I'd thank you to respect that. I've given you enough of my time, I think, so unless you have some specific points to clarify I'd like to get on with some quite important work"

OK, thought Pete, so you want to play hardball?

"You said you were headhunted by United Midwest?"

Mahoney was caught off guard, but recovered quickly. "You don't give up easily, do you? An opening came up and I applied for it. Obviously as I was successful they must have thought I was the right man for the job"

"And was Mike Johnson involved in the selection process?"

"I don't know, but I can see what you're getting at. He certainly didn't interview me, if that's what you mean. That would have been an obvious conflict of interest as we were previously colleagues. In this business there are more forms to fill in and more people watching you like hawks than you can possibly imagine. I'm sure the Human Resources department here will furnish you all the appropriate paperwork, but I should warn you that they can be very protective – we all work for the same company and we look after each others' interests.

Indeed, they might insist on a court order, given the aspects of confidentiality"
He leaned back and folded his arms. Such an obvious display of defensive body language wasn't going to put Pete off. He'd sat opposite tougher nuts than this one.
"Indeed. And I should warn you, 'Sir', if we're into warning each other, that our next interview might be at Eastleigh police station if you keep giving me the run around. And I'll tell you something else, the coffee's nowhere near this good in the interview rooms down there, and you'd be lucky if you got a cup twice a day if you're a reluctant interviewee. I'm investigating a suspicious death, and if I think there's anything in this building that will help me solve it then I'll get a court order within the hour, but it won't be just for your HR department, I'll close the whole place down while I look for what I want. I hope that's clear enough. I'll see myself out".
He got up to go.
An alarmed Mahoney stood up with him, suddenly flustered.
"Look, I'm sorry Inspector, that was unnecessarily rude of me. All this stuff involving Mike has got me wound up. I didn't mean to sound so pompous, and I certainly don't mean to be obstructive. I do apologise".
Pete sat down.

“I did get a written recommendation from Mike. As a matter of fact I wasn’t actually headhunted by an agency, it was Mike who put me forward. It’s all above board, though. The bank has a scheme which encourages staff to bring people on board from other companies. The staff can get up to fifteen percent of the first year’s salary in commission if the bank hires someone they recommend. I know that sounds a lot, especially if the salary is in six-figures, but the recruitment agencies charge up to forty percent. All the banks have schemes like that - it’s an accepted form of poaching from one another. But once the recommendation results in an interview, the staff member is excluded from the process. I can assure you that I got the job on my own merit, Mike wasn’t involved in my appointment in any way.”

“OK, apology accepted, But you knew Mike quite well, and he was in with the same crowd as you. Could he have gone overboard with his gambling, maybe got involved with another syndicate? One you didn’t know about?”

“Absolutely not. Mike was very careful with his money. From what I’ve heard about these syndicates...” Pete cleared his throat and looked sceptical...”No, really,” Mahoney continued, “from the little I know of them you need a lot of investment to beat the odds”

“But not if it involves an accumulator bet” offered Pete, remembering the discussion at the bookies.
Mahoney could hardly disguise his amusement.
“I’m sorry, Inspector, but that’s the very last type of bet a syndicate would touch”. He paused and corrected himself. “Assuming what I’ve heard about them is true”. Pete was beginning to think the room was bugged, Mahoney was being so careful.
“And what, may I ask, have you heard about them?” Pete prompted.
“That they spend a lot of money on research to find a bet that is a near certainty, then they invest a lot of money so that the return is worthwhile. If it’s a corrupt syndicate they will find a way to influence the outcome, maybe through bribery, but the odds have to be very low otherwise the win would be picked up by one of the various regulatory bodies. To imagine them fixing half a dozen races to make a fortune from nothing is just, well, unimaginable”.
Pete took the point. “OK, well I needed to ask anyway. I’ll let you know if there’s anything else. Now I will see myself out, and let you get on with whatever it is you do that’s so important”.

It was a bright autumn morning and Pete thought it an ideal time to check out the Bournemouth connection again. The incident with Carl Swann at the Artful Dodger was still fresh in his mind, and he could see a world of difference in the club scene that Carl and Spike Palmer inhabited and the lazy contented world of the Cricket Club and the retirees sleeping in the afternoon sun. That both these worlds were different sides of the same seaside town was a conundrum that Pete wanted to look at again, so with that in mind he found himself parked at the pier approach in Bournemouth just after midday.

Without leaving his car he could see the calm sea stretching out from the flat sandy beach, split almost exactly in half by the majestic pier. In the distance to his right he could just make out Old Harry Rocks, a distinctive rock formation piercing the deep blue water, and the beginning of Dorset's beautiful coastline. He and Jenny had holidayed near Lulworth Cove, further around the headland, once, and the stunning scenery in that area had been an influence on his decision to transfer here from Bristol. On his left the sea's horizon met Hengisbury Head, completing the semi-circle of this huge natural bay. His view turned inland, and up from the pier he could see the large houses which used to be the holiday homes for rich Londoners. Indeed, the home of Lily Langtree, King George's mistress, was not far from here, and was now run as a boutique hotel. Hotels and guest houses had taken over the seafront area, with a few blocks of purpose-built holiday apartments casting their shadow behind them. The pretty town gardens were centre of this bustling town, with bowling greens and bandstands to entertain the traditional aging visitors, with fireworks displays at night and the unique sight of dozens of sculptures built with candles, to be illuminated by the holidaying children as night fell, bringing an innocent kind of magic to the onset of nightfall. Opposite the gardens was the shopping centre, a total necessity for any town that hoped to offer anything visitors could want. From the large department stores through the pharmacy chains and cheap chic outlets to the pound shops, there was something for everyone, but all the storefronts bore the same couple of dozen names that you could find in any high street in Britain. So you could travel a few hundred miles and shop in the same stores you visited every Saturday, Pete thought. How comforting.

He got out and walked down the Pier Approach to the gardens. He thought about a walk along the pier, but thought better of it. That would be the only place in the town that you would only find tourists, not locals. He turned and walked along the path through the gardens. The park benches were mainly occupied by older people, sitting watching the world go by. A few children paddled in the little stream, watched over by young, but well-dressed, mothers. None of them looked old enough to be nannies. Definitely middle-class here, not rich. Bournemouth wasn't Hyde Park, after all. There were dozens of deck chairs positioned around the central bandstand, being tidied by a team of council workers. There was no band there yet, but a notice proclaimed that there would be a concert of "Old Time Favourites" at three o'clock. The grassy areas away from the paths were occupied by groups of students, lounging in the sun and looking pretty relaxed. Of course, these weren't real students – the university campus was too far from here. These were English students, or rather foreign students being taught English in the numerous 'English as a Foreign Language' colleges in the town centre. Pete could hear a lot of English being spoken – it was the Lingua Franca of the students, but the number of different foreign accents was quite amusing. He was listening to a group of young boys discussing the Chelsea football team's chances in the Premiership, trying to decide whether their accents were Spanish or Portugese, when he heard a guitar playing.

He was drawn by that sound to a group near the Crazy Golf,

sitting under a tree. They were mainly young girls, maybe Sixth Formers from Bournemouth School for Girls, or maybe language students from nearby, but they were sitting quietly in a circle around a young man strumming away on an acoustic guitar. He was singing "Mr Tambourine Man", definitely not The Byrds dreamy version but the Bob Dylan one, plaintive but poignant. Pete walked up and stood at the back of the group. As one by one they noticed Pete. Looking distinctly out of place in his suit and tie, they became self-conscious and stopped singing. The guitarist, in contrast, seemed unaffected by Pete's presence and continued singing until the song was done. As he stopped, his audience sensed that the show was over, and slowly drifted away. The man had long, sandy hair and a tousled beard, and was dressed in a loose tee shirt, shorts and sandals. He didn't seem to mind the interruption. His listeners would return soon enough when his visitor left. He looked up questioningly at Pete, who spoke first.

"Dizzie James, I assume?"

CHAPTER SIXTEEN

"Obviously you're not a park warden. They all wear brown raincoats. So do the deckchair attendants. You're not from one of the schools, you don't look clever enough to be a teacher. So you must be a copper"

Pete smiled at Dizzie's assessment. "No flies on you, are there son? Yes, policeman born and bred, no disguising it from someone who's seen a few, like you"

"If you know my name then you know I've never been arrested for anything, and I don't intend to be. Getting caught is for mugs, and the best way not to get caught is not to do anything bad". He smiled charmingly. Pete could see why the girls hung around with him, despite his singing.

"So are you willing to answer a few questions?"

"Why not? If I think you're about to uncover some grand crime I've committed, I'll just clam up"

"I'll try to remember to look out for that signal" Pete smiled back good-naturedly. It was hard not to. He sat down next to Dizzie, although he certainly felt out of place wearing suit. The carefully tended lawns in Bournemouth seemed to invite sitting, lying down, curling up into a ball, almost anything but standing up. He thought he'd seen a 'keep off the grass' sign

somewhere, but imagined that it would be difficult to enforce.
"Do you know a chap called Mike Johnson?"
Dizzie looked as if he was trying hard to recall the name. "No, don't think so. How old would he be?"
"He was forty-two. He was found dead last week."
"Oh. Tough. That's a bit young to die, even for an older person." He looked pointedly at Pete. "Any reason you're asking me?"
"Well, he actually died in Eastleigh, but your name came up amongst others he might have had dealings with down here. He died in suspicious circumstances, and that's why I'm asking questions. How about his wife, Kathy? Two years younger"
"Well, as you might have noticed I don't hang around with a middle-aged crowd. Are they part of the Bournemouth scene? Folks that age mainly live out of town, up towards Ringwood or over Broadstone way. People who live in the town are usually students in digs, or old folk in care homes. So what were this Kathy and Mike couple up to that got him killed then? Were they part of that Ashley Heath wife-swapping crowd I heard about? I tell you, you can't walk through that town without getting lost in Pampas Grass on the front lawns. You look like the swinging type, I'm sure you know what I mean".

Pete smiled, not knowing whether to be flattered. "No, nothing like that, Kathy was from Bournemouth but Mike wasn't. They didn't even live down here now. They moved from Bournemouth a while ago, but they used to be part of the Cricket Club crowd here."

"That rules them out of my circle of friends then. Bunch of stuck-up twats. I got tossed out of that club last year for bringing in my own bottle of vodka. The price of their drinks, small wonder – I bet they all do it. And they didn't even have a decent cider on tap, just that awful Stella stuff and something with a toffee apple flavour. I didn't want to go back there anyway. They wanted me join up, pay a subscription or something. Whatever next? Sitting through a game of cricket for days on end? So this Kathy bird, you said she was a local girl. What was her name before she got hitched to the dead man?"

"Bateman. Kathy Bateman. Lived in Queens Park"

"Oh." Dizzie's eyes lit up. "I've shagged her"

Pete was quite naturally taken aback by Dizzie's directness.

"I see. And I thought you didn't mix with the middle-aged crowd?"

Dizzie was all smiles. "Not normally, of course. But this was a few years ago. She must have been, what, about thirty. So she still had all the important bits sticking out at the right angles, carried herself pretty well. And she had a fair bit of energy, from what I remember. We only did it a couple of times, round the back of the Winter Gardens up against the wall after a show, then when the run finished we sort of lost touch. How is she these days?"

"She's a widow. How do you think she is?" Pete resisted the urge to shake his head and tut-tut.

"So you had a relationship with her. How did this happen then?" he continued.

"She was in the Parkstone Light Opera Club and I was with the junior wing of the Poole Little Theatre. My parents got me to join up, and I didn't really fancy it, but it was a way I could get out of piano practice. They were convinced I should end up being a jazz pianist, which is why they named me after some ancient jazz musician. I was seventeen when I ran into Kathy, so plenty old enough to be legal – in case you were going to ask that question. Anyway, most of the women in Am Dram those days were just looking for an excuse to be out in the evenings away from the old man. The bloke would be working all day and come home just wanting to put his feet up in front of the telly, and the missus would be ready for a night out, so a couple of times a week rehearsing fitted in quite nicely. The normal blokes who do Am Dram are as old as the hills, so the women who were after a good time had to make do with us young studs. I like to think we didn't disappoint them. As it happens, Kathy Bateman had a pretty good voice. Not surprising when you saw where it was coming from. I seem to remember it was 'The Sound of Music'. I played the teenage Rolf and she played Sister Maria, but she was certainly no novice"

He grinned inanely at his own joke. Pete was unimpressed.

"And you never met Mike, her husband, or had any contact with Kathy after she left Bournemouth?"

"No. As I said, I've never heard of this Mike Johnson. And as for Kathy, there are plenty of lonely women in this town, young or mature. No need to revisit old pastures. Ever."

Pete sighed, but tried not to sound like he was being judgemental.

"So tell me. Were there any drugs involved when you knew Kathy?"

"No, never. I was just trying out a few things myself, just E's and stuff, and I didn't have any spare cash to splash out on getting a bigger high. As for Kathy, she was always afraid that taking drugs would damage her chances of stardom. You know, affect her vocal cords or fuck up her brain or whatever. I never knew her to get high. She didn't need to really, she got her kicks from enjoying life, whether it was shagging me or tap-dancing on stage. I used to envy her, really. I was never any good at tap dancing. Then we both moved on."

"So you wouldn't know if she was a cocaine user?"

"No, I wouldn't, but I would bet the Kathy I used to know would never even have tried it"

"How easy is it to come by here in Bournemouth?"

"Not my scene, I already told you. I would guess if you've got enough money you can get anything you want. Me, I'm happy just singing my songs and getting laid. Both those things are free and legal, at least for now"

"So you don't know a chap called Spike Palmer?"

"Of course I do, everyone here does. Well, we did, I should say. We went to the same junior school, then he went on to Poole Grammar and I went to Bournemouth Boys. His folks had ideas above their station. I think they ended up in some mansion over at Canford Cliffs. It was a shame about Spike. He had everything going for him but he just loved living on the edge. Got himself filled with coke a few weeks back and drove his bike into a wall at sixty miles an hour. Real waste. He had a lot of talent, we jammed together a few times, but he was better than me. A great keyboard player, but he had more fun living the high life and never took himself seriously enough. In his time, he was a bit of a fixer, could get you anything if there's enough cash involved. And the more risk the better for him. Used to drive his brother Des crazy with what he did. Des was always bailing him out. Pity he's gone though. The world needs more characters like him."

And with that Dizzie picked up his guitar and strummed the opening chords of "Blowin' in the Wind"

As Pete drove back from Bournemouth it was late afternoon, and the stream of commuting cars was herding in the opposite direction. From here he'd go straight home rather than back to his office, but he'd already decided that another discussion with Kathy Johnson would be in order. Maybe a reminder of her wilder days in Bournemouth could nudge her into revealing how Mike Johnson had come by the cocaine, assuming she knew. It was worth a try, he thought. He'd been considering who was the most likely suspect of those people he'd talked to so far. The obvious ones were the shady characters like Carl Swann, but he couldn't rule out the gambling connection yet, so Spike's brother Des was still in the frame, and anyone associated with him. Closer to home, There were Kathy's neighbours who had to be rank outsiders, and people he worked with – or had worked with, he reminded himself, thinking about Karen Peterson. Kathy herself couldn't be considered, she had a strong alibi for the night of the death, the sports club would confirm that. And anyway the fact that the murderer lifted Johnson up to the noose made it certainly a strong male he should be looking for. His thoughts hadn't clarified too much as early evening found him pulling up outside the Eastleigh Travel Lodge.

"Is Mrs Johnson in her room, do you know?" he asked the girl on reception, flashing his ID.

"No, I'm afraid not, but then we wouldn't expect her to be. She checked out yesterday"

"Oh. Did she say she was going back home?"

"To be honest, she didn't, but she was in one hell of a mood. She'd had a right go at our manager. She said she'd had a burglar in her room and was being spied on and followed by someone. Called the manager all kinds of names and said she'd sue the company for incompetence. Well, we all know about her husband and the suicide and everything, so the manager tried to calm her down, but she was sure someone had been in her room."

"And had they?" Pete was starting to get concerned.

"There's no way of telling. We keep the key cards in the rack behind me". She turned and indicated the pigeon holes. "But the desk isn't manned all the time, so it's possible someone could have borrowed the key and put it back again. The manager said there was no sign of a forced entry, and Mrs Johnson said that nothing was actually missing, but she was quite distraught when she finally left. Mind you,....." She hesitated.

"What?"

"The cleaners are pretty sure her bed wasn't slept in, but there were signs that two people slept in the room opposite, which was supposedly single-occupancy" She blushed slightly.

Pete didn't pretend to be surprised. "Everybody's a bloody detective these days" he sighed. "And I'm sure you wouldn't mind giving me the name of the person registered in that room?"

"It was a Mr Jack Martin, but don't tell anyone I told you that. It could cost me my job"

At that moment Pete's mobile rang. It was Dave, back at the station.

"Where are you now?" Dave asked.

"I'm at the Travel Lodge, but Kathy Johnson has already checked out. I spent the afternoon with some dropout down in Bournemouth, after a tip-off from Andy. As it turns out, he knew Kathy Johnson in days gone by, but I don't think he can be the source for Mike Johnson's cocaine. I do think that Carl Swann has got some questions to answer. He gave Andy and me the runaround, quite literally, last night, so I might have to pull him in. On top of that, when I got here the receptionist says there might have been someone going through Kathy's room the other night. If that's true, it was lucky she was in someone else's bed at the time. I think there might be more to this 'Being Stalked' story than I thought. Anyway, you called me. What's the latest?"

"The reason I was calling you is that I think we've had a bit of a breakthrough. The results have come back from the lab – you know, the tests on the Johnsons' cars and garage. The SOC boys found some DNA in the garage and they've come up with a match on the convicted criminals database"

Pete rolled his eyes. "I knew I should kept chasing that bastard when I saw him last night. Now I'll have to get some heavies down to Fratton Park and drag him out of the social club"

Dave went quiet. "You chased him in Bournemouth? Last night? I thought he would have been at work by then."

"What do you mean, at work? He hasn't had a real job for years." Pete paused. "We are talking about the same person, aren't we? Carl Swann?"

Dave said “No, not Carl. I’m talking about Terry Walton. He works at the Monte Carlo casino in Southampton.”

CHAPTER SEVENTEEN

The secret of giving a good blow job, she was thinking, is a steady rhythm. Of course you do need to keep your teeth out of the way, but really, once you've got yourself in a comfortable position you just have to get to a steady beat and keep it there as long as it takes. Breathing on the off beat is quite important too, she corrected herself, as making yourself gag kind of kills the moment. Still, if you can keep your mouth open for about ten minutes, like waiting for that teeth impression stuff to set in the dentists, you've got it made. After all, most of the stimulation he's getting is from the idea of what you're doing, not so much the sensation. That's why it's important for him to watch what you're doing and to hear those little moans you let out every now and then.

She'd talked about it with her girlfriends. The kind of subject that comes up at most Anne Summers parties. Most of them did it when necessary, but she didn't know any woman who actually enjoyed it. They thought the same as her, that it was a man-thing, and they did it if that man deserved a special treat or was in danger of wandering off to get it elsewhere. Few of her married friends did it. They agreed with her, it was one of those special tricks you use as bait when you're trying to get him to stay – once he's living with you he'll be staying anyway, so why bother? One wife who liked to stray occasionally just for kicks said she always did it rather than 'normal' sex, just so she could tell herself that she was still being faithful to her husband. After all, if a US president could claim that he wasn't having sexual intercourse using that technique, so could she! Certainly none of the girls said they got any pleasure from it other than pleasing the bloke – one said it was like having a can of squirty cream rammed down your throat, with no control over when the button gets pushed. Squirty cream, eh? If only!

She'd been daydreaming a bit, and she hadn't noticed that he seemed to be approaching take-off, making a few grunting noises in time with her moans, which she managed to make without even thinking about it. It was about time, too, as the floor was beginning to make her knees ache even through the thick-pile carpet. She found her thoughts drifting off to what she'd need to buy at the supermarket on the way home. It would be late, but she knew that if she didn't get any food in her husband certainly wouldn't, even though he'd been home at six from his own job. Never mind, at least she could afford it. Her boss would add a couple of hours overtime into her pay check for the blow job, considering it "performance above and

beyond normal office duties". She smiled to herself. I suppose it is, really, she thought.
As his rhythm increased, so did hers, pushing her head right down and then up again for a quick gulp of air and letting out another moan. She could hear his breathing getting heavier and louder, and the leather chair he was sitting in behind the desk started squeaking in time with the beat. The floor she was kneeling on now joined in, and there seemed to be a loud thumping in her ears at the same time. Surely that's not his heartbeat I can hear, she thought – he'd better not keel over with a heart attack, I might not be able to get up with him slumped over the desk and me beneath it. The thump-thump-thump got louder and seemed to be encouraging her to put everything into one final effort, so she gamely held on and pushed her head down as far as she dared, moaning even louder on the upward movement. She thought she could hear shouting – maybe it was that supermarket daydream again?

There was a loud crash and Pete Thomas burst into the room with two burly policemen behind him, red faced from smashing the main door in when their knocking and calling went unanswered. They all stopped and surveyed the scene before them. Des Palmer was sitting behind a huge leather desk, with his shirt wide open but wearing nothing else, as far as they could see. He was as red-faced as the policemen, had been sweating heavily and was out of breath. Everyone went quiet. Palmer looked shocked, then confused, then really angry. He put his hands flat on the desk and started to rise.

"What the hell do you think – " he began, but was interrupted by a loud thump from under the desk, and a couple of pencils on the desktop jumped with the impact.

"Ow!" came a muffled voice. "That was my fucking head. Watch what you're doing, Des, will you?"

Des sat down again. There was a long pause. Slowly a woman's head appeared from under the desk, facing Palmer's navel. Her hand appeared next, and proceeded to rub the top of her head while the four men watched in silence.

"Feels like you're not up for it anymore, sweetheart" she continued. "Maybe we'd better catch up tomorrow instead?"

Palmer had recovered his composure slightly. He looked down at her and smiled.

"Yes, maybe, Marybeth. But in the meantime perhaps you can make a cup of tea for these gentlemen?"

She turned her head slowly and registered the presence of the three visitors.

"Oh" was all she could muster. She got out from under the

desk, dusted down her skirt and walked primly through the door they had just barged through. She tried to close it behind her, but somehow the latch didn't fit anymore. Palmer waited till she'd gone, then bent down and lifted his trousers back in place. He took some time finishing dressing while his company waited patiently.

"Now what the fuck do you think you're doing?" he finally snarled at Pete.

Pete had had time to recover from the shock of the situation, and felt that a reasoned manner would keep him on top of this encounter.

"Mr Palmer, we're looking for Mr Terry Dalton in connection with a complaint from Mrs Kathy Johnson"

"Johnson? I don't know a Mrs Kathy Johnson. Oh, wait a minute – from the other night? You mean that madwoman is the reason you broke my door down?"

"We were concerned for her safety. There was a possibility that her life was in danger, and no-one answered our knocking or responded to our shouts. In the circumstances, " he allowed himself a slight grin, "I'm sure we don't need any formal report of this intervention. We'll reimburse you for the damage we've caused"

"I don't give a crap about that – why are you looking for

Terry?"
"I'm afraid I can't give you any details, just to say we need to speak to him urgently"
"But why the hell would he be here?" demanded Palmer.
"We assumed he'd be working here today"
"In the middle of the afternoon? You Plods need to get more clever with your ground work. We don't open till six, and that's when Terry should be here".
"OK, so where is he now?" responded Pete, ignoring the sarcasm.
"Probably at home in bed. But I can't see how he can be mixed up with this Johnson woman. We'd never heard of her or her husband before she came round the other night causing trouble"
"Did you ask Terry if he'd ever met the Johnson's before?"
Des hesitated. "Er, no. I don't suppose I did. She seemed to have it in for me, for some reason. Something about her husband and some gambling problem, but I checked in my system before I even spoke to her, and neither of them have ever been members here"
"Maybe it was a connection through Terry? offered Pete. "Was he in the gambling business before he worked here?"
"No, not as far as I know. He'd been working at a bank before

he came here. In their credit collections department. That's his speciality, chasing bad debts"

Pete raised his eyebrows. "Do you know the name of the bank he worked at?"

"Yes, it was National Westminster on Richmond Hill, Bournemouth". Pete was disappointed. There was no link there to Mike Johnson's career.

"And would Terry Walton have any connection with Bournemouth Cricket Club or the Artful Dodger pub in Bournemouth?"

"Well, that I don't know. He's lived down there a while so I would guess he's been to most places. Maybe you can ask him when you go and call on him at home."

"I didn't know he lived in Bournemouth. Where, exactly?"

"Near the town centre. 15 Derby Road. I've never been there, so I can't give you directions"

"We'll find it, don't worry. Thank you for your cooperation and sorry again about the damage. Have a good day"

Pete turned and went through the broken door, followed by the still-silent policemen. He paused at the reception desk, where the receptionist was preparing tea for them.

"Don't worry about that now, Marybeth, thanks all the same. You can get back to your other duties now."

Outside, he was straight on his mobile to Andy in Bournemouth.
"Yes, Andy, he's not here. We stumbled across some mid-afternoon entertainment which upset Mr Palmer, but I daresay he'll recover. Unless the teeth marks are deep. What? No, it doesn't matter, I'll explain later. Look, can you get a bunch of blokes over to this address in Bournemouth, pronto? See if Walton is there or if there's anywhere he might have taken Kathy Johnson? I'm going back to the Johnson's house in Eastleigh, see if she's turned up there"
He hung up after giving Andy the address in Derby road and told his two officers to go back to work. He'd come in a separate car, and as he left Southampton he gave Dave a call "hands-free".
"Dave, I'm on my way back to Eastleigh. I've left Andy chasing after Terry Walton, I don't want to be home too late. Did you have any luck going through those names I gave you, to see if there's a potential source for the coke?"
Dave's laugh could be heard distinctly through the car radio speakers.
"If he's got a source like that he's keeping their relationship off the social networks and away from the gossip-mingers, and I

wouldn't blame him! Still, I did check them all and there's nothing likely. I made a few enquiries about that cricket club, though, through a mate of mine down there. He reckons they were under close surveillance by Hampshire Drugs Squad for a while. They even had an undercover man working there and the local police, including Andy, weren't in the loop. As it turns out they couldn't get any hard evidence together and they closed down the operation because of the cost. They were pretty sure, though, that anyone who drank in there could easily score cocaine if it was needed."

"And did they have any idea, even if they didn't have evidence, of who the supplier was?"

"They did. They reckoned it was Ken Rawlings, the manager of the bar."

"But if he was the supplier for Mike Johnson's hit last Tuesday, Johnson's been keeping his habit from his wife for a good couple of years"

"Actually", replied Dave, "It needn't be a habit at all. Don't forget I'm a member of the Police Drug Information group in Hampshire, so I keep informed about that stuff. There are plenty of casual users of Class C drugs, most of them perfectly ordinary folk, and these days you can even find someone using the harder stuff without them ever getting hooked on it. They just use it when they want to escape, and you'd never know they were users any other time"

Pete had a quiet twenty minute drive back to Eastleigh in which to reflect on what Dave had said. Did that mean that everyone he knew had tried drugs? That they knew how to get hold of them now if they wanted to? Including hard stuff like cocaine? Was Dave himself a 'casual' user? How about Jenny, his own wife? What kind of world were we letting kids grow up in? Probably just as well they didn't have any kids of their own, he reflected. Then instantly regretted the thought. No, it would have been great to have kids, it just never happened. Those lucky enough to have them just had to protect them as best they could till they were adults themselves.

"It's been a long day, Pete" he said to himself as he pulled into Briar Crescent.

CHAPTER EIGHTEEN

Andy was on his mobile as the back-up van arrived with a dozen or more uniformed officers, who stood at ease around the parked van and several squad cars that were already in the street. Derby Road is a pleasant tree-lined avenue near the centre of town, with numerous elegant houses set back from the road and fronted by manicured lawns. Several "For Sale" and "To Let" signs indicate the transient nature of the residents there, but for many years the street had suffered more from its reputation, for being the centre of the prostitution business in Bournemouth. The houses on that street had seen more than its fair share of police raids, and residents often blamed those raids on the reputation rather than any firm evidence of wrongdoing. To add insult to injury, most raids were carried out in the early hours of the morning, in the hope of nabbing drug peddlers in the same net as the kerb crawlers. It was unusual, then, to see this much activity in the early evening, so the local kids were out in force, standing well back from the police van, but ready to cheer on whoever the police were chasing – after all, he could be their dad as far as they knew.

"Right, reinforcements are here and we're just going in" said Andy into the phone. "Hang on a minute Pete" he paused. The team had gathered round to await instructions. Andy looked at the layout of the house and its neighbours, then addressed the team.

"You four go around the back down those alleyways. You two stand guard at the neighbours' gates, that side and that side, in case he's seen us and is jumping houses. Stop anyone who wants to leave their house, get their names and check ID. If they don't have ID, bring them round to the van and we'll check them against the mug shots. The rest of you follow me when I go knocking on number fifteen's front door. Don't forget he's a tough nut and might even be armed. No heroics, just stand back if he gets nasty and we'll get the dogs in. Once we're in the house, have a look for any signs of the Johnson woman. Check all the rooms, flag up anything unusual, but don't mess anything up in case we need to get SOC in."

Pete was walking up the drive to Kathy Johnson's front door. The sun had not long gone down and there was a chill in the air. In contrast to the scene in Bournemouth, here there was no-one on the streets, not standing, walking or driving. There wasn't even the usual sensation of being watched through curtains. The road was simply devoid of life.

"Andy. there's no sign of anyone at the Johnsons' house" he

said into the mobile. “Let’s keep this line open so I know what’s going on”. He rang the bell and waited. There were no lights on, but he could see that the door was slightly ajar. Pete had his flashlight at the ready, switched it on and pushed the door open with it.
“Anyone home?” he shouted into the gloom.

“OK boys, let’s go!” Andy yelled, and marched up to the door of number fifteen. No-one answered his ringing on the doorbell. He was about to pound on the door when he noticed the door was half-open. He lifted his arm to signal “quiet” to the group behind him, then reached to his inside pocket for his latex gloves. He wasn’t going to be the first one to contaminate any potential crime scene. One glove was on and the other halfway there when the door was suddenly pulled back and he was confronted by a tall, plump but not unattractive woman in a dressing gown. She folded her arms and stared at him.
“Mrs Walton?” stammered Andy, caught slightly off-guard. The woman didn’t seem surprised to see him, just curious, and stared at his semi-latexed fingers.
“And what are you, a fucking gynaecologist?”
Andy reddened. Then recovered. Officialdom beats humanity, and a sense of humour, every time.

“We’re here to look for Terry Walton. I have the necessary paperwork” he announced, waved a sheet of paper at the bemused Mrs Walton and turned to the waiting team. “Alright, in you go, boys”. And with that, half a dozen uniforms barged past and started combing the house from top to bottom.

Pete had trodden on broken glass as he entered the house. A pane had been knocked out of the door, near the lock. He walked into Kathy’s lounge. The curtains were drawn so he kept his flashlight on and shone it around. The room was in a complete mess, drawers open and contents spilled over the carpets, papers everywhere. A glass cabinet in one corner had been smashed to the floor, there was glass everywhere. He went on into the kitchen. The same story here. All the cupboards had been searched, doors left open and debris everywhere. Each room in the house, the garage included, had been rifled and left in disarray. He checked every room to make sure there was no sign of Kathy Johnson, and with some relief noted that there were no bloodstains to be seen.

Mrs Walton seemed quite amused.
“I must say, that’s about the quickest response I’ve ever had from you bastards, but why the fuck are you all running around

the house? He's hardly likely to be here, is he?"
"But he does live here, doesn't he?" asked Andy, his latex gloves safely back in his pocket. "You're his wife and this is 15 Derby Road?"
"Of course he lives here, normally. And this is the address I gave you people when I phoned an hour ago".

Pete had seen enough of the house, he'd need to get some forensics here soon. He was wondering why it had gone quiet at the other end of the phone.
"Andy, what's happening there? Someone's turned over the Johnson's place. I'll need to call in SOC. There's no sign of Kathy here. Have you collared Terry Walton yet?"

Andy could only just hear Pete's voice. He'd lowered the phone from his ear while he spoke to Mrs Walton. He raised it again and spoke into it.
"Just a second, Pete". He addressed Mrs Walton. "Did you say you called us an hour ago?"
"Yes. That's why you're here, isn't it? I reported him missing"
Andy stared at her. "Right. Hold on a minute love". He walked back to the road, talking to Pete as he went.
"Bit of a cock-up here, Pete. Seems he's gone missing"

"Well I don't suppose that's a surprise, everything considered. See if there's anything else you can find out, check the wife isn't hiding anything and get the boys back to the station. I'll check with Kathy's neighbour to see if she knows anything" He hung up.

As Pete was crossing the road to Gloria's house, Andy was checking that the heavy mob had found nothing at the Walton's house. They'd had a valid reason to enter the premises, so it was a good opportunity to pick up anything incriminating, but there was nothing. He told the men to stand down, then turned back to Mrs Walton.

"So when did you notice he was missing?"

"When I woke up at lunchtime" she replied. "He hadn't come home last night"

"But in his line of work was that unusual?"

"Not on a night when he'd be at the casino, no – but he doesn't work there on a Tuesday. That's Sea Scouts night"

Andy did a double-take. "Sea Scouts? You mean he works as a bouncer most of the week, then goes sailing with teenage boys on a Tuesday?"

"He's always done it. His own dad was a sailor and Terry wanted to join the merchant navy from school, but his dad wanted him to concentrate on his career, so Terry was in the

Sea Scouts in his spare time. After a few years he was made a Sea Scout leader" she added quite proudly.

"To concentrate on his career? What kind of career do you call being a paid thug for a casino?"

She looked offended. "I'll have you know that Terry's a qualified accountant, and he's got a degree in Economics. He does the books for the casino, which has a multi-million pound turnover and some pretty complex tax obligations." She seemed surprisingly knowledgeable. "As for being a thug, he's also an amateur weightlifter, ex-county champion, so Mr. Palmer pays him extra to double up as his heavy. He never actually has to do anything thuggish, as you would call it, and you can check his record if you haven't already done that. He's a strong-looking bloke, so usually just the sight of him makes most troublemakers back down"

Andy considered it time to stop wondering how any of this fitted together.

"So where is the local Sea Scout Hut?" he asked.

"You mean the boathouse – they're Sea Scouts, remember?" she corrected. "That's over at Christchurch, near Wick Ferry, just next to Warner's holiday camp".

Gloria answered the door just seconds after Pete knocked.

She'd been watching across the road as he'd walked up to her house.
"I won't stop long, Gloria" he started, "I just need to know if you've seen Kathy"
"No, I haven't, but to be honest I wouldn't have seen her if she'd come back. I've been round at my friend Brenda's most of the afternoon. I didn't want to be here if that horrible man came looking for her"
"So that phone call you made - there really was someone following her from the Travel Lodge? And you've seen this man?" Pete reached for his pocket, where he had a photo of Terry Walton from the files.
"No, not really. I mean I didn't see him, he stopped at the end of the road". She sounded disappointed that she couldn't be more helpful. But then her eyes lit up as she realised that indeed she could help. "But I know what car he was driving"
"And what would that be?"
"A silver BMW. Maybe I should have said in my message? It was at the end of the road when Kathy asked me to phone you"
"And did you see a licence number?" Pete already knew the number from the car registration database, but needed to confirm that it was Walton's car that Gloria had seen.
"I didn't see it at all. It must have been waiting around the

corner". Gloria was suddenly deflated. "But Kathy knows about cars" she rallied, "So I'm sure she was right about what type it was"
"So what car was Kathy herself driving when she came here? Her own car and that of her husband are still impounded at Eastleigh police station"
"Oh, it was a very nice one, the one she came here in. It was bright red, but very classy. I think it was new. Must be a hired car if you've got hers, don't you think?"
Pete sighed as he realised he hadn't thought this through yet. "Gloria, do you think you could make me a cup of coffee, please – black no sugar, while I'm waiting for a call to come through?"
At last Gloria could feel useful again, and wandered off to the kitchen as Pete dialled a number at the station.
"Chloe, a couple of things. Firstly, can you get an SOC team over to Briar Crescent, Eastleigh. The Johnsons house. It's been broken into and rifled. I'll need the whole place put under the microscope again. More urgently, though, I need you to check with all the car hire companies in the area, find out if they've rented a car to Kathy Johnson today. I need that info ASAP, so quick as you can, please, and call me back as soon as you have it".

Ten minutes later Pete was running out of polite conversation with Gloria when his phone rang.

"Yes Chloe. A red Citroen DS3 cabriolet?" He made a note of the licence plate number. "Thanks for that. And SOC are on their way? Great. See you tomorrow"

"You're right, Gloria, she was driving a red car. I've just double-checked"

Gloria beamed. "I don't often notice cars, I must say, but as red is my favourite colour I couldn't help but notice it. I was right about it being a hired car as well, wasn't I?"

"OK Gloria, let's forget about the car for now. Maybe it's got nothing to do with where Kathy is. I've just come from the house and she's not there. In fact there's no sign she's been there tonight." Pete thought it best not to mention the state of the Johnsons' house. "Do you have any idea where she might have gone if she didn't come home?"

"No. Oh dear, I hope nothing dreadful has happened to her. I think I'm her only friend. Well, me and Graham. She didn't know many people around here. But perhaps she had some friends at that sports club she goes to? One of them might have let her stay at their place"

Pete's eyes narrowed as he followed a thought.

"Yes, I believe one of them might have" he replied.

It was nearly dark when Andy got to the Wick Ferry car park in Christchurch. It was out of season, so even though the neighbouring holiday camp was open there were few lights on, just the bar and a couple of the cabins. Once out of the car, he could smell the distinctive salty air of the nearby mud flats, and could see by the pale moonlight the waters glistening at the river edge. The silence was broken only by the clanking sound of rigging cables and mooring lines as the evening breeze started to pick up. The winding outward route to the sea was deserted and all those boats staying the night were now safely moored. The evening tide had brought back that afternoon's amateur sailors, who had long since finished winching their hobby boats up the steep slipway on their trailers, hitched to the family four by four and driven home for dinner. The regular evening strollers had finished watching all this housekeeping, fed the swans and ducks that had gathered with them, then wandered off for a romantic dinner at the distant Ferry Inn pub. Andy knew that in the summer months this huge car park was always full, but tonight, next to the large black hut to his left, there was one solitary car left.
A silver BMW.

CHAPTER NINETEEN

The Travel Lodge lobby was busy with customers at this hour, early evening. Road-weary businessmen dragged their overnight bags past Pete as he waited patiently for the receptionist to be available. He'd noticed that it was the same receptionist as the last time he'd been there – Sarah was her name, he'd seen on her name tag. Obviously it was company policy to have name tags, helps the customers feel they know you already, and always useful in case of complaints, or even praise. He'd been on a course about dealing with the public, and remembering names the second time you meet someone is very important. It makes people feel closer, more wanted, more relaxed, more likely to remember things for you. Interviewing witnesses is a big part of the policeman's job, so getting them to recall details they didn't even know they'd noticed is a skill in itself. Pete looked around him as he sat in a comfortable chair next to yet another potted plant. There was a hubbub of noise from the bar, but the restaurant was deserted. Early enough for a few after-work drinks then, but not yet time to move on and eat. Eventually the reception desk had no customers. Sarah looked up brightly and said "And how can I help you this evening, Inspector Thomas?". She must have

gone on the same course.
“Hello again Sarah” Pete responded as he stood and approached the counter. “Did Mr Jack Martin come in yet?”
“Oh, yes – he’s been in, but he’s already left. He went out in his running gear, so I suppose he’s gone over to the sports club.” She suddenly realised why Pete might be looking for him. “Oh, what I said about there being two people in Mrs Johnson’s room, I didn’t mean to get anyone in trouble.”
“No, you won’t. As it happens I know they met at the sports club, and it’s Mrs Johnson I’m looking for. I’ll look for them both at the club”. He left as darkness started to fall.

Meanwhile, at Wick Ferry, Andy had mounted the steps of the Sea Scout hut and tried the doors. Locked. He walked back down the wooden entrance staircase and over to the parked BMW, tried all the doors. Locked. Through the gloom he shone his torch on the hut and around it. No sign of life. An involuntary shiver caught him as the night mist started to fall.

It took just a couple of minutes for Pete to reach the sports club. There was a young man at the reception desk this time. As with the female receptionist, he probably doubled as a personal trainer when required. How is it, he thought, that young people can keep themselves so fit when they want to? Pete flashed his ID again and asked if Jack Martin had signed in.

"Yes he has" the young man replied, all professional smiles.

"And Kathy Johnson?" Pete asked hopefully.

"I'm afraid not"

"OK, so where can I find Jack Martin, and what does he look like?"

"He'll be on one of the running machines. Tall chap, skinny. The gym is through the door on your left, changing rooms opposite. Oh, maybe this won't apply, but you're an unaccompanied guest, so I have to tell you. Can you not use any of the training equipment unless you've been inducted by one of our instructors? She smiled.

Pete was wearing a suit, white shirt and a tie, black lace-up shoes. He smiled back.

"I'll try not to" he replied as he followed the signs to the gym.

It was packed. TV screens on all four walls had pop videos blaring out heavy-beat music while on different screens, with the volume muted, you could watch football replays or the real-time ticker tape of share prices and other financial news updates. Most of the occupants of the gym, however, seemed to have their own Ipods and were staring into space as they exercised, ignoring the loud music. At one end of the gym, in a much quieter area, burly men and sturdy-looking women were lifting massive weights. In the middle were a variety of muscle stretching and cross-training machines and nearest to the entrance were a half dozen running machines. There was only one such machine occupied, by a tall skinny man running at a steady pace with a constant thump-thump, thump-thump as his trainers hit the rubber conveyor belt. He was on a program that showed on a screen the rise and fall of some imagined country trail as the conveyor belt increased and decreased its gradient to match. Pete wondered why people didn't simply run outside if they wanted it to be that realistic. He walked to the front of the machine and addressed a gently perspiring Jack.

"Jack Martin? Inspector Pete Thomas. I need to talk to you. It's quite urgent" He flashed his warrant card. Jack looked troubled and pressed the stop button on the machine, gently slowing his pace with the belt till he was walking.

"I just need to warm down for a minute. Hope you understand Inspector. Risk of cramp, etcetera"

Pete smiled indulgently, wondering how the phrase "warm down" came into being, as the machine finally came to a stop. Slightly out of breath and red in the face, Jack motioned Pete to follow him and they ended up in a quiet corner of the changing rooms, Jack mopping his brow with a hand towel and taking a swig from the water bottle he'd had strapped to his wrist.

"So what's this all about" he asked, calmer now but a bit more defensive.

Pete went for a bit less formality. "Well, the thing is, Mr Martin – do you mind if I call you Jack?"

"Not at all" replied Jack, visibly relaxing as anticipated. "But the thing is what?"

"Well I don't want to cause you any embarrassment, but I do need to check something with you. I believe you know Kathy Johnson?"

Jack's face coloured even more. He hesitated a second.

"Not really", he bluffed, "I've seen her just once since we met at the bar here. Oh, and we had breakfast once when we bumped into each other at the Travel Lodge. I didn't even know she was staying there. She wanted to talk about that awful business with her husband"

"And that first time you met her, it was on the night he died, wasn't it? Last Tuesday."

Jack paused. Obviously the inspector already knew a great deal.

"As it happens, yes, it was the night he died. But at the time we didn't know that"

"No, I daresay." Pete leaned in a little closer. "I suppose if you had known, it might have affected your performance in the back of her car that night. Which, I might say, needn't become public knowledge if you cooperate with me. Do you understand?"

Jack looked shocked, then slowly smiled.

"I'm sure I'm not the first bloke who's found something to distract him when he's working away from home, and as far as I know it's not illegal"

Pete was glad that a little guesswork had saved him having to wait for the DNA analysis from Kathy's car to come back. But before he could continue, Jack added "But I take your point, it would get quite messy, so I'll tell you everything I know, which probably isn't much. What seems to be the problem? You said it was quite urgent"

"Well, the thing is, we don't know where Kathy is at the moment. I don't suppose she's hiding out in your room back at the hotel?"

"No such luck, although my body would probably rather have a night on the running machine than another one with Kathy just yet, if you get my drift"

Pete did, but gave Jack a look that said "You're not the lucky

bastard you think you are – I certainly wouldn't give up my cosy "once a fortnight" for a passionate one night stand"
Somehow it felt less than convincing.
"So when did you last see her?" Pete continued.
"When she checked out yesterday morning. We were at breakfast together. I admit we didn't just bump into each other, although no-one would have known we'd spent the night in the same room." Pete resisted a sympathetic smile. "She said she was going to stop playing detective, leave it to the professionals. In fact, she was on her way to see you. But then, before we'd even finished breakfast, she saw that bloke from the casino"
"Terry Walton? How do you know him?"
Jack explained about the trip with Kathy down to the casino in Southampton. The confrontation with Des Palmer, the wrestling match between Kathy and Des, then Kathy and Terry, and finally him dragging her away before it all got too nasty.
Then he related the story of the following evening, as Kathy apologised for her behaviour but then got involved in a fight with Carl Swann outside the Travel Lodge.
"Blimey!" exclaimed Pete. "She even got herself mixed up with the thug from Fratton Park? How did he know where Kathy was?"

“Apparently Kathy had paid a visit to his wife, but I didn’t ask too many details.”
“Yes, he’s a nasty case, that one. The woman he lives with has got some connection with Mike Johnson, maybe even with his death. How did Kathy manage to see him off?”
“Well, I helped her a bit. That Carl Swann is a bit of a monster, but he’s never boxed or done any martial arts, so I weighed in and he went running”
“For which, I assume, our Mrs Johnson was most grateful?”
Pete paused, aware that he was losing his objectivity. “Sorry Jack, there was no need for that. I must say, though, she certainly doesn’t know any boundaries, tangling with the likes of him. But back to the problem of Kathy being missing. There still has be some connection with Carl, but I can’t see him kidnapping her. After all, he could hardly take her back to his place. He’s got a woman and a kid at home. To be quite honest with you, we’ve reason to believe that Terry Walton has something to do with Kathy’s disappearance. That’s why I was rather hoping she was still with you. We’re getting a little concerned that we can’t locate her.”
Jack looked concerned. “So what can I do to help?” he asked.
“Tell you what,” replied Pete, “let’s go back to the first time you met Kathy, in the bar at the sports club. Is there anything

she said or did that evening that might give us a clue as to where she is now?"

Jack took a gulp of water and tried to focus. He hadn't exactly been taking notes at the sports club, but he could remember most of the details. Nights like that didn't happen often enough.

"Let's see, then", he started. "She was sitting on one of the sofas, doing the Telegraph crossword, drinking a shandy. She didn't look like she was expecting anyone, and I watched her doing her crossword for ten minutes or so. She had her gym bag next to the sofa and her purse and car keys on the glass table. I made a light comment, she gave me the cold shoulder and then we got to chatting. I sat next to her on the sofa and we nattered away like we were old friends, right up to closing time. We talked about living in this area, about making friends. She doesn't seem to have many. She knew a couple of pubs I've been to in the New Forest, and a few good restaurants like the Spa Hotel and Chewton Glen. There wasn't anywhere she mentioned that sounded significant. If anything, her previous life back in Bournemouth sounded more her style, and she seemed to be missing that. I got up a few times to get drinks in, made sure we had a tab running – I didn't want her to think I was hitting on her" Pete smiled neutrally. "And we didn't move from there. When the barman – Sam is his name - said he was closing up, we both got up to go. I had my sports bag and she had hers. She picked up her purse, the car keys and her newspaper." He squinted as he concentrated on recalling the detail". There was an odd thing about the car keys"

"What was that?"

"They obviously wouldn't fit in her purse, and that was because there was this huge pink metal tag on the key ring, really out of place, with a brass Chubb key attached to it. I couldn't help but notice, so as we were drinking up I asked her what the Pink Elephant was – that was the name on the pink tag, which was in the shape of an elephant. She was quite coy about it. "That's my insurance policy" she said. That was all. I didn't have a clue what she meant, so I dropped it. Well, events kind of overtook us, if you know what I mean"

"I think I do" sighed Pete.

"So what is this Pink Elephant?" asked Jack. " Are they some kind of Insurance company?"

"No, they're a storage company, renting lock-up units. There's a big one here in Eastleigh. A lot of people store stuff just before or just after they move, but I wouldn't have thought they'd carry the key around with them all the time." He'd been making notes while Jack spoke, and paused to underlined something. “So you left the bar and went to her car?”

“You seem to know the story already, although I don’t know how. I can’t imagine Kathy has told you every detail.”

“No, she hasn’t, but don’t forget we’re investigating a suspicious death here, we have access to a lot of information, and I’m not telling anyone how much we know and how we know it. But I think that’ll do for now, I’ll let you get dressed.” He noticed Jack’s relieved look. “But we’ll talk again soon, I’m sure”

“Was it her footprints on the window?” asked Jack.

CHAPTER TWENTY

The old hut was in complete darkness, and the door was locked, with an additional very sturdy padlock for security. Andy shone his flashlight through one of the windows and could see a large empty hall, with some small rooms off it. The torchlight slowly scanning the walls revealed nothing unusual. The old wooden steps creaked under his weight as he slowly descended them. Next to the steps was a ramp leading up to some double doors, probably so that boats could be towed out of the hut over to the slipway. He climbed the ramp and tried the lift-up door. Firmly locked. As he walked around the hut, he shone the torch on all the windows. There was no sign of activity, and no lights on anywhere, even though it was now quite dark outside. Andy paused and listened, in case there was any delayed reaction to his descent of the creaking steps or his trying the doors. He could hear only the wind whispering through the trees and the distant clinking from the boats. As he reached the back of the hut, he found another set of steps leading up to a flimsy-looking door, also padlocked. He mounted the steps and as he rattled the door the fittings came loose. Obviously the security on this side was just for show – this was the entrance most frequently used. He pulled the door open quietly and stepped inside. His torch illuminated a row of bright yellow kayaks mounted on a trailer, ready to be towed through the lift-up doors and down the ramp. On the wall were various maps – Christchurch harbour, Bournemouth bay, the Solent, and sheets of tide tables. A handwritten notice in black marker announced "Don't get caught out in the bay at high tide – the current at the run gets VERY strong!" Must mean something to the boating people, Andy thought to himself. There was a long list of names with each name assigned to various duties such as rope storing and boat cleaning, signed at the bottom by T. Walton (Skipper).

He walked into the main hall and shone the torch around. Nothing there - maybe I'll check the rooms off, although it's all a bit creepy, he thought. He was walking towards the farthest door when suddenly a figure sprinted out of one of the other rooms, making for the back door. Andy wasn't a great athlete, as his chase through Bournemouth town centre had shown, but he kept himself in trim at the police gym and had good reactions. He let the flashlight drop and dived to his right in a head-first rugby tackle, grabbing a foot and bringing its owner crashing to the floor with a yelp. The person was small and skinny, but very energetic, lashing out with feet and flailing with hands to try to get free, but without making any sound

except a muffled squeal.
"Just stop your kicking, will you?" shouted Andy. "I'm a police officer and you're going to answer some questions". He now had his arms around the suspect's waist and quickly twisted one arm behind his back in a half-nelson, sitting astride him to pin him to the floor. He shuffled them both around the room until he could retrieve his flashlight and shone it on the suspect's face squashed against the hard floor. It was a boy of about thirteen, dressed in jeans, trainers and a navy blue sweatshirt. The boy still didn't make a sound but was breathing heavily. Andy relaxed the pressure on him to roll him over, and then saw the Sea Scouts emblem on his sweatshirt. Making sure the boy couldn't struggle free, Andy reached into his jacket and took out his ID, shining the light on it.
"I'm Detective Constable Andy Withers, of Dorset Police. I need you to stop struggling and then I'll ask you some questions".
Seeing the police badge and Andy's photo seemed to calm the boy, who spoke for the first time.
"Well, you can't blame me for putting up a fight." he whined, "There are some weird people around. You should have shouted out who you were instead of creeping around. Let me up and I'll be good. Look, I'll even show you where the light

switch is"

Andy cautiously let the boy up and stayed close while he walked to the wall and put the lights on. There were a couple of chairs around a table in one corner. Andy led the boy over and they sat opposite each other.

"OK" began Andy," now tell me what you're doing here with all the lights off'.

"I mean, I know I'm not supposed to be here on my own, but it's so boring at home. Anyway, because I'm one of the Sea Scouts this hut sort of belongs to me partly, especially 'cos I'm a patrol leader. So hanging out here helps look after the place, stops tramps and squatters getting in, you know? I mean, so I treat it kind of like my den, you know?"

Andy was used to interviewing young suspects, so the copious use of 'you know' and 'I mean' didn't seem unusual. "But where is Mr Walton? Has he been here tonight?"

"Terry Walton? Skipper? Oh, he left after all the other lads went, about an hour ago. I mean, that's what he does every week after the meetings, you know? Usually, I pretend to leave before all the others, then I hang around the playground up the road and sneak back through the back door, you know? I hide in the back room over there till about ten then go home to bed"

"But what do you do in here by yourself?"

"This." The boy replied, and brought out a Nintendo DS from under his sweatshirt. "Like my Mum and Dad are really strict about playing video games, they won't let me have it on at home, so I sit in the back room and play it"
Andy was taken aback. "So you sit in the dark on your own?"
"Of course, I play the single-player game. There's no WiFi here."
Seems innocent enough, Andy thought, but then worrying doubt crossed his mind. "Tell me, son, does Mr Walton ever stay behind with you? Or has he ever come back and found you here – the two of you here by yourselves?"
"No, why? Oh, I get it – you want to know if he ever tries any funny business, like wanting to play with my knob? No, he's not like that. And he's never offered to show me his either, before you ask. I mean, there's a lot of that type over at the bogs at Hengisbury Head, but nobody goes over there after dark, you know? And one of my mates says there's a bloke who hangs around the mini-golf in Boscombe giving kids sweets if he can flash at them. They just grab the sweets and run off, call him a perv for his trouble! Anyway, Skipper would be on the register if he was like that and got caught, then he wouldn't be allowed to run the Sea Scouts. That would be a shame, 'cos he's pretty good at it. Know what I mean?"

Andy was amazed at the child's view of the world, but encouraged by his ability to put it all in his own order of proportion.

"So is that Terry's car outside, the BMW?"

"Yeh,of course. It's the one with the Sea Scouts sticker in the back window"

"But you said you'd seen him leave"

"I mean, I did, but not in his own car. He must have gone off with that woman."

"Which woman?"

"The one who turned up when Skipper was locking up. I saw them from the playground, you know? She'd parked her car next to his. She was yelling and screaming at him, then he walked over to her and started shouting back. They were between the two cars, so I couldn't see what was happening, but there was a lot of noise, you know? I thought he was going to kill her"

"So what did you do? Did you think about running for help from a grown-up?"

"Give me a break, mate! Grown-ups. You only get them in Enid Blyton stories. No, course not. My old man and me mum scream at each other like that all the time, don't mean nothing. I mean, I thought he's big enough to take care of himself, so I

hid back behind the hut, waiting for it all to calm down, then suddenly it stopped"
"And you didn't see where they went after that?"
"No, I just heard a car door open, then close. I mean, two car doors open and close, then I heard a car driving away. Then I came back to the hut and saw that Skipper's car was still there, you know? I looked around for him and shouted out his name, but he'd obviously gone off with her. They must have made it up after their fight like me mum and dad, usually after he's whacked her one."
Andy felt his concern rising. "But you didn't actually see him do that?"
"No I didn't. So anyway, I came in and finished playing my game as usual till I heard you turn up. I thought it was Skipper coming back so I hid. Then you came in with a torch, and I thought, I mean, Terry never uses a torch, you know? So I thought it must be some old perv, so I tried to run for it"
"What kind of car was the woman in?"
"A Citroen DS3, soft-top. I'm pretty good at cars, you know? I'm going to get a Lexus when I get to sixteen. I mean, I might have to get a job first though"
"What colour was this DS3?"
"Couldn't see. They all look the same with these yellow lights

everywhere. I mean, probably red, maybe blue?"
"Did you see who was in the car, or who was driving?"
"Nope. Too far away. Sorry"
"Well, that's a start, anyway. Hold on while I pass this info on to my colleague" Andy dialled Pete's number.

"Now what?" Pete grumbled when he felt the phone buzz. He and Jenny had just finished dinner and was starting to doze off with the evening paper sliding off his lap. Jenny was watching the evening news with the sound turned down slightly, to facilitate his habitual after-dinner "dozing off". He saw who it was and spoke into the phone.
"Yes, Andy?" He listened while Andy described the scene at the Boathouse and the encounter with the boy. "And he reckons it was a Citroen DS3, red or blue? That'll be the one that Kathy rented – it's red, by the way - while we've got hers in the pound. Did the kid hear any of the conversation? Any sounds of a fight, then – screams or anything?" Pete listened while Andy described the fight and the ensuing car doors slamming. "Sounds to me like she's had to go along with him, maybe he's got her to do the driving. Look, there's not a lot we can do tonight. Get the usual from the boy and send me a report by email. And thanks for going down there, especially on your

own in the dark with a villain like that around. I owe you one."
Pete hung up and looked over to his ever-interested wife.
"Turns out this casino thug that I told you about is also a sea-scout leader, so Andy went looking for him down at Wick Ferry, in Christchurch."
"That's an interesting hobby, Sea Scouts. Maybe you should try being a Boy Scout leader yourself?" Jenny smiled.
"Me?" Pete looked aghast.
"You've always said you'd like a night out with the boys" she replied, trying to keep a straight face.
"Oh Ha bloody Ha " he slowly got her joke.
"But I must say, it's a funny hobby for someone who works in a casino" Jenny said, seriously now. "Although it would be a great alibi if he's having a bit on the side – he goes off all saintly, teaching boys how to tie knots or whatever, then on the way home he stops in at his fancy lady's for a bit of the other. With all that going on, it beats me how he'd find the time to murder anyone"
"You know, sweetheart, you should write some crime stories for those women's magazines. Real life isn't anywhere near as exciting as what goes on in your mind. Anyway, as you know, he's just a suspect at the moment. Funny thing is, it looks like the murdered man's wife has gone all Miss Marple again and

gone down there to confront him, because she's convinced he topped her husband. Andy has a witness down there who says that Walton and Mrs Johnson were arguing in the car park, then they both went off in her car. I just hope nothing nasty has happened to her"

"So do you have to go out again?" said Jenny, trying to sound as if she didn't mind if he had to.

"No, I've already got an all-points for that car of hers, not much more I can do tonight. I'll leave early and go down to Portsmouth to that Pink Elephant storage unit I told you about. If anything happens I'm sure everyone knows where to find me". And with that Pete turned his newspaper to the sports page.

Back at the boathouse Andy was preparing to call it a night. At least he'd passed some useful information back to Pete, and had a witness to ask some more questions tomorrow.

"Ok son, I'll have to take your name and address in case we need to get back to you".

As Andy stood up and released his hold, the boy leapt up and dived through the still-open back door, and was out of sight in seconds. With a sigh, Andy followed and shone his flashlight beam in the darkness, and could see the boy scurrying past the playground and on towards the Mudeford housing estate. No point in chasing him, thought Andy, he's well gone. He returned to the car park to check out the BMW. Unsurprisingly, it was still locked. There was nothing to note in the area around it, so Andy phoned in a report to Dorset dispatch, asking them to send a patrol over. He would wait for them and then ask them to stay with the BMW till he could get a forensics team there the next morning. If Walton returned to the car, they were to apprehend him, but, he emphasised, they should approach him very, very carefully.

CHAPTER TWENTY ONE

The Pink Elephant storage facility in Eastleigh is a foreboding building, set on a business park opposite a friendly-looking car hire company, but looking more like Alcatraz than a drop-off for cardboard boxes. Although the facade is bright pink in keeping with its name, it is surrounded by fences topped with razor wire, bathed in spotlights and under the scrutiny of CCTV cameras. A friendly-looking pink elephant next to the brand name adds just a touch of lightness to the grim appearance. The entrance consists of an electric sliding gate with a keycard lock, which opens with the card each subscriber is given when they rent a unit. This is to allow vans and trucks to bring and take the sometimes bulky contents of each unit whenever the customer needs it. The facility is open seven days a week from 8 a.m. to 11 p.m. Once inside, the customer has access to a selection of hoisting and carting vehicles so that he can store and retrieve on any of the three floors without assistance. The building inside the compound is compartmentalised so that the customer's keycard will only allow access to specific floors and sections, and ultimately he can only open the door of the specific unit he has rented. The units vary in size from four metres square to ten metres square, and each is a sealed box with a three metre high ceiling. The facility is meant to look intimidating and impregnable, but really isn't. A determined burglar would simply rent a unit under a false name to store his break-in equipment then cut through a few fairly thin walls to his booty.

Pete was at the storage facility at eight-thirty, and had a quiet walk around it to check out its perimeter. It all seemed pretty secure, maybe too secure for the kind of stuff most people would store there – furniture between house moves, collections of knick-knacks from previous marriages, clothes that didn't fit anymore but just couldn't go to the charity shop, bikes they'd bought to keep fit but that they were scared to ride in traffic, collections of things bought cheap on EBay but no-one wanted to buy at an inflated price. The list was endless, but all the stuff had one thing in common – only the owner knew what was in there. After taking ten minutes to walk a full circle, Pete approached the gate, warrant card in hand. There was a sign next to the key entry slot which read "For assistance push button". So he did, and looked up to the camera above the gate.
"Help you?" came a metallic voice through a speaker below the button.
Pete lifted his ID to the camera.

“Pete Thomas, Portsmouth CID. I’d like to speak to someone in charge.”

“That’ll be me today. Jamie Furclough, Assistant Manager, Hampshire area.”

“OK, Jamie, I’d like to speak to you then. Can you let me in, please?”

“I could, but that wouldn’t be much help, I’m afraid. I’m in Winchester”

“Is there nobody the other side of this gate, then?”

“No, we don’t keep staff on each site, it’s all run from here”

Pete could feel frustration building. And his neck was starting to ache talking to the camera above him. He moved closer to the camera, as if that would emphasise the seriousness of the situation, and pointed up to the perimeter fence.

“So what about all these cameras? Who’s looking at the monitors at the other end?”

“Well, I am” replied Jamie. “Or at least some of them. I just flip from site to site and the cameras get chosen at random unless I request something specific. There’s really not much goes on that I need to look at. I’ve been here three years and we haven’t ever had a break-in. The cameras and the fences, the barbed wire and the electric locks, they’re all quite good deterrents.”

"You said about all the sites. How many are there, say, within thirty miles of here?"

"Winchester, Portsmouth, Southampton, Farnborough, Basingstoke. That's five within half an hour's drive. It's big business, you know"

"Yes, thanks for the company sales pitch. Now if I give you a name you can tell which site has their stuff stored in it, I bet?"

"It's company policy not to give out private information like that"

"Listen son, I'm getting a pain in the neck talking to this camera, so I'll make this quick. I'm conducting an investigation into murder and kidnapping, and you can either help me or explain to your bosses why they're being prosecuted for obstruction. I'm pretty sure it would be this site I'm interested in, but if I needed to see who came to any one of those five sites last night, I'd need to come to you in Winchester?"

"Yes, and you'd need to do it today." Jamie hesitated, and adopted a friendlier tone. "Sorry, Sir, I don't want you to think I'm obstructing you. You're welcome to come up here any time you want. But if it's CCTV footage you're after, you'll need to come soon to be sure of finding what you want. We recycle the recordings every couple of days."

Pete put on his best headmaster voice. “Well don’t recycle any more till I tell you you can. I’ll get a court order if I have to. Give me your address in Winchester and I’ll be there in an hour.”

After taking down the address, Pete marched back to his car rubbing his neck. This was not a very good start.

Dave had been reading Andy’s report from the previous night when he got the call from Pete to meet him in Winchester. The report didn’t really have much substance, just that Andy had found an abandoned BMW at the car park of Wick Ferry in Christshurch, and a child had told him that someone had driven another car away, maybe a red or blue Citreon DS, at about 9:30 pm. The report noted that a woman had been seen arguing with Terry Walton earlier. The patrol that Andy had brought in had reported no visitors to the parked car all night, and he was now getting the car towed back to Bournemouth car pound for further investigation. SOC had already forced open the car doors, but had found nothing suspicious. They would have some detectives interview Terry Walton’s wife and Des Palmer and pass on the results later in the day. Andy confirmed that the details of the Citroen had been circulated in both Dorset and Hampshire counties.

The drive to Winchester was only twenty minutes and the Pink Elephant site was easy to find on the outskirts of the town. Pete was waiting for Dave as he arrived at the gates, having walked around this site like he had the one in Eastleigh.
“It’s like a wormhole” observed Pete.
Dave struggled to make any connection.
“I mean,” continued Pete, “you can be standing in a certain place, then drive under an hour and stand somewhere else. And then you can swear that you’re still standing in the same place. It’s as if there’s a hole you’ve dropped through and it’s taken you back to where you started”
Although it sounded a bit like Alice in Wonderland, Dave decided it must be some science fiction that Pete was reading, overflowing into real life. He just nodded as if it made sense.
“Here we go again” said Pete, pushed the button next to the “For assistance push button” sign and held his ID up to the camera.
“Me again, Mr Furclough, as promised. Can you let me in now?”
There was a buzz and the gate started sliding back. It waited till they had both walked through and began closing again. A man of about twenty five, dressed in a security-type uniform, came

out from a side door under the Pink Elephant sign to meet them. They shook hands and introduced themselves. Mr Furclough said he was happy to be called Jamie, and led them to his small office, which had a bank of five TV monitors above a desk with a kind of mixing unit on it. There was a printer on one side of the desk. The printer was loaded with continuous stationery and was printing a single line as they sat down on a few guest chairs that Jamie had pulled up.

"What does that do?" asked Dave.

"Every time the gate opens at any one of the five storage sites, it prints the date, time and card ID. It's what we call the entry log" he answered proudly.

"That's pretty useful" observed Dave

"And I guess you don't burn that log every couple of days?" offered Pete dryly.

Jamie was quick enough to see the dig.

"No, we print on top of the old logs, then use both sides" he answered straight faced, then "Just kidding!" when he saw Pete's double-take.

"OK" continued Pete, "Let's get down to business here. We're trying to trace someone who is known to have a key to one of your storage units. She was last seen around 9:30 last night and I know your facilities close at 11 pm, so we'd like to know if she came here before you closed. Can you check the log for entries last night around ten pm?"

"Dead easy. We store the logs for each day when we change shifts at eight in the morning. Yesterday's should be right here". He picked up a box from the cabinet and started leafing through the printout.

"As I thought, not much traffic at all. I take it you just want entries from those five sites?" he checked through the list, counting mentally. "There are four entries. Two here in Winchester, one in Farnborough and one in Eastleigh. Is Eastleigh the one you're most interested in? Ten-fifteen last night"

"Yes, let's try that one first. Can you find the CCTV footage for that site for that exact time?"

"With the magic of technology,....." Jamie faltered when he saw the unimpressed looks from the two policemen, and went quiet as he searched with the keyboard.

"Here we are!" he announced, and all three watched the main monitor. It showed the main gate at Eastleigh, although it could have been any of the sites. The word "Eastleigh" was helpfully shown at the top of the image next to the date and time. There was nothing happening, then they could see the main gate opening slowly and a woman walking towards the building

entrance. She stopped just before passing under the camera and looked up at it.
“Bingo! That’s definitely Kathy Johnson” observed Pete.
“What’s she doing? Why hasn’t she driven in?”
Kathy stopped in her tracks and looked behind her. She seemed to be gesturing to someone outside the gates, and pointed up at the camera. She then turned and walked out of shot under the camera.
“Maybe she’s not the one who was driving” volunteered Jamie, “and whoever was didn’t want to be in range of the cameras.”
“Good spot.” commented Dave. “Are there any other cameras inside?”
“Yes” replied Jamie, “one on each floor, but I’ll need to know which floor she went to. Just a minute”,
He checked the paper log and wrote down a number on a post-it pad, then keyed the number into a keyboard on the desk. A PC monitor on the desk flashed up a page of information.
“Michael Johnson, 12 Briar Crescent, Fareham – Unit 342” he read aloud, then keyed something into another system, obviously linked to the CCTV footage, and the image on the main screen changed to a view of a corridor with doors leading off it. The date indicator at the top of the screen showed the previous day’s date, but the minutes indicator was ticking

through at great speed. Sped-up images appeared occasionally of people coming in and out, but as the time passed 20:00 there was nothing for a while. Suddenly a woman's image appeared from below the camera, and Jamie hit the control to run at normal speed. The three of them watched as Kathy walked down the corridor and opened a door, then went inside. A few minutes passed and she reappeared, this time carrying a large holdall. She locked the door again and walked towards the camera. As she approached it she seemed to be mouthing the same words over and over.

Pete repeated the words as he watched her.

"HELP ME! HELP ME! HELP ME PLEASE!"

And she was gone.

CHAPTER TWENTY TWO

As Pete and Dave walked into the office, Mary Shackleton, the on-duty dispatcher was talking to Chloe Perez, one of the DCs assigned to the case.
"Ah, I was just updating Chloe on the all-points notice, Pete" Mary explained. "We've circulated the latest photos we have of both Mrs Johnson and Mr Walton, and description and registration of her hired car. No reports yet. We've sent out alerts to all the ports and airports with their passport details and photos. Do you want us to feed any kind of breaking news report to the media?"
"Not just yet" replied Pete. "We don't know quite what Terry is up to, we don't want to spook him into something silly if he sees his mug on a screen in the local chip shop"
Mary nodded and headed off towards the Control Centre, as Pete called his team together for an update.
"OK, gang. You'll have all read the reports so far, including the one from Andy about finding Walton's car and the boy who said he saw a woman in a red Citroen. As we don't know where the two of them might have gone, we'll just have to wait till they're reported in. The storage facilty where we saw Mrs Walton on CCTV is about thirty miles east of the Sea Scouts

car park in Christchurch, so they may be headed towards the ferry for France at Dover, or the Eurostar at Folkestone. Meanwhile, now is a good opportunity to hear some input from each of you".

They all settled into chairs in a semi-circle facing Pete, who stood next to a whiteboard on which was written the names of the main characters in the investigation, headed up by Mike Johnson (deceased) and his widow Kathy. A map of South East England showed the location of significant events in the case.

"As you know, Dave Seddon and I have been chasing Kathy Johnson and the man who now seems to have kidnapped her, Terry Walton. Finding the two of them is the main priority right now as we're obviously concerned for her safety. However, there are quite a few loose ends to chase up on. Let's start with her latest boyfriend, this Jack Martin. Chloe, I think you were looking at him?"

"That's right guv" she replied, flipping open her notebook. "He seems a genuine kind of bloke, I've spoken to people he works with and from his previous project. Certainly no form and his name doesn't raise any flags on any of our systems. Seems it was just bad luck he happened to hit on Mrs Johnson on the night her husband got killed, and then he was dragged into the action at the casino because he felt he owed her something"

“I could do with that kind of bad luck on a first date” mumbled Raj, a young DC sitting next to her. She smiled “You’d have to have a first date, before that could happen Raj”
There were a few smiles. Chloe continued with her report.
“Maybe he’s tried it on a few times before, when he’s been on the road. He was bound to get a ‘Yes’ sometime. There are plenty of singles out there who aren’t really singles. Take my word for it, I’ve met a few. Anyway, I’ve made some discreet calls, to both professional and personal contacts of his, and he seems to be on the level. One thing I should mention, I suppose, although it hardly seems worthwhile. I went through his work history with the guy from the agency that employs him. One of Jack Martin’s previous clients was Ladbrokes, the bookies, although he was just a programmer on some accounting system. No sign of any trouble there or at any of the other places he’s worked.”
“OK” nodded Pete. “How about this Des Palmer. Mr Casino. Him and his secretary give a new meaning to the phrase “desk job”. He’s got plenty of form, I suppose?”
“Well actually, no” replied Chloe. “He’d have had trouble getting a licence anyway, if he’d had serious form. He’s squeaky clean as far as we’re concerned, and he’d probably want to keep it that way if he’s making a good living out of the

Casino. I've checked their annual reports – it's a very healthy business and he pays himself a six-figure salary. Terry Walton isn't badly paid either, and as a qualified accountant he could get a lot more if he went to work up in London. It's difficult to see him as a kidnapper, though. I can't see what he would get out of it, unless Mrs Johnson knows something that he can't let her tell anyone else about. The people I've spoken to who have worked with Walton describe him as a gentle giant, and that kind of fits in with that Sea Scout hobby of his. He does, though, seem to have a bit of a temper, which showed itself when he had to eject one of the blackjack players a couple of years ago. It didn't stop with Walton showing the guy the door – there was a real set-to in the car park and the bloke ended up in Southampton Infirmary. That's when Walton was arrested for GBH, although there were no witnesses and the victim refused to press charges. Everyone says he's a reformed character, now he's got a family to look after."

"Yes, I met Mrs Walton and the family on our visit to Derby Road" chipped in Dave. "A fine-looking woman. Rough as you like but not short of brains or deadpan humour, and she's been round the block a few times. On balance, I think I'd rather face Terry than her in a fist fight"

"At least we know where we are with those kind of people"

continued Pete. He flipped over some pages in his notebook. "And while we're looking at the Bournemouth connection, I've had some input from Andy Withers. He's been checking on the previous circle of friends and colleagues of the Johnsons there. Nothing really to report, so if there was something going on there before they moved up to Eastleigh, no-one knows anything about it. As you know, I met that Dizzie bloke myself in Bournemouth Gardens, and I've never met anyone more aptly named. I don't think we're going to get anywhere by pressing him or his mates, but I've asked Andy to keep a watchful eye on them. Likewise with the cricket club crew, not much pressure we can apply, but there's the possibility of a drug link there, with a chap called Ken Rawlings being a name to watch out for, and as we know Johnson was stuffed full of cocaine when we found him."

Chloe raised her hand as if she was in class.

"Yes Chloe?"

"Well, Sir, I've been checking all the names that have come up so far, and this Ken Rawlings fellow actually has a connection with Tom Baxter, the American you met at the bank. They both belong to Brockenhurst Manor Golf Club, quite an exclusive club in the New Forest. I can't find out if they've ever played together or even if they've ever met, but I thought I ought to mention it”

“Thanks Chloe. A few more puzzle pieces out of the box then, and even if they’re not edges or corners, who knows? They might be the link we’re looking for later on”

The room went silent while everyone tried to understand Pete’s jigsaw puzzle analogy.

Pete cleared his throat and continued.

“So, as we’re back in Hampshire, what about our financial services friends? What do we have on Dan Mahoney, the Merchant Banker, if you’ll excuse my rhyming slang?”

“That’ll be my man then” volunteered Raj. “Real wide boy. Didn’t do much academically but seems to have had a meteoric rise in the finance sector despite that. A lot of his experience seems to have been of the “sitting next to someone who did that” kind. Went from college to local government on a sponsored trainee programmer course, then left before they could get any work out of him. His gift of the gab seems to have carried him from one employer to another, each one happier to give him a glowing reference than to admit they shouldn’t have hired him. I’ve spoken by phone to a lot of people who have dealt with him. They all think he’s due for a fall sometime soon. However, he’s got no criminal record, even though he’s been known to hang around some rather dodgy characters in Bournemouth and the South Coast. He actually still lives with his Mum in Poole."

"And the Misses McCarthy and Saunders?"

"Both fast-track from the internal graduate program. Amanda McCarthy was from Oxford with a first in Maths, Rowena Saunders from Brunel with a 2.1 in English and Politics. They entered the graduate scheme at the same time. As you might know, these schemes take the cream straight from university and give them four assignments of six months each in high profile departments. If they get through that they're almost guaranteed a Vice President position within five years."

"Vice President? Crikey, that's a hell of a fast track!" exclaimed Chloe. "It's taken me five years to get the 'Trainee' tag off my job title!"

"Don't be over-impressed, Chloe. At the latest count, there were over three thousand Vice Presidents at Mid Western. It's just a pay grade. In fact, Tom Baxter is a Senior Vice President, and there are only about two hundred of those at the bank. He's probably on a salary close to half a million pounds, though."

"Did he have anything to do with the Karen Peterson affair?" asked Pete.

"Not as far as I can tell. It was between Mike Johnson and her and that Nigel Broome chap. I've checked up on Broome, he's working at another bank in Manchester, never comes down this way. As for Karen, her husband left her six months after the kid was born, and Carl Swann moved in soon after that."

"So obviously I have to ask", Pete continued, "Is Mike Johnson the father of Karen's kid?"

"There's no way of knowing. Karen hasn't applied for help from the Child Support Agency, and she's not living on benefit"

"Do we know if her husband is paying maintenance?"

"He says she hasn't asked him, and as he doesn't see the kid he doesn't see why he should"

"Fair enough, but maybe there's some history between him and Mike Johnson from before. Do a bit more digging there, Chloe. But if the husband's not paying, how's she supporting the three of them in Fratton Park? Carl Swann doesn't look like he's earning big bucks"

"Maybe we could ask him" smiled Raj. "He's down the nick"

Pete's jaw dropped. "What, Eastleigh nick? Where?"

"He's in a cell. Been there since yesterday lunchtime. Drunk and disorderly in Portsmouth. We had him brought to Eastleigh when we saw his name come up on the wire. He's probably sober enough now to talk to us."

"OK, but let's finish up here first" Pete continued. Anyone else we need to talk about?

A hand was raised at the back of the group. Mandy Baines, new to the station, but experienced, having transferred from Reading a few months earlier.

“Yes Mandy?”

“Mike Johnson, sir?”

Pete looked puzzled. “I didn’t really think he’d have a lot to say anymore”

She smiled. She was used to the black humour surrounding this kind of investigation. Sometimes it was the only way to distance yourself from the real life blood and tears in these cases.

“No, I mean the search of Mike Johnson’s home and office computers. That’s something I had Lemmy Brokic from technical services take care of yesterday. He checked the Johnson’s home PC but there was absolutely nothing of interest there. There was the usual file containing all his passwords for social networks and the like. A couple of dodgy videos, some pirate but harmless software and some very boring email. Logging on to his facebook and twitter accounts didn’t show up much either. The Internet history was still intact and showed no sites visited of any note going back six months. There seemed to have been no attempt to erase any files, no disk reformatting, no defragmentation. Lemmy did a hex dump and scan in case there was anything hidden, but it all looks clean. He then went down to Midwest Bank, where Rowena Saunders had told him they were keeping Johnson's work laptop. Lammy did exactly the same kind of analysis on that and came up with nothing. He did ask if he could look through Johnson's desk and office filing, but they told him that it had all been archived! Johnson's office was already occupied by his replacement, apparently. They certainly don't cry for long over lost colleagues. Lemmy has asked Rowena to get Johnson's stuff back from the archives, she'll let him know when he can have it"

"In his dreams he can have it" remarked Pete. "But well done for following that line through. Now, can you all just check that we have alibis established for every person in the frame? Tuesday night, between early evening and midnight, when the body was found. Follow up on the alibis for the time of death you've been given by each of the characters you've been assigned and let me know if there's anything that doesn't look right. Kathy Johnson and Jack Martin seem to be alibis for each other, and we can confirm most of that time with the barman from the sports club. The knitting pattern twins, Graham and Gloria. Raj, can you check which pub Graham was supposed to be in that night and see if anyone can vouch for him there. We know that Terry Walton goes walkabout every Tuesday night and we've got an APB for him and Kathy Johnson, so obviously he's number one suspect, but we need to eliminate any other 'persons of interest'. We know that Carl Swann can't be relied on to know where he was, but as we've got him in the lockup, there's an opportunity to check out his habitat."

Pete looked over at Mandy.

"Mandy, could you drive over to the Legion Club in Fratton Park and do some digging to see if anyone can remember Carl being in last Tuesday night? If we can give him an alibi despite himself, that will get him off the list of contenders and we can concentrate on Walton. In the meantime, Dave, you come with me and we'll see if we can jog his own memory"

CHAPTER TWENTY THREE

Pete and Dave had driven the half mile down to Eastleigh police station together and were now were standing in the corridor outside the interview room, ready to question Carl Swann. Dave was trying to explain why he thought Carl, and not Terry Walton, was now the prime suspect.
"Look Pete, there's something fishy about all this - If all the signs point to Walton that says to me that it might not have been him. Carl here, he's a career criminal. That's got to be worth something. Maybe that's the only reason he ran when he saw you and Andy in Bournemouth, maybe not. His only other option was to brave it out and have to answer questions about how he can afford to be down there in the first place. If he is involved in this Johnson affair, he must be in league with someone else down there – you said he was dressed up for a night out. He must have some contacts in the Bournemouth crowd, maybe something to do with the Moon in the Square pub or the Cricket Club, but in any event I'm certain he knows what this is all about. He's already connected to the victim through his girlfriend, and I bet he's got a cast-iron alibi for the night of the murder, through some dodgy friends or relatives who'll testify he was with them all night. Nothing more

suspicious than a solid alibi, in my book. On top of that, he's built like a brick shithouse, so he'd have no trouble lifting a body to the top of a stepladder."

Pete seemed less than convinced.

"It's all a bit tenuous for me, Dave. Of course he's capable of it, and once we find out what was at stake maybe he'll be in the frame, but I can't see him as too likely right now. He's as thick as two short planks, always on a bender and has a wicked temper – just remember the bruises on Karen's arms. I can't see him as a master criminal, or being able to keep quiet about it if he was. There's no evidence of forced entry at the Johnsons' house, so Johnson must have let the killer in or the killer had a key. Swann and Johnson never met, so why did Johnson let him in? I can't see Swann having a key. Before you say anything, yes, the same might be said for Terry Walton, but at least if there's a gambling connection it's possible that Johnson knew Walton and let him in. Anyway, let's try to push Swann out of the frame or higher up the pecking order. We'll keep it low key in there, see if we can get him placed at any of the key places and times"

They entered the room, set the recorder going and introduced themselves. Carl seemed awake but wary as he answered questions identifying his name and address.

“So, Carl” Dave began. “Do you know why we want to speak to you?”
“Haven’t a clue, mate. I know I drank a bit too much last night and the plods brought me in, that’s all. Then they said they had to bring me over to see you, and here I am. Well, I’m OK now so can I go? I expect you have to follow the rules, so you can give me the speech about not causing any more trouble, then I’ll be on my way”
“I’m sure that’s what we would usually do, Carl, but it’s a bit different now, what with a murder investigation going on.”
“You’ll have to fill me in, then. I don’t know anyone who’s been murdered recently” He smiled at his own joke.
“But Karen knew Mike Johnson from the bank she worked at”
“Of course she did, but I never met the bugger. That was all before my time, and if I had met him I would have given him a piece of my mind, but I didn’t, so what’s it got to do with me?”
“It’s Mike Johnson’s murder we’re investigating”
“Oh. I thought he topped himself. That’s what Karen told me.”
“OK, let’s move on, Carl. Do you remember where you were last Tuesday night?”
“I don’t even know where I was last night. I remember I saw your friend here,” he nodded towards Pete, “in Bournemouth last week. I would have stopped for a chat. I quite like that

bloke you were with, Andy, from the nick down there. He's a local boy. He knows we're not all the low-lifes you lot think we are. As it happened I remembered somewhere I had to be, so I left in a bit of a rush."

"You're not kidding" Pete intervened. "You left your pint on the bar and ran off like you were trying to qualify for the next Olympics"

"Well, I keep myself fit. Of course, compared with you lot I must have seemed bloody fast....."

"Yes, well," continued Pete, "we weren't too interested in talking to you then, but we are now. When was the last time you were over at Eastleigh?"

"Oooh, haven't been round that way for months. Bit too posh for me. No night life, no clubs and stuff like that. They all stay in and watch telly, go to bed at nine with a cup of cocoa"

"So you wouldn't have been anywhere near the Travel Lodge recently?"

Carl hesitated. He looked up at the camera filming the interview, and down at the machine recording his answer. He paused a few seconds. Then it seemed he'd made a decision.

"Ok, well, you obviously know I was shouting my mouth off again, so yeh, I was there. But no harm was done. In fact I could have called you lot and got the other bloke done for

GBH"
"Yes, we already know the details, as you said" continued Dave. "But we want to know what it was all about"
"It was that bloody Johnson woman. She came down to our place in Fratton Park causing trouble. Her and her husband – yeh, I know, her dead husband – they're all bloody troublemakers, I've had enough of them"
"But what had they done to you? As far as I know that's the first time that Kathy Johnson had even met Karen Peterson"
"But she must have known what her husband was up to"
"And what was he up to?"
Carl looked frustrated. Then suddenly angry. He stood up and raised his voice
"Well that's the fucking problem, ain't it? I don't pissing-well know what the two of them were up to. I've had a go at her a couple of times, tried to knock it out of her. That's what she needs, a good belting every now and then. But she's just a tough nut, says there's nothing in it. And I still get to look after her bloody kid once a month while she has a sleep-over on Tuesday nights. Good job the legion club's only down the street, so I can come back and check on him every couple of hours, otherwise I'd have to stay in and babysit, wouldn't I? And all I get out of it is a bit of pocket money, so I can stay on

the cider and end up in the nick every now and then."
He sat down again, suddenly very sorry for himself. Pete and Dave looked at each other, and Pete nodded for Dave to continue.
"So Karen was meeting Mike Johnson on a Tuesday once a month?" said Dave.
"Was she?" Carl looked confused, then boiled over again. "Is that what your telling me, they were having it off while I was a fucking childminder?" He got up, Dave came round the table to restrain him. "I'll fucking kill her, I will!"
"No you won't" said Pete. "Because she wasn't. That was a question Dave asked you, not a statement. We thought that was what you meant when you said she was away on those Tuesday nights."
Carl sat down again, calmed just as quickly as he'd been enraged. "No, I didn't know where she was, just that Johnson was paying good money for something she was doing once a month. But she came back on the Wednesday, about midday, just as I was getting up, and cooked me breakfast. Whatever she was up to it bought me a good Full English. Anyway, I know she wasn't shagging him. She knew better that to screw somebody else. I told her before what would happen if she ever did that"

"So what happens now, now that Johnson's gone?" asked Pete.
Carl reacted as if he hadn't thought of that.
"Christ! No more cooked breakfasts."
"That's probably the least of your problems. Who's going to pay the rent and everything? Is Karen expecting something out of Mike Johnson's estate for her kid?"
Carl laughed.
"Don't be twats, eh? You know damn well that kid's not Johnson's"
"I'm afraid we don't, Carl. Karen wasn't exactly forthcoming on the subject"
"Well take it from me, he's not. When I first shacked up with Karen I made her get a DNA test done on the kid. Her ex-husband, that Barry, cooperated. I suppose he was hoping it wasn't his, but it turns out it is. He's got plenty of money so he sends a cheque every month. I thought you lot were supposed to be detectives"
He smiled again at his own joke, then suddenly looked miserable.
"His money won't keep me in booze, though. I might have to find some work for cash"
Pete looked questioningly at Dave, who shrugged as if to say "This is getting us nowhere".

Pete stood up to go.
"Carl, I'm letting you go for the moment, but we'll want to talk to you again. Try to keep sober and out of trouble. Tell Karen we'll be talking to her again soon, so stay around."
Pete announced the end of the interview for the tape and switched it off. He and Dave then both left the room, leaving the door open for Carl to find his own way out.

The Royal British Legion Club in Fratton is one of hundreds of social clubs set up originally for the benefit of ex service men and women. The British Legion itself continues fundraising, primarily through the sale of poppies in the weeks leading up to Rememberance Sunday, on which the sacrificies of British service personnel are remembered. There is, however, no requirement any more to have been in the military to join a Legion Club, so the clubs have become a de facto social club in the more deprived areas of Britain. The club at Fratton Park is a fairly modern brick building just off the high street, with very little parking as most of its clientele walk there. It was a cleaner looking building than Mandy had been expecting as she parked and entered through the main doors. A disinterested man at the desk looked up from his portable TV and asked if she was a member. Mandy flashed her ID and said she'd like to

speak to whoever was in charge.
"That'll be me, love, at this time of day. Tom Chomelewski at your service. The cleaners have already been in to tidy up after last night's bingo session. Not much else happens till the bar staff get here at twelve, then we're open till eleven tonight, but there won't be many people here till nine as it's not a weekend. Apart from the serious snooker players, who are here most of the afternoon hidden away in the games room. Plus the usual half dozen long-term boozers. They'll sit around in a corner getting tanked up on cider or lager, or at the bar boring the staff with their life histories, then stagger home to sleep it off well before the family people get here early evening."
"Would one of those long-term boozers be Carl Swann?"
"Sometimes. Depends how much cash he's got. Anyway, this is a social club and we're all part of one big happy family. So all I can tell you officially is that Carl is a member of this club. We don't keep records of when anyone is here or how much they drink. That would be a bit 'Big Brother' wouldn't it?"
"So if I asked you whether Carl was here last Tuesday you wouldn't tell me?"
"I wouldn't know, so I couldn't tell you. I daresay if Carl wanted someone here to confirm he was here at a certain date or time, he would have told you who that person was, and that

person would swear blind that Carl was here."
"And I daresay we'll ask that person as soon as we find out from Carl who he is" smiled Mandy. She looked past the man into the drinking lounge. The grill was down over the bar and there was no-one sitting there, just a few sets of cheap-looking seats arranged in fours around card tables, waiting for domino teams or whist drive members to take their places. She remembered well those days when, as a child, she had been taken into such social clubs for "Family Nights", when the wives were allowed to join in the evening drinking sessions because they were allowed to bring the kids in with them. In those days the wives would otherwise be expected to stay at home with the kids while the husbands went out drinking. The kids would spend the evenings sliding across the dance floor on their knees, treading drinks and crisps into the carpet, and screaming to go home because they were tired. Maybe in the twenty-first century it's different, she thought. But maybe not. As her thoughts drifted, her eyes wandered around the foyer and settled on a list of the club presidents, dating back to the nineteen fifties. One name jumped out – Kenneth Rawlings, president 2005/6.
"Do you know that man, Ken Rawlings?"
"Ken? Yes, he was a board member here for years, then

president. He ran the bar for a few years before he moved"

"And where is he now?"

"He runs the bar at the Cricket Club in Bournemouth"

CHAPTER TWENTY FOUR

"I'm going to grab a sandwich then make my way back to the office", said Dave as they left the Eastleigh police station. "Do you want anything or are you going home for lunch?"

"I said I'd be home" replied Pete, "unless something crops up. You go and get your sandwich and I'll give you a lift back, I'll have something later if I can't get home" He turned and was walking towards his car when a Rolls Royce swept into the parking lot at speed and started heading straight at the two of them. Dave panicked and dived to his left, jumping up on the low wall surrounding the car park. Pete held his nerve and stood still, daring the driver to run him down. At the last second, the car swerved, braked quickly and glided to a halt in the visitors parking space. Pete breathed a deep breath, then marched over to meet Des Palmer as he got out, with his secretary friend easing out of the plush passenger seat to join him. Dave sat on the wall and lit a cigarette.

"What the hell do you think you're playing at?" Pete bristled, "You could have killed us both!"

"Not in a great machine like this", smirked Palmer. "It turns on a sixpence and has pinpoint braking, in the right hands that is. Sorry if I scared you. It's terrible when people arrive suddenly

when you're not expecting them, isn't it?"
Pete smiled grudgingly. "Oh, fair play to you, I suppose, you evil bastard. So let's call it even, shall we? So anyway, good morning Mr Palmer". He smiled at Palmer's companion "Marybeth, isn't it?" She smiled dutifully as Pete continued. "I hope you're not here to sample the food at the Eastleigh police cafeteria. I hear it's liver and onions today"
"Morning Inspector" replied Palmer, his honour restored, "And you can call me Des, like everyone else does, since we've met in such intimate circumstances" Pete smiled at the self-deprecating irony. "No, we've just come to pick up Terry's car. We had a call from your Bournemouth lot to say they'd finished with it and I could pick it up here."
"But Terry lives in Bournemouth, wouldn't it be closer to get it collected there?"
"Are you kidding? This is a company car, it's not Terry's own. Till we find out what's happened to him, I'll have the car back. I didn't get where I am my giving cars away, unless it's in a blackjack game. Anyway, I'm glad I almost bumped into you, maybe you can tell me how you're getting on finding him and that woman"
Pete ignored the jocular tone. "At the moment, we don't know very much, but I'll tell tyou what we do know in case you can

fill in any gaps. We think your Terry Walton and she are in a red Citroen DS which she's rented. It was last seen at Wick Ferry, Christchurch, where Walton has his regular Tuesday night Sea Scout meeting. We assume Mrs Johnson followed him there, maybe from your casino, maybe from his home in Derby Road, to confront him about whatever business he was up to with Mike Johnson."

"She may not have had to follow him, after her visit to the casino. His car was parked next to mine, and it has a Christchurch Sea Scouts sticker in the rear window."

Pete hadn't been aware of that but tried to brave it out. "Of course there is that possibility also. Anyway, we have an all points bulletin out for them and we're hoping to intercept them soon. And that's all I can tell you. But maybe you can tell me something. Your late brother, Spike. What could have been the connection from him to Mike Johnson? Was it the cricket club in Bournemouth? Is there a gambling connection, even if it doesn't involve your casino? How about drugs? Did your brother supply cocaine ever?"

"That's quite a list of questions, and I don't have any factual answers I'm afraid. I'm sure other people will have given their opinions, and here's mine. Spike was a great guy. He was good at everything he tried and he had a lot of admirers. Of course,

some people were jealous so he had enemies too. He just wouldn't have cared about them. He went and did what he wanted, and lived life to the full. Sadly, that involved getting high occasionally, and he died as a result. I've never heard of anyone being sold drugs by Spike, but I also don't know where he got his. As for a connection between Mike Johnson, they might as well have come from different planets. I don't think Spike would have liked the bloke if he'd known him, but I'm pretty sure they never met, despite sometimes frequenting the same hangouts. And gambling, forget it. Spike gambled with life. He would have laughed at anyone trying to make money from gambling, like he had little respect for my Casino business, despite it being financially successful. As for sport, he only cared about results if he was a participant, and he never played unless he could win. Does that answer your questions?"
"Yes, in a way it does, thank you. Would you be that positive about any link between Terry Walton and Mike Johnson?"
"No, of course not. I've known Terrry a long time, but we don't move in the same social circles. He also had a career before I hired him, and I don't know anything about who he knew back then. He's always been dependable, if just a little secretive. But I respected that."
"So you couldn't completely rule out the possibility that he's

kidnapped Mrs Walton?"
"No, I couldn't, though I'd say it's unlikely they've eloped together, after the row at the casino. Unfortunately my best guess is that she pushed him too far and he smacked her one to keep her quiet. Then to avoid messing up my car he drove off in hers. He doesn't like himself when he's lost his temper – he almost ended up in prison the last time – so he's probably gone off to the wilds of Scotland for a few days to calm down."
"Why Scotland?"
"Or Wales, or the Isle of Man – it's just somewhere far away from here."
"Not France?"
"Never France. Terry was as British as the Queen. Only more so. He doesn't have German ancestry.He dislikes foreign food, foreign languages, foreign students, you name it. No, he'll be in the UK somewhere."
"And what do you think he's done with Kathy Johnson?"
"With a bit of luck she woke up on the journey with a sore head and he's dumped her at a motorway service area somewhere. She'll turn up soon, I hope. On the other hand, he's quite resourceful. You might never find her."

Pete was driving back from the car park discussion with Des

Palmer, Dave beside him tucking into a sandwich. Pete's phone rang. He put the call on the loudspeaker. It was Raj, who'd been sent off to Parkway railway station to explain the parking ticket found in Johnson's car, dated a few months ago.
"Yes Raj" answered Pete, trying not to sound impatient. He knew finding Kathy and Walton were pivotal to the case, but until they were found his team had plenty of other work to do filling in the missing gaps of the case, so he wanted to encourage all contributions.
"I've been at the station looking for evidence around the date and Timestamp on that ticket" began Raj. "Unfortunately, there's no CCTV in the car park itself, but there are cameras on the platforms. I've been with the security guys here going through the images from both cameras. I've got to say there are a hell of a lot of people using this station. But anyway, I'm pretty sure I didn't see anyone who definitely was Mike Johnson, but of course he might have been looking the other way"
"That's a pity, Raj." He smiled at Dave, who returned the look with his mouth still full. You had a good look at the people waiting for the train to Fratton Park?"
"Yes, you'd be surprised how many people come through that station, the platforms are crammed full from seven in the

morning till gone nine. I'm surprise really there aren't more people falling on the track. It's like some Japanese bullet train when the train pulls in, and there are hardly any seats left anyway, so most of the people end up standing all the way. Anyway, I checked each train out, looking at everyone who came on to each platform, even zooming in on the entrance turnstiles in case he came in late and jumped straight on. As we didn't know his destination I had to go through the tapes several times concentrating on the people getting on the train. But that's when I saw her."

Pete was suddenly interested. "Saw who?"

"Well I was checking the train going to Fratton Park. That's a local, so there weren't many people actually getting on it, and there was an express coming in just after it, so people were crowding around ready for it. Then I noticed that another train had come in on the opposite platform, obviously coming from stations on that same Fratton Park line, so I switched to the camera on that platform. I happened to be looking at the exit, thinking that maybe Johnson would be arriving there and struggling through the crowd of people getting off the train – there's only one entrance, you know, it's the exit as well. And there she was, going through the turnstiles on the way out"

Pete was getting frustrated, but said calmly "Saw who, Raj?

Who did you see?"

At that instant a loud noise rattled the railway station and echoed down the phone, obliterating anything that Raj was saying. It subsided after a few seconds.

"Sorry about that guv, anyway it was her. Karen Peterson. She was carrying a big holdall, and she didn't have her kid with her."

"Wow. Thanks Raj. Well done, a bit of extra thinking from you there. I don't suppose you saw which direction she took after she'd gone through the turnstiles? Or if she met someone?"

"No, the camera doesn't reach that far. Sorry." Raj sounded despondent, as if it were his fault.

"No, you've done great, Raj – a good result, that. Can you collect the tape of her and bring it back with you? We're waiting for the others to check out alibis, so we'll put all this together when you get back."

Pete ended the call and turned to Dave, explaining what Raj had found out.

"So, the parking ticket was just that," Dave commented. "He was parking there just to pick up his girlfriend from the train. But where were they going?"

"That's the question" responded Pete. There's nothing out there. It's not like Southampton Central where there are restaurants to wine and dine her, then plenty of hotels for afters. There's just the car park. Not even a pub nearby, if I remember correctly. And it's bloody noisy. I almost had my eardrums burst when an express train shot through"

"An express train? No, it wouldn't have been that. Every train, both express and local, stops at Parkway." Dave had done his research on the train timetable. "That would have been an aeroplane going over"

"Well it was bloomin' low if it was"

"Of course, it was. It would have been taking off, or landing. You just have to walk over a footbridge from the station and you're in Southampton airport"

Pete, who rarely flew anywhere, was obviously surprised by the news.

"So maybe that was it! he gasped. "Maybe it's something to do with the airport or flights from it. I'll call Raj back and get him to check the passenger lists from the same day as the parking ticket, maybe he'll find Karen Peterson, Mike Johnson or both!"

CHAPTER TWENTY FIVE

Jack was worried. He hadn't really expected to hear anything from Kathy, given how brief their relationship had been, but he had felt a little disappointed when he hadn't seen her at the gym for a few days. Even though she was frustrating to be around, with her wild accusations and constant fear of being followed, still there was a tinge of excitement in all this, and she wasn't bad in bed either. He'd been having trouble focussing at work, with his project assistant having to correct a few poor assumptions he'd made in the revised plan. He'd have to tread a bit carefully, he didn't want his work to suffer. Hell, they might replace him as Project Manager and he'd end up in some god-forsaken place like Sellafield again. He wouldn't forget that horrendous weekly commute and all those lonely weeknights wandering the streets of Whitehaven in the rain looking for an open restaurant or a bar that didn't go completely silent when a stranger walked through the door. To alleviate his worry, he'd taken the bold step of phoning Eastleigh police station and asking to speak to Pete Thomas, but was told that DI Thomas wasn't available – he could speak to Detective Dave Seddon who was working on the same case, if he wanted to. So he did, told Dave who he was and asked if there was any progress. Naturally Dave was wary of giving out any information, but did say that they were concerned about Kathy's safety, as she appeared to be in the company of a Mr Terry Walton, whereabouts unknown. Jack reacted silently. Walton, the bodyguard from the casino. The one who Kathy had seen through the restaurant window, and who had broken into her room. That phrase 'in the company of' seemed to imply some kind of liaison. Obviously she and Walton had met up somewhere, and now neither could be found? But he couldn't imagine Kathy having a romantic night with Walton the way they had. Surely her standards were a bit higher than that? She must think more of Jack than to go off shagging someone else within days, musn't she? Then he thought back to the episode at the casino – her screaming accusations, then her crazed attack on Des Palmer followed by her laying into Walton, when he tried to pull her off Palmer. No, that was no romantic foreplay, he smiled to himself, she was beating the shit out of them both because she was so upset about her husband's death, and who could blame her? So, hold on. Let's look at this another way. Maybe this was some kind of revenge trip for Walton himself, after being attacked so viciously by Kathy? That's why he'd been following her. Just to find a moment when she was alone so he could put her in her place. It had nothing to do with her husband's connection with Palmer, or whatever led to his murder. It was just Walton's own pride after being humiliated by a woman. He suggested this possibility to Dave Seddon, who told him that it was a police matter. Very patiently but firmly, Seddon told Jack that they would involve him if they needed to, and ended the call.

So Jack had gone to the gym again after work, more to jog out the frustration he was feeling than to get into shape. Maybe he did feel something for Kathy, it wasn't simply a quick grope in the car park? No, he didn't want to go there. He was very happy in his marriage, even if he was just home at weekends and holidays. This was just a bit on the side, nothing more. Just thinking that hackneyed phrase made him angry with himself. No, of course he had feelings for Kathy. He wasn't that shallow. He'd never had sex with a woman without having feelings for her, just as he would never dream of using the services of a prostitute. As for Kathy, he found her fascinating and incredibly attractive, but he would be happy not to stay in touch once it was over. And of course it would be over soon enough. But then he'd like to be the one who ended it, and if that sounded too male macho, then too bad. So here he was climbing the steps to the gym entrance again, hoping more than a little that she would be there, having put Walton in his place instead of the other way round.

As he entered the gym, Jack could see that it was another quiet night. The same receptionist was on duty as his last visit, and Jack had his usual cheery banter with her. He'd previously found out her name was Vicky, and after a few meaningless exchanges he took the plunge and dared to ask if Mrs Johnson had been in.

"No, funny thing that" Vicky replied. "She used to come in every night regular as clockwork, but I haven't seen her at all this week"

Dave leaned forward and eyed the computer screen.

"She couldn't have come in without you knowing?"

"Oh, of course she could if she wanted to. If there was a crowd of people coming in at the same time, the turnstile would be open and she wouldn't need to swipe her card if she didn't want to. Same as on the way out. They're supposed to do it so we know if anyone's left inside if we have a fire alarm, but it's a waste of time really. Last time we had a fire drill no-one had time to print off the list, so we couldn't check who was there anyway!"

"So on that Tuesday night when her husband died, she must

have come in at about six?" he looked inquiringly.
Vicky didn't really have much else to do, so she played along and entered a few keystrokes.
"No, it was about eight o'clock when she came in. She went straight to the bar"
"Oh, of course, she said the class she was going to had been cancelled"
"No, that wouldn't have been it. The only class she goes to is Martial Arts, Mondays and Thursdays"
"Oh," Jack felt a little uncomfortable. Maybe it had been easier for Kathy to say she'd missed a class, rather than admitting she'd spent all evening in the bar.
"So what does she do the other nights she's here?" he asked.
"Weights. She's one of those power lifting nutters, there's a big group of them do it together. They get quite obsessive. I know she looks small and she's a woman, but she could lift a sack of coal over her head without a murmur"
"Oh." was all Jack could muster. No wonder she was unafraid to lay into Palmer and Walton. Maybe there was some previous business with the two of them that she was sorting out, and he'd got dragged into it by mistake? No, he already knew her better than that. She hadn't met either of them before that episode at the casino, he was pretty sure of that. "So she went

to the class on the Monday, not the Tuesday. Can you tell what time she came and went that night, the Monday?"
"No problem." She tapped away again. "In at six, out at ten"
"But of course those are just the times her card was swiped, aren't they?"
Vicky smiled.

Pete and Dave had continued working into the evening while most of the others had left. They were standing in front of a large scale map of the Solent area.
"Yes, I know Fleet services is the most obvious choice to drop someone of from the motorway" Dave was saying, "But we've already sent a couple of squad cars there. They went through the shops, restaurants and toilets, made a couple of announcements over the tannoy and checked with the forecourt staff. No sign of Kathy, Walton or the car. They certainly didn't fill up with petrol there because the forecourt cameras record every licence plate number in case of drive-offs. We had the guys check over the fence, the rear of the services area leads onto farmland, but no sign of anyone going that way."
"Has anyone checked on Walton's history, to see where he might go if he feels cornered?" Pete inquired.
"Yes, boss. He's spent a long time in Hampshire and Dorset,

but he’s originally from Edinburgh. Chloe phoned through to Scotland and they checked out any relatives. Seems the only living one lives in the town but swears she hasn’t heard from Walton for a couple of years now”
“I don’t like the feel of this, Dave. The longer she’s missing, the more worried I get”
A noise from the corridor outside broke the strained silence. The door to the office opened and a breathless Raj walked in. He looked suitably surprised to see them.
“Burning the midnight oil, are we? I thought only us juniors had to work that hard!”
Pete smiled good naturedly.
“No, there’s not much on telly tonight, we thought we’d have a boys night in. There’s some popcorn in the fridge and we’ve rented a DVD of Fast and Furious” Pete kept a straight face. Raj hesitated a moment, then recognised Pete’s sense of humour, took off his coat and dumped a sheaf of printed papers on the desk in front of them.
“OK, I think I might have something here” he began. “ I went over to the airlines booking desks at Southampton Airport, as you asked. There are ten of them if you exclude the ski package companies. On the day of the parking ticket and CCTV of Karen at the railway station there were twenty-three flights.

Three of them had already left before the time on the ticket, and the remaining flights belonged to six different airlines. I went to British Airways and Air France first, then Flybe, leaving the smaller airlines till last. At each one I asked for a full roster of passengers boarding – I thought I should just ignore "no-shows""

Pete was a patient man, but this level of detail was perhaps best left till the next morning.

"Just tell us what you found, eh, Raj?" He smiled kindly.

"Well, yes I will, because it will surprise you two as much as it surprised me" beamed Raj triumphantly. "I'd gone through every flight, including the minor airlines, a total of over a thousand names, with no sign of Karen Peterson or Mike Johnson, although their surnames are quite common. I thought maybe I'd have to go on to the "no-shows", when something hit me"

"Which was?"

"I'd seen a familiar name on the list of Petersons and Johnsons and it had stuck in my mind, so at the end I went back to find it again. I thought at first I'd made a transposition error as I'd written it down, so I had the airline print off the ticket details and the CCTV photo of the person checking in"

"And whose name did you find?"

“The name on the ticket was Kathy Johnson”

Pete drew a breath.

“Wow. And did you find out when the return leg was? She must have been back by early evening when she had the row with her husband.”

“The return flight was the next day”

“So Kathy didn’t take that flight?

“Well actually, no.” He pushed across the desk a printout of the grainy image captured by the CCTV. It clearly showed Karen Peterson standing at the check-in desk.

CHAPTER TWENTY SIX

It didn't take much organising to bring Karen in. The local uniforms from Fratton Park had arrived around breakfast time and had found Karen at breakfast with her child. Carl was evidently in bed still, sleeping off yet another busy night at the Legion Club. Karen said she preferred to leave him asleep, and called her Mum in from just down the road to look after things. Her mum didn't seem worried by her daughter being taken away in a squad car, maybe she assumed it was something Carl had been up to again. She simply carried on feeding Karen's child her breakfast. As for Karen, she sat quietly in the back of the squad car with a policewoman, and didn't ask any questions or say anything during the short trip to Eastleigh. Pete and Dave were waiting in the interview room. Karen was asked if she wanted a solicitor present, but declined. A cup of tea was offered and accepted, then the interview began.

"Karen, do you know why we've brought you in?" started Pete.
"I'm guessing it's to do with the Johnsons" she replied.
"There's all kind of rumours I've heard about her being kidnapped and things. I suppose you want to hear if I know anything about it"

“Well, do you?”
“Sorry Inspector, I don’t. I don’t even know that bloke who they say has taken her, Wallace is it?”
“Walton. Terry Walton. No, we’ve checked his background against yours and there doesn’t seem to be much in common, although I think your Carl might know him from way back. No, it’s more about your little day trips to France”
Karen stiffened, then settled back into the chair and folded her arms defensively.
“And what do you want to know?”
“For a start you can tell us what you were doing taking a flight once a month to Bergerac in France, and staying overnight. We know already that you took the plane from Southampton, using a passport with Kathy Johnson’s photo and your name. We also know that Mike Johnson had time off work to meet you at Parkway station before your flight. So you can tell us what it was all about.”
“OK, simple enough. You know already that I used to work at the same bank as Mike, and that there was a row about me getting a promotion over some bloke called Nigel Broome, who incidentally was a right prat. Anyway, I got the job and not him, and I was making a good job of it, I thought, but it was a lot harder work than I was used to. I had to go on corporate

training courses and visit other branches, a few overseas trips – New York, Paris, that sort of thing for a few days at a time. So after a few months my home life started suffering. My husband at the time – Barry was his name, in case you don't already know that - he thought he should be doing all the bread-winning and I should be starting a family. So to keep him happy I let myself get pregnant and that made the job even more difficult to do well. I know I had maternity leave if I wanted to, but before I could even tell anyone at work officially that I was pregnant, he up and left me, the sod. Said he'd met someone else at a corporate team-building seminar up in Birmingham and had to be with her. I said what about the baby and he said just get rid of it, it was a mistake. I said too fucking right it was a mistake, mate, and you're going to be paying for it the rest of your life, because I'm not having an abortion. So he went, but not before I'd got a solicitor involved and made him do the right thing financially. All this time, Mike was the only one at work who knew I was pregnant, and he was a real friend. Just after the birth, I moved down to Fratton Park to make a new start. I joined the British Legion club because my Dad used to run the bar there, and that's where I met Carl, who's a real swine but loves me and the kid dearly."

Pete interrupted. "Sorry, did you say that your Dad used to run

the bar there? Does he not anymore?"
"No, he runs the bar at the Cricket Club in Bournemouth. He told me that you'd been asking questions over there. His name is Ken Rawlings. Peterson was my married name, I kept it for the baby's sake"
Pete had been making notes. "This doesn't get any simpler, does it? So what about your relationship with Mike Johnson?"
Karen continued. "After I'd left the bank Mike and I kept in touch, just occasionally meeting up for lunch or whatever"
"Whatever?"
She sighed. "You know, you ought to keep a clean mind if you're going to do an unbiased interview. Yes, whatever. We never had a relationship. How many more times do I have to say it? So one day he asked if I'd like to earn some easy money on a regular basis"
"I'll keep my mind clean on that one as well, then. What did he want you to do?"
"Just pick up a bag from him at Parkway station car park. He'd give me a return flight ticket on the Flybe airline and enough money to stay over in Bergerac. For doing that I'd get five hundred quid, so it wasn't hard to say yes"
"And what did you do in Bergerac?"
"Well you probably know because you're all so clever and you

can read timetables that it gets there just after one in the afternoon. Mike had arranged for a taxi to pick me up and take me to a bed and breakfast place, then I could go shopping in the afternoon. The B&B was run by retired English couple. You'd be surprised how many English people live out there now, and anyone who's still French has to be able to speak English, and my not speaking French wasn't a problem at all. I got to stroll through the parks, take little boat trips up the Dordogne river, visit that big chateau on the hill at Montbazillac, do some wine tasting. It was a pity I couldn't take my kid, but really she's too young to appreciate that kind of thing. The only specific thing I was told to do was to eat at exactly the same time at night at the same restaurant, "Le Vieux Porche", overlooking the river on the old quay. I must say, they do a very decent coq au vin, and their profiteroles are to die for. Anyway, at exactly nine o'clock each night I was there, this chap would come in carrying a briefcase, walk over and kiss me on both cheeks as if we were old friends then sit down opposite me. He would make some small talk with me, but he never ate anything, just ordered a cocktail, which I had to pay for, of course. I would have my holdall on the floor next to me, and I'd have to tell him when there was no-one watching. Then he'd reach down and take a plastic bag out of the holdall and put it in his briefcase. We'd chat a bit more, in fact we got to know each other quite well, and he was quite a looker, so the time passed quickly enough, then he'd get up about an hour later, kiss me again on both cheeks – they do that a lot, don't they, the French? - and leave. All very cloak and dagger, eh? I'd had enough wine for a nice night's sleep, and next day I just made my way back to the airport and home"

"And did you know what was in the bag?"

"I'd be daft not to have had a peek, wouldn't I? As it happens, Mike told me. Money."

"Money?"

"Ten thousand euros, each trip. Apparently as we're all Europeans now you can take as much cash out as you want, but if it's more than ten thousand euros you have to fill in a form. Mike didn't want to fill in the form, so he kept the amount under the limit and I had lots of trips to make. He was quite an expert on the financial regulations, you know. But I suppose he would have been, wouldn't he, being manager of the Money Transfer department at the bank. Although I was getting to grips with a lot of it myself since I got promoted in the same department. Maybe I should have worked harder at that, who knows where I might be by now. So he explained that this carrying of banknotes within the EEC is all legal and above board, so I didn't have to worry about anything. And that's the story of my trips to France. Nothing sinister, and no sexual involvement either side of the channel for you to get off on. Now is there anything else I can help you with?"

Pete looked at Dave, who merely shook his head.

"Did Mike or this other bloke explain why he was squirreling out ten grand a month to France?"

"Of course. Mike told me he was planning on buying a house out there for his retirement. The way he explained it, to get enough money there without being liable for tax he had to invest it over there slowly. He said there were too many regulations about transferring money across and he didn't want anyone else knowing about it"

"Particularly his wife?" observed Dave.

"He didn't say. I didn't really know Kathy very well, just through Mike. I always thought he was too good for her though. She's a bit too full of herself. As for the French bloke, well he was definitely French, had a lovely accent but spoke good English and he was dressed like some French men's perfume advert. Smelled as good, too. He told me he was doing Mike a favour by putting the money in a deposit account till Mike had enough to buy the kind of place he wanted. He said that a lot of English people go there and buy something in a hurry, then realise it needs too much work or its too remote or its got too much land to look after. He seemed to be a good friend of Mike's. He said they used to work together in Bordeaux, so I assumed that's where Mike's account was. Anyway it was just part of the small talk, I wasn't really interested, and I don't think he was really. I was just the courier. So can I go now?"

"And what about your passport?"

"That was another thing that seemed a bit strange. Mike insisted that I use a new passport that he'd got for me, in the name of Kathy Johnson, but with my photo. We'd gone off together to the quays shopping centre the day I said I'd do it, just to get the photos done in a booth. It was quite exciting really, like having an affair but without having to do anything seedy, if you know what I mean. When it came to arranging the flights he explained that he'd had to book all the tickets in her name, for some reason, so I'd need to pretend to be her at check-in. Of course when I went through immigration at either end I used my own passport, otherwise that would have been illegal, wouldn't it? Mike did explain that technically I didn't need a passport at all, as we're in Europe, but the airline insisted on the names being the same on the ticket as any ID you use, and as the UK doesn't have identity cards like the

French, I'd have to have this other passport."
"Didn't you think you might be breaking the law by doing that?"
"Oh, no, Mike explained that it would all be OK, I'd just have to show my real passport if I got stopped"
"I think you'll find that Mike knew a lot less about immigration law than financial regulations" observed Pete.
Karen looked crestfallen.
"You mean I might be in trouble?"
"Yes I think you might be. Where did Mike get the false passport?"
"He said he could get loads of them, from some bloke he knew up in London. He said that most of the eastern Europeans working in Britain are on false passports, they're dead easy to forge and you could get one from this bloke for a couple of hundred quid, you just need a valid passport in someone else's name and a photo"
"Do you remember this bloke's name?"
"No, Mike never said his name. What happens now?"
"For now, we'll let you go till we need you. But you'll have to give us both passports, and you'll certainly face some legal action for having a false one. I hope the money you got from Mike hasn't all been spent yet. You might need it for a

solicitor"

As they left the interview room Pete was handed a note by the dispatcher.
"A sighting of the Johnson car?" asked Dave hopefully.
"No such luck, Mandy Baines wants me to call her. It seems she's down at the coroner's and has the final version of the autopsy report. Come on, let's do this on the squawk box"
Dave followed Pete into a vacant interview room, closed the door behind them and they both sat. Pete dialled Mandy's number on the conference phone on the table and the ringing sound filled the room. Mandy answered.
"Yes Mandy, it's Pete Thomas"
"Thanks for calling back, boss. I thought you should hear this as soon as you could"
"OK Mandy. Dave is here with me on the speaker phone – what have you got?"
"It said in the original report that time of death was estimated at between six pm and midnight. If you remember, we asked at the time why it couldn't be more accurate, and the coronor's office told us that there were some conflicting results from their tests. Well the latest report goes a lot further. The forensic team has done some computer simulation to find out what

would lead to such conflicting results, and the best model they've come up with is this – "

There was some shuffling of papers, then Mandy read from the report.

"Our revised time of death is twenty four hours earlier than our first estimate. We believe that the corpse had been frozen and then left to thaw out."

There was a stunned silence from Pete and Dave.

"Forensics are over at Briar Close now, checking out the freezer in the garage"

CHAPTER TWENTY SEVEN

As they arrived back at the office, Pete was intercepted by the duty sergeant, who, unusually, had a broad grin on his face.
"You've got a visitor Pete" he indicated a set of chairs against the wall.
There, dressed in a tailored pale lilac jacket and a matching skirt with a hemline to catch the eye, sat Amanda McCarthy, from Mid Western Bank. A man in a pin-stripe suit sat next to her, shuffling papers from a briefcase resting on his knees.
"Ms McCarthy," Pete greeted her and shook her hand, "How nice to see you". He turned slightly towards the duty sergeant and winked smugly. "Shall we find a room, and can I offer you a drink?"
She stood and the man next to her stood with her, having hurriedly tidied away his papers.
"May I present Mr Alexander Philpott?" The man shook hands with Pete. "Mr Philpott is a corporate solicitor, representing the bank's interests." Pete came back to earth and showed them both to an interview room, not missing the reciprocated smug smile from the duty sergeant as he went through.

"How can I help you, Ms McCarthy?" Pete started, once he'd

handed out plastic cups filled with the police station's version of coffee. That'll remind them how good they've got it at the bank, he was thinking.
"This is a bit of a sensitive matter, Inspector, so if it's possible I'd like to keep the conversation off the record for the moment" Amanda replied.
Pete smiled kindly, then continued. "Ms McCarthy, I'm leading a murder investigation. As far as I'm concerned any information which leads to the apprehension of the culprit is a valuable asset and one which I'm entitled by law to have. If there is anything you know about the circumstances leading to Mr Johnson's death then I suggest you share it with me, otherwise if I find out later that you've been withholding relevant you would be liable to prosecution for obstructing the course of justice." He looked across at Philpott. "And I hope you'll be taking notes, sir. This will be an informal interview unless I deem it necessary to record it, at which time I will do so."
He addressed Amanda. "Now, in previous conversations with you and your colleagues I got the impression that you only knew Mr Johnson at work. It seems to me that you worked very closely together and I'm beginning to think that your visit here is to admit to me that you know Mike Johnson on a

personal level and in fact you may know something about his demise. So. Is there anything you would you like to tell me about your relationship with Mr Johnson?"

Amanda looked shocked, then hurt, then angry. She said nothing for a few seconds, then, having collected herself, she addressed Pete calmly.

"Inspector Thomas. It's a great pity that in this time of budget constraints the police force has had to cut down so drastically in its training of senior police officers such as yourself. Any basic interpersonal skills education would have steered you away from such a confrontational start to our conversation. Your bullying tactics might work on some scumbag selling pirate DVDs at Ringwood market, but not on me. I'm just glad I had the foresight to bring a colleague with me to witness your crass provocation."

Philpott was quietly scribbling notes, but said nothing.

"Now," Amanda continued, "before I say anything else, are you able to offer protection of any sensitive information I give you?"

Pete stuck to his guns. His approach might be old-fashioned, but he knew from experience that getting someone to get emotional made then less careful about what they said. "If you mean that you prefer me not to tell Mrs Johnson about your affair with her husband, then you certainly don't have my protection"

Amanda laughed. The sound of it lit up the room and Pete felt guilty that he'd tried to needle her.

"I suppose I shouldn't be surprised at your assumption, Inspector. After all, the newspapers would have all of us bankers as cheats, both financially and morally. No reason to suspect that you wouldn't jump on that bandwagon. For the record, no. I have never had an affair with Mike Johnson or anyone else at that bank or any other. That information you are free to publicise to whomever you want. In fact, as my personal situation is a matter of public record, I can tell you that I am already in a civil partnership with another person at the bank. Someone you've actually met"

Pete was a little wrong-footed. He paused, thinking back to his few visits to the bank – Dan Mahoney? Tom Baxter? Surely not? He thought he might as well know, even if it wasn't relevant.

"And that someone is?"

"Rowena Saunders, the lady you met from Human Resources. We've been together for about two years now. Obviously I'm not really a person of interest to you in this case, or you would have researched a little deeper and had that information

already."
Pete started writing notes because he couldn't think of anything else.
Amanda continued "So can I tell you why I'm here so you don't have to guess?"
"Go ahead" Pete continued writing something illegible.
"OK, but forgive the techno-speak. It's been brought to my attention that there are some discrepancies in the FX trading portfolio. Specifically, there were some Swaps that matured a week or so ago that were meant to result in a positive Forward position in one of our Euro nostro accounts, but the settlement proceeds have been paid through a Eurobond purchase ledger."
Pete looked up.
"I'm afraid I couldn't spell most of those words, so I won't write down what you've said. Can you tell me what has happened so it can be understood, even by an under-trained policeman?"
Amanda smiled. She knew she had him beaten intellectually, and her 'techno-speak', although almost correct technically, was designed to sound more complicated than it was, just to belittle him. She'd had her revenge for the demeaning arrogance of Inspector Thomas's approach, and now she would be reasonable.

“Of course. It means that a transaction was set up some time ago, to convert an amount from one currency to another at a date in the future, known as the settlement date. If you do such a deal you can get a better rate than waiting for that date to arrive. Of course, the exchange rate could go in your favour or against you, but with a bit of skill and experience you can usually make a profit on the deal. Anyway, come the day of the settlement, the proceeds of the deal was moved somewhere unexpected”

“But surely you can just get it moved back?”

“Normally, yes. But in this case the money was used to purchase Euro Bearer Bonds. These are actually pieces of paper, like old-fashioned bank notes, for which any bank in Europe is obliged to pay cash to whoever cashes them in, without any proof of identity or ownership”

Pete had followed the simpler explanation of the problem, and was already thinking back to the conversation he had with Dan Mahoney.

“Wouldn’t your expert security man, Mr Mahoney, have caught this the day it happened? On the settlement date?” Pete was pleased with himself for using the correct term.

“You would think so, but it looks like none of the normal exception reports show this transaction, which is very strange, to say the least. The IT department are looking at the source code for the exception reporting programs, in case they've been tampered with. Dan's stand-in is very worried"

"His stand-in?"

"Yes, Mr Mahoney has had two weeks holiday scheduled for a while. It started ten days ago and we're unable to contact him. He was staying the night in a hotel somewhere in the UK, then on to his holiday home in Italy. As you have counterparts in other countries, we were hoping you'd be able to help us to contact him so that he could advise us, without this affair being made public – sorry, that was a poor choice of words, but this is the only affair I'm actually involved in". She smiled sweetly.

Pete considered what Amanda had asked. "I'll do what I can, but this doesn't have any obvious connection to the Johnson murder case, so I'll route it to the appropriate department. Presumably you can give me the address of his holiday home? I'll make some calls and have someone try to track Mr Mahoney down. I'm sure he'll be as upset by the news as much as you are – he seems quite a dedicated and professional chap. Apart from that, I'm afraid this murder case takes precedence, and if you can't add anything that will help us with that, I'll be happy to show you both out." Pete stood up to leave.

"Don't you even want to know how much money is involved?"

Amanda stayed seated.
"OK, just out of interest, how much are those Euro Bonds worth?"
"Twenty million Euros"
Pete smiled. So even bankers had a figure that they would consider 'a lot of money'.

Chloe had been asked to check on progress at the murder site. She was patiently waiting outside the Johnson's house in the sunshine when Gloria wandered over.
"I see you're all back again, then" Gloria observed. "Is it about the break-in? Pete Thomas told us about it" she added after seeing Chloe's quizzical look. "He said they'd left it in a heck of a mess."
"No, it's not actually" replied Chloe. "We've got some technicians chasing up something in the garage where Mr Johnson's body was found." She thought for a few seconds about how to ask the next set of questions. "We're looking at everything that was in that garage, just to complete the picture. For example, there are a couple of bikes in there. Were either Mr or Mrs Johnson keen cyclists?"
"No, I don't think so, Mike was always too busy for exercise, and Kathy had her gym. I suppose they must have had bike

machines or something similar there. I never saw them get those bikes out on the road."
"And the workbench? Was Mike a keen do-it-yourselfer?"
"Oh, no. He would have brought someone else in to change a plug. I remember thay had a leak in the kitchen once and Mike came over to get Graham to show him where the stop-cock was, so he could switch off the water till the plumber could come. In fact I'd be surprised if he had any tools at all"
"There was a small toolkit on the workbench"
"That must have been new. And I've never heard it called a workbench before. That's where they would dump all their used pots and pans until one of them could be bothered to wash them up"
"OK" Chloe was jotting down notes and brought up the next item as if it was on a list of things she had ready to ask. "And the freezer, how often was that used?"
"Never, as far as I know. It came with the house when they bought it, and I don't think Kathy ever used it. The fridge freezer in the kitchen was big enough for them. I don't think Kathy cooked that often, didn't see it as a priority. She gave us a very nice meal whenever we came over to eat, as I already told you we did sometimes, but I always thought it had been prepped by Marks and Spencer and all she did was warm it

up."

At that point the men in plastic overalls came out of the house and started changing. They had a box with specimen bags in it, and loaded it into their van.

"Thanks for your help Gloria" Chloe closed her notebook. "You'll hear if we've made any progress" She waited for Gloria to take the hint.

"OK, I'll be off home then" Gloria couldn't hide her disappointment and made her way back across the road. As soon as she was out of earshot Chloe turned to address the head technician.

"Find anything?"

"The freezer's been well cleaned, but we've found some traces of fluids in the bottom seams. They'd have been frozen along with whatever produced them, but now they've thawed out. We've done a preliminary test and the source is definitely human."

CHAPTER TWENTY EIGHT

It had been a very quiet night so far. Ken O'Hara and Dev Stretta were passing the time halfway through the night shift by talking about their nights out with the guys, and what they got up to. They were comparing some of the funniest moments in some of their friends' stag nights. Ken had been at a stag party in Dublin with some of his Irish mates where the groom-to-be had become so drunk that when the bar had closed they'd had to leave him where he was, sitting on the pavement near a cycle rack. For safety's sake they'd removed his wallet and tied him to the cycle rack with his own belt. He'd been woken up at six the next morning by the dustmen, who had tried to lift him up after waking him. It took four of them to pull him up to his feet, and the cycle rack, still attached, came with him. The dustmen thought it was hilarious, until the man felt for his wallet, found it missing and started accusing them of taking it. They couldn't stop laughing at the sight of him chasing their dustcart down the street, with a six-foot cycle rack dragging behind him. Luckily one of the more conscientious of his pals had been on his way back to check on the groom and explained to him what had happened. Now it was Dev's turn, and he was recounting a tale involving a "lady-boy" stripper who they had booked for the stag celebration of a mate of his. The stripper had made a grand entrance fully dressed as a busty blonde, had then stripped to his panties and had done some pretty outlandish things to the groom, who was so drunk he hadn't a clue it wasn't a woman. The stripper, for his grand climax, had then revealed his "prize possessions" for the groom and his audience, to rapturous applause from all the lads who, of course, had been in on the joke from the start. The video taken by one of them was the highlight of the best man's speech a week later, to the horror of the bride and her family.

All the story-telling and meaningless chatter were part and parcel of police motorway patrol work. The circuit on the M3 between Surrey and Hampshire was pretty routine most of the time, you just drove South from the M25 junction till you hit the M27, then you had a coffee break at Rownham Services, turned round and went back again. Keeping a steady seventy mile an hour speed, you would get very few motorists daring to overtake. After all, the squad car was so obviously police, with its fluorescent yellow stripes and roof-mounted light bar, you'd have to be blind or incredibly drunk not to see it. Tonight they'd started the shift after rush-hour, so there wasn't even a traffic jam or fender-bender to take care of. Of course, that wasn't always the case. Sometimes they would have to attend road traffic accidents, and would pray that the paramedics would arrive before they did. Some of those sights were not to be forgotten. Or they would get a call about a minor accident that had turned into an argument and sometimes violence between road-rage drivers It was quite amazing how far the disagreement could get before the police arrived at the scene to calm things down.

The radio crackled.
"Control to Lima Six, report your position please"
Dev reached forward and took the radio handset.
"Lima Six to Control, we're just past junction 13 heading South towards Winchester"
"Lima Six, take the next exit at Otterborne and park at junction 12 northbound ready to rejoin the motorway. The cameras at Chandlers Ford have spotted a vehicle on the urgent list. A red Citroen DS." She detailed the registration number of Kathy Johnson's hired car.
Although most people are familiar with CCTV cameras snooping on them in banks, supermarkets and high streets, with the UK being the most densely populated country in the world of such devices, few are aware of the extent these cameras are used on Britain's roads. A system of interconnected cameras at

strategic points on Britain's motorways records the registration number, date and time of every car passing beneath it. Since 2005 Project Laser has implemented over two thousand ANPR (Automated Number Plate Recognition) cameras, and plans are well advanced to convert all other CCTV cameras to recognise car plate numbers. Currently the system can hold one hundred million number plate 'reads' per day. The ANPR data centre links to the Police National Computer in the same location, North Hendon in London, which passes lists of 'vehicles of interest' from burglaries, petrol court drive-offs and other police investigations. An alarm is raised if such a vehicle passes under an ANPR camera

"We believe the driver to be one Terry Walton, wanted in connection with the murder of Michael Johnson in Eastleigh, Hampshire. He is accompanied by Mrs Kathy Johnson, who we think has been abducted by Mr Walton. The car was doing 86 mph at Chandlers Ford, so should hit junction 12 at 22:17. Keep well back so he doesn't spot you, then pursue and apprehend. Radio in when you have visual contact, then keep us informed of progress. I have notified DI Thomas, who is running the case, and we can patch in to him if we need to."

"Understood, Control. On our way now"

"Lima Six, Mr Walton is possibly armed and extremely

dangerous. Do not, I repeat, do not tackle him if there is imminent danger to yourselves. An armed response unit is on its way from Guildford to Bracknell, and will take over from you if the suspect hasn't been stopped by exit 3"
"Thank you Control, that's very reassuring. We'll keep you posted."

Ken gunned the engine and they made it to junction 12 at ten past ten. They parked on the slip road running on to the motorway, out of sight of the streaming traffic but with the engine running.
"Nice to get a bit of action, eh Dev?"
"Dunno, mate. I'd rather do a few speeding tickets or a couple of blow-in-the-bags than face someone with a gun or a knife"
"Well, like the nice lady said, we don't approach him if there's any risk to us. We've got that Tasar in the boot, but it wouldn't be much good if he's got a gun, so we'll stay well back and wait for the cavalry"
They waited without saying another word. The kidding of just a few minutes ago had been replaced by a nervous silence. They both concentrated on watching the cars go by. Even at motorway speeds, they could clearly read the plate numbers.
A dark Citroen sped past.

“That’s him!” They both said at the same time. Ken rolled the squad car down the slip road and into the slow lane, quickly gaining speed until they were a few hundred yards behind the other car. Dev had notified Control that they’d made visual contact. The instructions were the same as before. Pursue and Apprehend if safe to do so. Even at this hour there was some traffic on the road, so Ken had to keep leaving the slow lane to overtake, while the pursued car stayed in the fast lane. After a couple of minutes they were in open countryside and the commuter traffic was less. So far, the car in front had maintained a good speed just a little over the speed limit. Suddenly the distance between the cars started increasing noticeably, so that Ken had to accelerate to keep pace.
“I think he’s spotted us” said Dev
“OK Dev, show time, eh?” replied Ken. “The traffic’s going to be a lot heavier after Farnborough, so if we’re going to take him peacefully now’s the time”
“OK, let’s do it” agreed Dev. He switched on the flashing lights and sirens.
The car in front increased its speed rather than slowing down.
“Bloody idiot thinks he can outrun us. Doesn’t he know I’ve been on the level five course?” Ken was obviously nervous but seemed fully in control. He slowly advanced on the other car,

flashing his front lights to reinforce their demand to stop. By now the traffic was mounting again, with cars joining the motorway from Fleet, the beginning of the nightly exodus to London for a good night out. The car in front didn't have the fast lane to itself now, but rather than slow down it was zipping in and out of the three lanes to overtake slower cars any way it could. The squad car kept pace.

"OK Dev, better get that armed response unit at the ready. They'll probably need a helicopter and some way of closing the Motorway further up. This bloke is seriously not interested in stopping"

Dev had the mike in his hand and was halfway through that message when they both shouted the same phrase.

"Holy Shit!"

The driver in front had misjudged the amount of space he had to get back into the fast lane, and at ninety miles an hour had clipped the rear bumper of a car in front of him. The poor driver of the impacted car had no way of controlling it as it spun around in the middle of the road twice and then hit the side of a truck which had slowed down when its driver had seen the flashing police lights. The pursued car almost went under the truck but managed to accelerate away from it in a giant sideways skid that took it towards the barrier on the central reservation. With a massive bang it's front passenger corner hit the barrier hit the barrier and pushed the car back into the motorway. The car crossed all three lanes and smashed sideways into the safety barrier on the nearside, then still at high speed it ploughed along the barrier with its nose screaming along the metalwork until it suddenly sprung free and shot back into the traffic lanes, but sever damage had already been done to the steering. The driver fought to regain control, trying to steer back in a straight line, yet still accelerating, but there was not much left of the car's front end. The Citroen swerved in an arc and hit the crash barrier again, this time head-on. Almost in slow motion, the car left the road and somersaulted into the fields below, to land on its roof in a cloud of dust.

Ken brought the squad car to a halt as quickly as he could, given that all around him seemed to swerving around, some slowing in shock, some speeding up to avoid getting involved. He headed for the emergency lane, and as soon as he could stop he started reversing towards the spot the other car had left the road. He didn't get far before he reached a line of cars that had also pulled over, maybe trying to help, maybe just rubber-

necking.
"OK, Dev" Ken yelled. "You take care of the traffic and I'll see if I can find them alive. I'll update control before I go, but you'd better get some flares out before this turns into mayhem!"
Dev was out of the car already and heading for the boot where they had their Hi-Vis jackets and a good supply of flares, warning lights and cones for exactly this situation. He handed a Hi-Vis jacket to Ken and started gathering equipment.
"Control, this is Lima Six, come in."
"Control to Lima Six, go ahead"
"The pursued vehicle has left the road" Ken gave an accurate GPS reading from his console. "Please alert fire and ambulance. I'll go and see what the damage is. I'll give Inspector Thomas an update from the scene"

Pete was watching Arsenal frittering away a two-goal lead in a champions league game. Between mutterings about wasteful possession and yelling at the ref, who fell for every dive thrown by the opposition, Pete munched at some Bombay Mix, served as a starter for their mid-week takeaway. Jenny was sitting at a small table in the corner, reviewing some legal papers and tut-tutting every now and then. The man in the van had already delivered the Meat Vindaloo and Vegetable Dansak, and Pete heard the satisfying sound of the microwave bringing them to serving heat. A perfect night, he thought to himself. A good curry, a good football match and who knows what else later? Life can be good.

The phone rang just as Arsenal had been awarded a free kick. Pete picked up the receiver and answered distractedly.
"Pete Thomas"
"Ken O'Hara here, sir. I'm at the scene of a Road Traffic Accident on the M3. We were pursuing a vehicle of interest, a Citroen DS rented in the name of Mrs Kathy Johnson. The car left the road at speed after hitting some other vehicles and ended up in a field. The Fire Brigade have made it safe, there's been no fire but the vehicle is on its roof. There was a male driver and a female passenger. Fire Brigade have freed them and they're both unconscious, some broken bones, but alive. An ambulance has taken them both to Basingstoke hospital, but their injuries don't appear to be life-threatening. One of the armed response unit chaps is going with them and will keep guard until they wake up or if there's any change in their condition. We're going back on traffic duty, but dispatch wants to know if you'll be going to the hospital tonight?"

The microwave pinged.

“No, I’m a bit tied up here.” Pete replied. “I’ll make my way over there first thing in the morning. Just get the hospital to call me if by any chance both of them die, so I won’t have a wasted journey”.

CHAPTER TWENTY NINE

"I thought you'd like to know we've found Mrs Johnson." Pete was saying. "She was involved in a high speed car chase on the M3 last night and she's currently in Basingstoke Hospital. I'm on my way now to interview her when she comes round, but I thought you'd like to know she's apparently ok"

Jack looked relieved to hear the news.

"Thank you Inspector, I appreciate your coming to tell me. I must admit I was getting a bit worried for her. What about the bloke who kidnapped her, that Walton chap?" Jack continued with his breakfast, having already offered Pete a cup of coffee from the Travel Lodge buffet.

"He's OK too, we've got them both under guard. We followed up on the information you gave us about the storage facility, and sure enough they'd been there a few days ago. We don't know why, but he seems to have forced her to there to pick up a holdall. We don't know where they've been since"

"What would have been so important about a holdall?"

"Well, we were informed yesterday that there's something else that's been going on, and there's a lot of money involved. I can't really say much more, but it involves the bank where Mr Johnson used to work"

“ Ah, does this have anything to do with Carl Swann? When he confronted us in the car park here, he seemed to think that Mike Johnson was up to something. He even thought Kathy might know something about it and would pay him to keep quiet. I’m pretty sure she wasn’t involved though.”
Pete smiled at Jack’s loyalty.
“That will be up to us to find out, I’m afraid, Jack. But we’re fairly certain at the moment that it’s nothing to do with Carl. His girlfriend Karen Peterson, on the other hand, is very involved in it. She seems to have been running errands for Mike Johnson once a month before he got himself killed. Day trips to France carrying bag loads of euros. Did Kathy never mention anything about France in the time she was with you?”
”No, but then we didn’t talk geography too much. Our specialist subject seemed to be biology.”
“And you can cut out the lewd double-entendres, thank you. I hear enough of those from the guys I work with”
“Sorry Inspector. But how can I help now – you seem to have the culprit under guard at the hospital”
“The thing is, Jack, I think I must be missing something. This story starts with Mike Johnson involved in some get-rich-quick scheme which goes wrong so someone bumps him off and tries to make it look like suicide. According to Kathy, they had a

row the previous night and she stormed out, spending the night with her sister in Weymouth, and only coming back here late the next day to spend the evening at the gym, where she met you. Now it turns out there's some discrepancy in the timing of Johnson's death, although I won't be giving out any details."

"Oh." Jack seemed surprised, "For some reason I assumed the row had been the night Kathy and I met."

"No, she'd been away most of that day. We've corroborated her stay with her sister, and there's vide footage of her filling up at a petrol station near Weymouth. It does mean, though, that we'll need to look again at everyone's alibi, not for the night of Johnson's death but for the previous night, the Monday. You know, you seem to be up to your neck in this sorry saga, and according to you it all started with a quickie in the car park on the Tuesday night, when you and Kathy Johnson met for the first time. That's either a lucky coincidence, or maybe it isn't". Pete paused to give Jack time to anticipate the next question, then asked it.

"Can you account for your whereabouts on the Monday night?"

"I was at the gym the previous night. Obviously I'm a stranger around here so I don't have anyone who'll be able to vouch for me. I could say you can check the sign-in records at the club, but I know for sure they can be fiddled."

“That’s the problem with all this technology stuff. If it’s not a picture, like at airports and high-security storage units, then the log doesn’t mean what you think it does. It could have been anyone signing in.” Pete paused and seemed to collect his thoughts before asking the next question.

“Tell me, Jack. Have you ever worked for Mid Western Bank?”

Jack smiled.

“Inspector, if you’re half the detective you’re supposed to be, you already know the answer to that question. No I haven’t. But you’ll also know that I’ve worked for other banks, and you’re guessing that I know how their security works. I bet that’s what you really want to discuss with me. I’m sorry if you think you’ve missed something about my chance meeting with Kathy, but deep down you know damn well that I’m not involved in the cloak and dagger stuff, whatever it is that’s going on. I’m just not devious enough”

Pete sighed.

“Yes, your right. I’ve checked out your profile and can’t see any connection between where you’ve worked and for whom with anybody or any place relevant in this case. Maybe there’s part of me that can’t believe you’d strike lucky like you did”.

“So let’s assume I’m innocent, and I’ll apologise later if it turns out I’m guilty” Jack grinned conspiratorially. “Now, what do

you want to know about bank security systems?"
"OK, so I was told by Dan Mahoney, the security man at Mid Western Bank, that to transfer money out of one of the customer accounts into their own it would take collusion between two employees, plus a lapse in the exception report reviews by the security staff. Does that sound about right?"
"Yes, that sounds about normal. Do you mean someone's managed to transfer out a load of cash from Mid Western? Is that what was in the holdall you said Kathy was forced to get out of storage?"
Pete sighed again.
"Look Jack, I don't know what was in the bag because we haven't found it yet. The car they were both in was really smashed up, and we've taken it to our forensic labs. As for the money, of course I can't tell you if Mid Western are missing any money. Even if I did, they would deny it. You'd have to pinch billions to make a dent in the bonuses they pay their staff, anyway"
"Yes, I know. I was a contractor working alongside some of the permanent staff at a couple of banks. They resented my being paid a premium rate, but as I told them, I had my own overheads to pay, like health, insurance, pension, holidays and all. They certainly didn't complain when they got fifteen

percent bonus at Christmas, and the high-ups got a hell of a lot more. But don't let me get on a soap box, even if you're a willing listener. Back to the question of running off with some money without anyone knowing. The best way to do a sly transfer would be to have a dummy employee ID. You log on as that employee, do the transfer and then authorize it under your own ID. Then it looks like there are two people involved. If you time it right, there will be an inexperienced person checking the security reports when then come out, and they won't notice the sudden appearance of a new ID. As far as I can see, there's not a lot of risk"

"So if you knew when the head of systems security was going on holiday, you could set it up so that the transfer would happen at the time he was away? You wouldn't even have to be around yourself if that transfer was the settlement of an earlier transaction."

"Like a Forward FX deal? Sounds like you've been brushing up on your banking procedures, Inspector. With a bit of planning, that timing wouldn't be difficult at all"

"But where would the perpetrator, let's assume it was Mike Johnson for the minute, get a dummy employee ID?"

"Probably the best way would be to re-use the ID of someone who has left the bank"

“Like Karen Peterson? This is suddenly all making more sense” Pete looked at his watch. “Look, I’ve got to go on to the hospital now, but thanks for your help”
“Just let me know if it turns out I’m guilty” Jack smiled, and went back to his breakfast.

The guard at the private hospital ward had been expecting Inspector Thomas.
“Morning Guv. I was just going to phone you. The woman has regained consciousness and the staff nurse says it’s OK to talk to her, but she’s in a lot of pain. The car landed on its roof so they both had to be cut out of the wreckage, but the guys at the scene say they were pretty lucky to survive the crash. The woman hasn’t even broken any bones, thanks to her seat belt and the airbags, but got herself shaken around quite a bit when the car rolled over.”
“Thanks, I’ll go straight in then. Is she in this room?”. He indicated the door behind the policeman, noting that there was another policeman stationed outside a door further down the same corridor.
“That’s the one, sir.” He followed Pete’s look to the other room. “The nurse said that the bloke down in the other room is in a much more serious way. He had his leg trapped in the

wreckage, so there are a few broken bones to mend. He's still unconscious, but he'll pull through ok."

"Fine. He'll be facing some charges when he comes to." Pete entered the room behind him.

There was just one bed, facing the door, with an array of monitors and drips on either side. The room was in darkness with the blinds drawn, but there was soft lighting around the bed itself and its linked instruments. There was a faint hum of machinery. Hooked up to various tubes and wires to the monitors and drips lay a young woman with a very bruised and swollen face. She was still as Pete entered the room, but her eyes opened when Pete closed the door behind him. As he moved towards the bed she tried to focus her eyes on him, then spoke in a feeble voice.

"Who are you?"

Pete had seen people mutilated and disfigured as a result of car accidents and violent attacks, leaving their faces swollen and almost unrecognisable. He had also heard people speak under the influence of a variety of drugs and painkillers. Neither of these were happening here, though.

"I'm Inspector Pete Thomas of Portsmouth CID. And who the hell are you?"

The woman, though groggy, tried to sit up, squinted at him as if

she should recognise him, then replied sleepily “I’m Pauline. Pauline James. Where’s Vinny?”
“I assume that Vinny is the bloke in the room down the hall. You’re both here in Basingstoke hospital after a crash on the M3 last night, and you’re lucky to be alive, both of you. You were in a Red Citroen C3 being chased by a police car. The car wasn’t yours or Vinny’s. What were you doing in someone else’s car last night?”
She took a few seconds to absorb the information, gathered her thoughts and spoke slowly. “We were going up to Hammersmith for a concert, so we borrowed a car. We do it all the time. It’s a lot easier than hitch-hiking and we can’t afford the train. Vinny just hot wires a car and we dump it back somewhere else in the same town the next morning when we’re done. Nobody gets hurt, they just don’t have a car for a few hours but they find it next day and the insurance company pays for the damage.”
“Except when you try to outrun a police car and end up crashing upside down in a field. You were lucky no-one else in that motorway traffic got injured, including my colleagues in that police car. OK, Pauline. So where was it that you hot wired the car last night?”
“In the car park of the big hotel in New Milton, the Chewton

Glen. They have a nice range of motors there. We've used them a couple of times now"

Pete pulled out his mobile and pushed the speed dial for Dave Seddon.

"Dave, it's me. That bastard Walton is still on the loose with Kathy Johnson. The two people in that car last night were a couple of joy riders. Can you check with forensics to see how they're getting on with the wrecked car? Make sure they prise open the boot and see if there's a bag full of money in there, but also get them to see if there's any trace of when the car was last used by Walton, any petrol receipts or anything. I'll be down in half an hour and I'll pick you up at forensics. We're going to the Chewton Glen hotel in New Milton." He paused while Dave asked him something.

"Because that's where the car was pinched from, although it seems a bit posh to be one of Terry Walton's regular hangouts"

CHAPTER THIRTY

They were driving at a comfortable speed across the New Forest heading South. The early morning mist had cleared and the vast expanses of moorland were starting to turn a little golden as the autumn approached. Occasionally there would be a wandering wild pony or a cattle grid to slow down for, but there was little traffic on the road. Pete often reflected that simply driving together was a great opportunity to talk things over without interruption. His wife would respond that it was the one situation where neither party could simply ignore the other, and that it helped that you had an excuse not to make eye contact. Far from being a long-suffering married couple, Pete and Dave worked well as a team and took care to hear each other out. They were discussing the case so far.

"I still don't get the connection with Terry Walton", Dave was saying. "I couldn't find anything in his past to connect him with Mike Johnson, but now it seems like they're part of some grand bank fraud. Let's suppose that Johnson set up this transfer but then got killed by Walton before he could collect. Why would he kill him? He was already in on the deal, and even if it was less than fifty-fifty he would have been a rich man”

“Maybe that’s it.” offered Pete. “Maybe Walton wasn’t getting a big enough cut. For one thing, I can’t imagine Walton having the brains to be in this on his own, despite his economics degree. He must have contacts somewhere in the finance sector if he’s going to get rid of those Eurobonds. Which, by the way, I don’t think he’ll have left in a car overnight. So maybe his contacts were getting greedy. Actually ....” a thought occurred to him .... “perhaps it’s them, his contacts, who arranged the murder? Although Walton’s is the only one whose DNA was found in the garage after eliminating friends and family. Or how about this? Johnson was trying to double-cross Walton in some way. Cut him out of it in favour of someone else? How about Karen Peterson? She knows a lot more than she’s telling us, that’s for sure. Her story about shipping out Euros a bit at a time sounded plausible at first, but this Eurobond transfer thing is on a different scale. Blimey, she would have had to make....” he paused while the calculation went through his brain....”she would have had to make two thousand trips to make the same money! That’s four hundred years in monthly trips.”

“Well no wonder her boyfriend wanted to get in on the deal,” Dave chipped in. “Carl knew there was something going on when he went after Kathy Johnson at the Travel Lodge. Maybe he just didn't know how big it was."

"Or maybe ...... maybe Carl isn't her only boyfriend?"

"You mean Walton and Karen Peterson are in this together?"

"Why not? Think about it. Say Mike Johnson lets something slip in one of his handovers at the airport? Something like, This is just small fry. One day I'll hit the jackpot and you can keep all the euros I've stashed away in France. I won't need them because I'll be out of here with the big one. So she thinks she'll get some assistance on the heavyweight side. She can't trust Carl, he's always getting pissed up and shooting his mouth off. So she goes back to one of Carl's old buddies, who gets involved in more than one way"

"So there's a connection between Carl Swann and Terry Walton?"

"I bet there is, we just haven't found it yet"

"Maybe it's the false passports angle. I've been trying to track down how Mike Johnson could have so easily provided a new passport to Karen Peterson. There's a possible link to some Eastern Europeans through the doorman at Carl's British Legion Club, by name of Tom Chomelewski, but it's tenuous at best. I've got someone working through the connections, but it's going to take a while"

"One of the chaps at Border Control down at Dover told me

that you can get a false passport for about a thousand quid as long as you provide a photo and a photocopy of a valid passport for them to copy. That's petty cash when you're talking about twenty million euros. Actually, that's just given me in idea. Get on to Raj and ask him to call everybody on the list of connections for Mike Johnson. He needs to ask if Johnson ever asked them to lend him their passport or let him have a copy of it. The Karen Peterson passport was a copy of Kathy's, with Karen's photo on it. It might not be the only one they had done, so if Walton was planning on leaving the country, and I don't mean to Scotland, he could have had a passport provided by Mike Johnson. So it stands to reason that if there are any other false passports they would be in the name of someone Mike Johnson knew"

After Dave had finished making the call to Raj, Pete continued. "And another thing. Assuming whoever killed Mike Johnson was the same person who stored him overnight in the freezer and then suspended him from the ceiling, he must have known Johnson quite well. Either Johnson let him in to the house or the killer already had a key. There were no signs of a struggle, so either they were taking cocaine together or the killer slipped it into a drink and covered up his tracks afterwards. When we get back we're going to have to check who else had a key to the house, other than Gloria from across the road, who we already know had one to let repair people and the plumber in."

They were approaching the Chewton Glenn Hotel. An imposing but quietly elegant building set at the edge of the New Forest but close to the sea on England's beautiful South Coast. Far from the rest of New Milton in Hampshire, which had a kind of neglected look typical of an out-of-fashion seaside town, the hotel simply oozed class. Once they had passed through the ornate gates and started up the drive through carefully manicured landscaping they could appreciate that this was a hotel for the select few. Pulling to a halt outside the main entrance, they were greeted from apparently nowhere by a team of welcoming staff, dressed in matching uniforms and ready to help. Pete shrugged them off, flashing his ID card and lead Dave up the steps to reception. At the end of an echoing entrance hall was a reception desk, behind which was positioned an impossibly smart young lady with a lovely smile, a kind of Travel Lodge doppelganger just back from the dry cleaners.

After Pete had shown her his warrant card, she excused herself and went to the back room, from which emerged a few seconds

later an equally smart but pompous-looking manager, who asked Pete how he could be of assistance.
"We apprehended a young couple last night who had apparently stolen a car from this hotel" Pete began, "And we'd like to talk to the people who arrived here in it"
"Presumably you already know the name of the person who owns the car? That might make it quicker to find them?" The manager was used to protecting his clientele from outside intrusions.
"I'd really prefer you to check your registration system?" Pete countered, and gave Kathy Johnson's hired car plate number. The manager clicked a few times on the computer at the desk and looked up.
"I'm afraid that car is nowhere in our system. None of our guests has ever registered with that car"
"Yes, I was afraid of that. It's a hired car so he may not have know the registration number, or worse may not have wanted anyone to find them here. I was trying to find these people through the car they arrived in because I somehow doubt he would be using his real name"
Dave thought of something.
"But if he'd been here before, he might have used his real name. If I were to give you someone's name, perhaps you

could tell me if that person has ever registered here, then you could tell me if they registered recently?"

"Normally I would insist that you have a court order for that kind of information" the manager sneered, "But I assume it would take you less than an hour. OK, give me the name."

"Terry Walton"

The manager went to work with his mouse.

"No, he's never stayed here"

"No, we thought it might not be his kind of stomping ground. How about Kathy Johnson?"

The manager clicked again.

"No, I'm afraid she has never stayed here either. Not under that name, anyway"

"How about Karen Peterson?"

Another few clicks.

"No, her neither"

"Well, we know they might be using false passports, so how about the name Mike Johnson?"

"No, sorry"

"OK, let's try a few more names. Gloria or Graham Marshall? Dan Mahoney?"

This time the manager didn't need any clicks.

"Mr Mahoney, why he's a regular customer here. I believe he

was here a few nights ago, on his way to his house in Italy." He clicked to make sure. "Yes, here we are, Monday night. His normal double room in the garden suite. And here's his car registration number" He wrote it on a sheet of headed notepaper and handed it to Dave with a smile, "He and Mrs Mahoney checked out on Tuesday morning"
"Well, that's a bit of a coincidence" replied Pete. "Wait a minute, are you sure it was the same one we're talking about? Can you describe Mr Mahoney?"
"Average height, tanned complexion, very handsome. Always dressed in a dark suit, Pierre Cardin if I'm not mistaken"
"Sounds like the one we know. I don't think Terry Walton could pass for him. And you said he's a regular customer?"
Just then Pete's phone rang. He looked at the caller's name. It was Raj. Pete clicked the end call button. Raj could call Dave about the passports if he's found anything. The news that Dan Mahoney stayed at this hotel couldn't be a coincidence. Pete opened his mouth to address the manager again and was interrupted a second time by his phone. Raj again.
"Excuse me for a second, please" Pete sounded exasperated as he turned from the manager and walked over to a quiet corner. "Yes Raj, what is it that's so important?"
"Sorry to interrupt you, Boss, but I thought you'd better know

as soon as we got the news. We've just heard from forensics. They'd taken Kathy Johnson's hire car in to check for prints and so on. It was in a bit of a mess after the crash, and the fire brigade cutting the doors open. They had a good look for that holdall you mentioned, even ripped the seats out. Then they forced the boot open."

"And?" Pete held his breath.

" They found a body inside"

CHAPTER THIRTY ONE

"It's Terry Walton, guv" continued Raj. "There's not a lot of blood. Looks like he's been hit with something that killed him outright. In fact, the forensics team are checking out a tyre iron thet was lying next to the body, to see if they can lift any prints."

Pete was speechless.

"Guv?" it was Raj, after a few seconds silence.

"Yes, I'm here" Pete had composed himself. "So he'd been dumped in the boot before those young kids made off with the car. Any idea how long he's been dead?"

"The pathologist isn't here yet, but my guess would be at least a couple of days. There was a hell of a smell and a lot of flies when they opened the boot"

"OK, thanks Raj, we'll get together back at the office later. I'm at the Chewton Glen trying to find out if they know anything about the driver of the car before it got stolen. By some coincidence, it's a hotel that Dan Mahoney has stayed in before. Can you contact Amanda – you know, Amanda McCarthy - at United Midwest and ask for the name of the hotel that Mahoney and his wife were staying at before his holiday? I'm pretty sure it will turn out to be this one."

"Sure thing, I'll get on to Ms McCarthy straight away. But wait a minute, boss. Didn't you tell us yesterday that Mahoney lived in Poole with his mother? Oh, and before you go, boss – we still didn't find that holdall you were looking for."

"No, I'm not surprised now." Pete's phone beeped. "Oh, it looks like there's another incoming call, Raj. Thanks for the update".

Pete hung up and took the next call. It was Jack.

"Look, Jack, it's nice of you to keep in the loop, but things are getting a bit hectic now, so can I call you later?"

"Of course" replied Jack. "It's just that something occurred to me about the Terry Walton connection"

Pete wasn't ready to share the latest news about Terry Walton with Jack. He hadn't quite recovered from it himself yet.

"And what's that?" Pete asked politely.

"Well, you were wondering if there was a previous connection between Terry Walton and Kathy Johnson. My guess is that you've somehow placed Terry Walton at the murder scene, and that's why you were concerned for her safety when he and Kathy disappeared together."

"OK, let's say we did place him at the scene. We were pretty convinced it was him that contrived the suicide, and that he even put the body in the deep freeze for twelve hours to get everybody's alibis to stand up. Unfortunately, despite what we thought was overwhelming evidence, we've just concluded that it wasn't him after all"

"Obviously you won't be telling me who you've got in the frame for it now, but I bet the evidence you're talking about was Terry Walton's DNA that placed him at Kathy Johnson's house."

"Er, yes it was. And so?"

"DNA from strands of hair? You've probably got about a handful, and wondering why Walton isn't bald already."

"That hadn't occurred to me, but yes, there was a fair amount of his hair on the floor. But how did you know that?"

"I was there when he lost it. I worked it out earlier today. That was why Kathy attacked him at the casino. She came away with a fist full of his hair. She must have put it in her pocket and scattered it around the garage when she got home"

"Fuck!" Pete apologised quickly and continued. "That's the one connection we couldn't make. How come you worked that out?"

"It was what you said about some guys having all the luck. I'd been thinking I'd been pretty lucky too, but then I suddenly thought – what if it wasn't that? Maybe she shagged me for a purpose. I thought at the time it was to get revenge on her husband, but looking back it must have been to provide her with an alibi. Then she got me involved in that trip to the Casino, and I'm telling you she was really convincing as a distraught widow. Terry Walton's boss and him were really seething, and they even threatened to have us both dumped in the river, so later at the Travel Lodge I really thought one of them must be after her."

"That's what we all thought, too. Although you didn't tell us that they'd threatened you both. There was all that business of the bloke following her – she was pretty convincing on the phone, and had poor Gloria well frightened, although no-one else actually saw the BMW that Terry was supposed to be following her in. I still don't know, though, how she would have known he drove a BMW"

"That's another easy one" Jack responded. "There were only three cars parked outside the casino when we went there that night. One was a dark blue Rolls Royce, one was a red Ford Focus and the other was a silver BMW. It was too early for customers, so those three cars belonged to the receptionist, Walton and Palmer. No prizes for guessing which one belonged to whom. Also, there was a sticker in the Beamer's back window, Christchurch Sea Scouts, which seemed a bit out of place but certainly made it stand out."

“And that’s how she knew where to find Walton. But surely the killer would have to be a man, and a strong one too, to be able to lift Mike Johnson into the freezer, then hoist him up a ladder and hang him the next day?”
“I’m not party to most of the information you’ve been collecting, Inspector, but you can check with the gym if you like. Kathy Johnson was a champion weightlifter and an accomplished martial arts devotee. She was certainly strong enough, and I saw myself that look of determination in her eyes, so I wouldn’t put anything past her, not even murder”
“Or double murder” said Pete, and hung up before Jack could react.

Dave was still talking to the manager at the reception counter, who was very concerned that any adverse publicity should affect their reputation. After all, the suspicious death they were investigating took place a long way from here, and the hotel could never have known that one of their guests was a fugitive. Pete interrupted the discussion to take Dave to one side and pass on the news about Terry Walton’s body being found in the wrecked car.
“Crikey!” was Dave’s reaction. “So it’s been her all along?”
“Certainly looks like it. And there’s another connection we

should have picked up long ago, from the Bournemouth Cricket Club"

"Which is what?" asked Dave.

Pete didn't reply. Instead, he walked back to the reception desk, taking a photo from his inside pocket as he did so.

"Do you recognise this woman, sir?" he asked the manager.

"Why yes, of course," he replied. "That's Mrs Mahoney."

"I don't think so. We all know her as Mrs Kathy Johnson"

CHAPTER THIRTY TWO

"Ladies and Gentlemen, there will be a short delay to boarding of flight EZY8373 to Brindisi. Please remain in the lounge pending further announcements"
Gate 34 at Gatwick had a full complement of passengers waiting patiently if uncomfortably on rows of plastic seating. A couple of young children were running around tripping over luggage and generally getting themselves over-excited, to the consternation of a few people and the complete disinterest of their parents. It was a grey day, but their bright orange transport was already waiting on the wet tarmac and the forthcoming flight to sunny southern Europe would raise the most dampened of spirits. Those who had been standing near the boarding gate slowly moved away to sit back down after hearing the announcement. Such delays were not uncommon on cheap flights, although most had experienced even longer delays with "full-fare" airlines. One man in particular seemed unconcerned as he sat reading a newspaper under the sign for "Speedy Boarding", an oxymoron if ever there was one.

"Mr Graham Marshall?" a voice came from behind him. There was a moment's hesitation before the man realised he

was being spoken to.
“Oh, yes. Sorry. I was elsewhere. What can I do for you?” The man turned and looked at the person speaking to him. It was a uniformed man with a photo ID hanging around his neck, maybe someone from the airline.
“Just a formality, Sir. Would you mind stepping into our office for a few moments? Your flight’s been delayed anyway. We won’t keep you a moment, if you don’t mind?”
The uniformed man led him to a door in the corner of the departure lounge, which he opened and let his guest walk through before following and closing it behind them.

“Shit.” was all Dan Mahoney could say. Sitting behind a desk was Inspector Pete Thomas.
“Hello Dan” said Pete. “Haven’t left for your holidays yet?”
Mahoney didn’t bat an eyelid.
“No, as usual the flight’s been delayed, as you know. I guess that gives you time to ask a few more questions – is that why you’re here?
Pete smiled benignly. “No. I think you know the game is up. You and Mrs Mahoney – and I don’t mean your mother – are going nowhere anytime soon.”
Dan sighed, and took a seat opposite Pete.

"So how did you find us so quickly, Inspector?"
That's better. We realised that you Mike Johnson had no problem in obtaining false passports, and we assumed Kathy would use a false one as well. Having already interrogated Karen Peterson we saw that she'd need a valid passport in someone else's name, even if it was her own likeness in the passport photograph. It didn't take long to find out that Kathy had 'borrowed' both Gloria and Graham Marshall's passports a few months back for some dreamed up on-line application. They both fell for it and wouldn't have thought twice about it until we asked them specifically if their passports had been out of their hands recently. After that it was just a matter of checking with the airline which flights 'Gloria' and 'Graham' had booked. We were surprised to see that you hadn't left the country yet."
"Another of Kathy's brainwaves. On the off chance that you'd found the car quickly after the money had gone out, she reckoned that you would concentrate on the airports and ferry terminals first. So we waited a few days in the hotel here."
" I assume that's the swag bag?" Pete looked down at Dan's holdall, the one he recognised from the Pink Elephant security footage. "Not a bad idea using that CCTV at the storage unit to plant the seeds of a kidnap in our minds. Kathy obviously knew

quite well the workings of those places. And she'd done such a good job of playing the victim that we were ready to believe Walton was waiting outside in the car and that she was acting under duress"

"Look, Inspector, I know this sounds crazy, but I didn't have anything to do with Mike's murder. I was happy just to run for it, but Kathy had this elaborate plan for the suicide, which meant no-one would suspect any foul play. That's why she planted the newspaper and the mobile phone, so you would think Mike was in debt with gambling"

"And that worked for a while, but our clever chaps at forensics soon saw through it and we had a murder to investigate. Even though Kathy was astute enough to decry the phone and newspaper as obvious plants, so that we'd never suspect it was she who planted them. So you're telling me you didn't have any involvement in rigging up Mike's corpse from the garage ceiling?"

"Of course not – what do you mean, his corpse? Surely he wasn't dead when Kathy hung him up in the garage? She said she'd drugged him first, but I didn't think she'd killed him with the cocaine"

"Maybe that's an elaboration she didn't tell you about. We think she actually killed Mike on the Monday night, then hid his body in the freezer and killed him again on the Tuesday to confuse the autopsy report"

Dan went as white as a sheet.

"Bloody hell. That is cold-blooded."

"And where did the cocaine come from? Was that Mike Rawlings from the cricket club?"

"What, Colonel Mike, Mr Military Man? He'd have you shot rather than see you high at his precious club. No, the coke came through Dizzy, an ex of Kathy's who she kept in touch with. You probably haven't met him yet"

"No, I've met him, he fooled me into thinking he was just a harmless stud. So what about Terry Walton?"

"What about him?"

"Why was he involved?"

Dan sighed. "Things started to get a bit problematic when you started looking for a killer. Kathy wanted you diverted, so she found herself a suspect. She'd already set up the name Spike on the phone that she planted, after she read about the bloke dying from an overdose. She'd worked out that you'd need to find a source for the cocaine that Mike had in his body, so when she read about Spike Palmer dying she thought that he could be the source. After all, he wouldn't be able to deny it, being dead and all. Then when she needed a killer as well as a drug supplier, she went to the casino where Spike's brother works and staged a fight with Terry Walton. She'd never set eyes on him before, she told me, but still managed to come away with a sample of his hair to drop on her garage floor."

Pete looked impressed. "But why did Terry Walton have to die?"

Dan was shocked. "He's dead? Christ. I didn't know that, honestly. Kathy told me she'd persuaded him to go on the run. She's given him a huge wad of cash and he was going to disappear"

"And so he did" observed Pete. "But he wasn't far away. His body was in the boot of the car that Kathy hired, and would still have been there now if some joy riders hadn't crashed it"

Dan's white pallour was turning distinctly yellow. He held his head in his hands.

"Christ! What kind of woman have I got myself involved with?"

"Maybe we can ask her. Where is she?" Dan looked up.

"Come on, Inspector, that's not funny. You must have her in another room like this round the corner. You just want to see if our stories match up. Why is that? Surely she's not blaming me for everything now? Let me see her. She must know it's the end of the road now."

Pete was getting concerned. "Trust me, Dan, we've checked everyone out there and Kathy isn't there. We know you both checked in online, but as you don't have any hold baggage you just have to go to the departure gate for boarding. We saw you sitting there and thought it best to grab you first, but there's no sign of Kathy. When did you last see her?"
"She went to the toilet about ten minutes ago"
Pete turned to the uniformed airline chap. "Can you put out an announcement, please? Will the person who has seat number blah blah, the seat reserved for Gloria Marshall, but don't mention that name, please come to the speedy boarding desk".
The airline man left and Pete addressed Dan.
"There's an armed policeman stationed outside that door. Don't go anywhere"

Pete heard the announcement as he walked towards the Speedy Boarding desk. He stood near the desk where he could see and hear but could not be seen. After a few minutes a young girl walked up and confirmed that she had the seat mentioned in the announcement. Pete walked forward, showed his warrant card and led her to a quiet spot.
"So, can you explain where you got this boarding pass, Miss?"
Pete was trying to sound unhurried, but he knew that time was

running out.
“Of course” the girl replied in a foreign accent, German perhaps. “I bought it. I was in the bathroom when a lady said that she had a big problem. She was supposed to fly to Brindisi with a friend of hers, but she felt that her friend was thinking it was going to be a romantic week away. She’d had second thoughts but she couldn’t tell him to his face. She wanted me to take her place on the flight, and tell her friend that she would join him in a few days. Except of course she wouldn’t, but he would be hoping he would understand and still get on the plane.”
“And why would you do this favour for the lady? Did she pay you?”
The girl looked sheepish. “Yes, of course. She gave me five thousand euro. I couldn’t refuse really.” “But what about your own flight? “ asked Pete. “You must have had a boarding pass to get through security”
“Yes, of course, I have a ticket to Dusseldorf, but I can get a flight there from Brindisi tomorrow. Just one day delay for such a sum of money seemed a pretty good deal.”
“Certainly beats any compensation an airline would give you. So where did the Dusseldorf flight board from?”
“Gate 28 down the corridor. The flight leaves in ten minutes”

CHAPTER THIRTY THREE

Christine Migletz was studying the little plastic card, trying to memorise the position to adopt in the event of the pilot shouting “Brace! Brace!” She was not a confident flyer, but neither did she enjoy long road or rail trips, so aeroplanes were a necessary evil if she was to see her grandchildren, now living in Brighton, a world away from Dusseldorf. The lady sitting next to her had been friendly but quiet, and was now absorbed in her book, and hadn’t even paid attention to the safety drill, even though it was in both English and German. There was a light tap on her shoulder, and she looked up to see the stewardess smiling at her. She handed Christina a folded slip of paper then held her finger to her lips, telling her not to say anything. Christina unfolded the paper top read a message in German. “Please, as naturally as you can, get up from your seat and make your way to the front of the cabin, without saying anything to the person next to you”. She complied, and as she walked forward down the aisle someone slid into her vacant seat, causing her neighbour to look up.

“Hello, Kathy,” said Pete Thomas, “I think you need to come with me.”

Kathy was brought into the same room and told to sit in the empty chair next to Dan, both facing Pete. Dave Seddon stood guard at the door. Before Pete could say anything Dan addressed Kathy.

"So where do you think you were going? You said you were off to the loo, but I bet you were leaving me to face the music on my own. You'd seen the police here, hadn't you?"

"Actually, I hadn't" she replied. "I just had a last moment change of plan, just in case either of us had been clocked. If that German girl had done what I paid her for, you'd have known already that I'd be coming out later. And by the way, Inspector, I hope you confiscated that money I gave her. I'd like that back, please."

"You never stop, do you Kathy?" sighed Pete. "As it happens, I couldn't see anything illegal about her accepting your money, so I sent her on her way. I even forgot to take down her name, so we can't chase her even if we wanted to. Now, Kathy, we've heard from Dan here about how you were the mastermind between the three of you. It was a bit of a surprise to him, though, when I told him how poor Terry Walton was found. Why all the charade about the Pink Elephant storage unit? Was all that just so you could pretend to be kidnapped?"

Kathy turned her head slightly to see a large uniformed

policeman now guarding the exit.
"It worked pretty well, as it happens, don't you think? I needed somewhere with cameras to make it look like Walton was behind it all, and I remembered that Jack had noticed the big keyring at the club bar. So I knew eventually you'd end up there, although I didn't expect it to be as soon as you did. By the time I waved to the camera Walton was already dead. I'd stopped at a layby in the New Forest to try and persuade him to join us for a cut of the money, but he'd have none of it. He was going to turn us in, but he thought he might get his leg over first. Typical bloke, but I could see what he was up to. We went into the woods behind the toilets, but I had a tire wrench from the boot hidden in my coat. He didn't stand a chance, but it was his own fault. I thought I'd better drop him in the car boot rather than leave him to be found there by some picnickers. Anyway, back to the Pink Elephant place. That's where bloody Mike would insist on keeping all the stuff he was planning to move out to France. France this, France that. Anyone would think it was bloody El Dorado we were moving to. He'd worked out there and loved it, and was determined to go back rich. He had this friend out there who would launder the Euros for him, but this arrangement with Karen Peterson was just a trickle feed. For god's sake, we would have been dead before

we'd have been rich and able to retire. He was just such a bore, couldn't see past his bloody nose. We all three joked about "The Big One", and then when we all figured out how to do it he didn't have the balls to go through with it. He just had to go, then, didn't he?"

"And how long have you and this one" he nodded at the silent Dan Mahoney "been screwing each other? Did Mike know anything about that?"

"No, he would never have guessed it either, the thick bastard. I met Mike when we were all in the same crowd at Bournemouth Cricket Club. He got hold of all the fake passports from someone he knew there, I never knew who. He kept them under the bed as if we were playing some kind of "Cluedo" game. Except for the one he gave to Karen Peterson. I suppose you've figured that bit out?"

"Yes, we picked her up again earlier this morning. So she didn't know anything about the big one?"

"No, nobody did. But how did you even know to look for us? I thought I did a pretty good job of looking like a kidnap victim."

"Just a bit of luck, really. A couple of joy riders pinched your car from the Chewton Glen after you left the hotel in Dan's car. They crashed it and ended up in hospital. Wrecked the car."

“Glad I took out the third party insurance then. So you already knew what was in the boot?”
“Of course. But why did Terry Walton have to get involved at all?”
“That wasn’t part of the plan. I thought the suicide would have been enough, with the missing money from his salary and the betting paper.”
“And of course you knew already how much Mike was earning and where the extra money was going?”
“Sure I did. I had Mike set up the account, but only in his name so I could claim not to know anything about it if the tax people started getting curious. It helped me when I later went all hysterical at the building society offices in Southampton. I assumed you’d find out about that sooner or later and it would add to my grieving widow image, but you never did, did you?”
Pete said nothing. It wouldn’t help to admit there were flaws in their investigation.
Kathy continued. “I’d planted the bank statement for you to find in Mike’s bedside table, and I knew that would set you on your way to seeing Mike as having a secret to hide. He arranged the trips for Karen but I told him to tell her I didn’t know anything about them. The fewer people involved the better, and all that. The whole thing started out as a retirement

plan for the two of us, but dopey old Mike couldn't get a promotion at work to make it worthwhile, so I got fed up and went for plan B"

"With your friend here. And why did you pick the Chewton Glen to dump your car and Walton's body?"

"Dan had stayed there a few times on business. Seems an idyllic location, and the staff are very discreet."

"They certainly are" smiled Pete. "But when we were putting a few names forward they recognised Mr Mahoney here quite quickly. It was a few minutes until I remembered that the personnel people at the bank had said that Mr Mahoney was unmarried and living with his Mum. So who was the Mrs Mahoney who had stayed at the hotel with him? Had we uncovered a little tryst?"

"Seems to be I've heard that word somewhere before. I bet poor old Jack wishes he'd never said it. So that's when you guessed it was me?"

Pete smiled again. "Well, it was a bit later, actually. I'd shown the receptionist photos of all the women I've interviewed so far in the case. Before she recognised yours she identified Amanda McCarthy as a previous "Mrs Mahoney", obviously a bit ambivalent about her sexuality, and then she confirmed that you were the latest"

Kathy lost it completely.
"You bastard!" she shouted, and swung a right hook at Dan that connected with his jaw before he could blink. The force propelled him backwards, he rolled once and collided with the uniformed policeman, who was taken off-guard and collapsed on top of him. Kathy saw her chance and went for the door. Dave Seddon had seen the move for the diversion it was, jumped across the desk and grabbed her, then got flattened by the well-practiced back kick she aimed at him. As Dave hit the ground Kathy was through the door and into the crowd. Pete had rounded the desk by then and helped Dave up. Dan Mahoney saw his chance and he was off too, leaving his bag on the floor and diving through the open door to freedom.
"Stop them!" shouted Pete to the guard who had been standing outside. The guard pulled his gun.
"Stop! Police! Stop or I shoot!" he shouted.
There were screams and a blind panic, fuelled by stories of terrorist attacks and random shootings. Women were grabbing their children, staff were diving for cover everyone was running in different directions. No-one did the sensible thing and lay on the floor. The policeman with his gun raised had no chance to aim at the escaping pair, although he would never have fired anyway in such a crowded place with danger of

ricochets and collateral damage. He holstered his weapon and gave chase, followed by Pete and a limping Dave.
The airport security was geared up to prevent unauthorized entry. Getting out unopposed was a lot simpler. No-one was expecting two people running fast the wrong way through the passport control section, the duty-free area and the hand baggage scanning units onto the airport concourse. They were too quick for the couple of armed policemen on regular patrol, and Pete arrived at the exit doors with Dave behind him in time to see Kathy at full pace heading for the nearby forest, with Dan not far behind, slowly gaining on her.
"Damn!" yelled Pete. "If they make the forest it'll be nightmare to find them!" he started running after them again. As he did so, Dan finally caught up with Kathy, and before Pete's astonished eyes he rugby-tackled her and brought her to the ground.
A couple of minutes later Pete, Dave and the armed policeman had retrieved the struggling Kathy from underneath Dan and handcuffed her. Dan turned to them.
"It's time we both faced the music, don't you think?"

Printed in Great Britain
by Amazon